LOVE NOTES

BY ROBBI RENEE

SYNOPSIS

"Jemma had me at hello... but she was somebody's wife."

Dr. Ezekiel Green is ready to make a fresh start in a new city after the divorce from his high school sweetheart. What was supposed to be a professional business dinner with a future colleague quickly transformed into a love-at-first-sight encounter... or so he thought.

Dr. Jemma Holiday was spirited, brilliant, beautiful, and another man's wife.

"Doesn't he know I'm somebody's wife? Does he care? Shit... do I care?"

Dr. Jemma Holiday had the perfect life, love, marriage, and family in the public's eye. But behind closed doors, betrayal and mundane monotony were suffocating. A marriage of situational necessity. What was supposed to be a pleasurable evening out with her sorority sisters

abruptly transitioned to the one-night stand of her dreams... or so she thought.

What's the worst that could happen?

PROLOGUE - JEMMA
MONROE UNIVERSITY, FRESHMAN YEAR 2000

My God! Quinton Tyler Holiday was - in a word, gorgeous. Creamy alabaster skin, captivating green eyes and curly dark brown hair. Like Michael Ealy kinda fine, just taller. His 6'1" athletic physique was complemented by sharp chiseled thighs and arms to match. Even the boy's neck… my goodness. Who considers somebody's neck sexy? Me. I'm somebody. It was thick and long and strong and beautiful. I was fixated on the bob of his Adam's apple when he spoke. I wanted to lick it...*among other things*.

"Jemma, this is my dumb ass brother, Q." My roommate Quaron introduced me, but I was focused on the distinctive divot in the center of his smooth bottom lip.

"Huh? What?" I asked, now embarrassed.

"Q, this is my roommate, Jemma Jule Warren." She rattled my full government name.

"What's up, pretty girl?" He winked, biting the corner of those juicy ass lips. His glistening green eyes peered around the dorm room, laughing at the mess we'd made.

Quinton was a sophomore track phenom, while me and his sister Quaron were freshman. I met Quaron or *Roni* as she preferred, during freshman welcome week at Monroe University the summer before school started. Actually we'd met before during our junior year in high school when we participated in a youth leadership program organized by a Black Greek sorority in our hometown St. Louis, but hadn't kept in touch.

Once Quaron and I realized that we were both assigned to Betty Shabazz Hall, we quickly conjured a plan to become roommates. Quaron's roommate was like Freddie from A Different World: quirky, talkative, and annoying. My roommate, on the other hand, was just mean as hell. She looked like the leader of a fight club or something, and I honestly was terrified. After a few days of plotting a plan, we convinced the resident advisor that Quaron was allergic to her roommate's burning sage, and I was seriously afraid for my life.

Quaron and I had the bright idea to *be creative* and paint our dorm room with yellow, orange and white stripes. We quickly realized that neither of us possessed not one creative bone in our bodies. We were in way over our heads and needed to call for backup - quickly. The orange was beginning to bleed into the white, droplets of yellow paint splattered on the furniture and we were covered in a tie-dye mess. Quaron's older brother lived across the courtyard in the male dorm, Malcolm X Hall. Although hesitant, she acquiesced and called her brother for help.

Quinton sauntered in the dorm room, confidence seeping from his pores. His athletic frame was perfectly fitted in Monroe branded track pants and a white tank top. Dude was sexy and I was immediately in love.

"I will help y'all with this shit under one condition," he offered, lifting his brow for consent to continue. We nodded. "The beautiful Jemma has to agree to go out with me this weekend." Quinton's bass-filled baritone made my belly roll.

"Get the hell out, Q. You are not about to dickmatize another one of my friends," Quaron shouted, emphasis on the word another. "If those are your conditions - kiss my ass, and no thank you!

"Mind your business, Roni." Quinton teased, his eyes focused on me.

Quaron was about to speak before I interrupted their bickering.

"Ok," I said, blushing. "I'll go out with you."

"What?" Quinton and Quaron chimed in unison.

"But I have a condition of my own." Quinton raised an eyebrow. "You must complete the job to *my* satisfaction. One crooked line, one drop of paint out of place, the deal is off." I smirked, crossing my arms confidently awaiting his response.

"I have no doubt that you'll be completely satisfied, beautiful," he said, licking his lips as he perused the length of my body. *My God.* "It'll be finished by tomorrow." Quinton extended his hand to shake mine.

"I can't believe you agreed to go out with my brother." Quaron pouted, resting against the perfectly painted striped wall. It was Saturday evening and I was getting ready for my date with Quinton. He and his friend Jamar painted the most beautiful strips on the wall behind the makeshift kitchenette we created in our dorm room. They even strung some lights across the ceiling adding some additional pizazz to the room.

"I couldn't renege on our agreement." I blushed, applying Maybelline charcoal black eyeliner. "You have to admit, our room is the bomb thanks to your brother."

"His ass had help. Are you going to go out with Jamar too? He put in just as much work as Quinton's dumb ass." Quaron rolled her eyes.

"Maybe *you* should go out with Jamar. Girl, he is fine," I laughed. "And why are you so hard on your brother? He seems cool." I vainly attempted to quell the rosy smile across my face at the thought of Quinton.

I'd been preparing for this date for the past four days. Experimenting with different hairstyles, makeup pallets and outfits ranging from a short mini skirt and heels to fitted jeans and a skimpy tank. Quinton quickly changed those plans when he called, instructing me to dress comfortably and wear tennis shoes.

"My brother is a hoe." Quaron continued, as I stepped into my acid washed daisy duke-ish jean shorts and an off the shoulder NWA t-shirt knotted at the small of my back. I rolled my eyes. She returned the gesture while motioning for me to sit in the vanity chair so that she could spiral curl my hair.

"And Jamar ass is fine, huh?" She tittered, then we jointly guffawed, slapping our hands in agreement.

"I'm a big girl, Roni, I can take care of myself. Quinton is harmless. And besides, we're just having fun." I peered at her reflection in the mirror.

"Ok! But don't say shit to me when he fuck you and snatch your virginal soul." She shrugged. "You've been warned."

I laughed at Quaron's dramatics. Yes, I was a virgin but I wasn't stupid. I had too much to lose. Namely, my full academic scholarship to Monroe University. I was a Monroe legacy. The only child of Dr. Gavin and

Maureen Warren; they'd raised the perfect scholarly ballerina debutante. In the words of my father, *disappointment is not an option, only discipline.*

So, it didn't matter that Quinton was standing outside of Shabazz Hall looking magically delicious in a black distressed Wu-Tang Clan t-shirt, jean shorts, black Jordan's and a matching hat turned to the back. I, Jemma Jule Warren, would practice self-control and restraint.

"What's up, pretty girl?" He winked, bringing my attention to the sparkle in those greenish brown eyes. Quinton reached for my hand pulling me into his firm frame and planted a kiss against my forehead.

Self-control. Restraint. Self-control. Restraint. I mused unconvincingly.

Quinton and I leisurely meandered across campus to the athletic building. He gave me a tour of the state of the art facility, but I honestly was a little confused. Our voices echoed throughout the hollow hallways. The building was fairly empty since school didn't start for another week. Was this his idea of a first date, giving me the history of the Lou Brock Athletic Complex?

"I saved the best for last." He grinned, ushering me through the tunnel towards the track.

"Oo-k," I huffed, bored.

Quinton's beautiful orbs lit up like a Christmas tree as soon as he stepped on the outdoor track. This was his haven.

"Welcome to my sanctuary." He beamed, reading my mind. Damn, that smile weakened my knees.

"Quinton what are we doing? Are we supposed to be here?" I nervously questioned.

"This is my track, pretty girl. All access 24-7," he chuckled. "Come on."

"And this is what girls like for a first date?" I smirked.

"I don't know. I've never brought a girl here. But I hope this is what you like, pretty girl."

"Can you address me as something other than pretty? I am so much more than just that." I rolled my eyes, ready to implement the emergency plan - faking cramps.

"My bad, sassy *smart* girl." He blushed. "Come on," he repeated, pulling my reluctant frame towards him.

Quinton motioned his head to the center of the field. I don't know how I missed the plush burgundy blanket, wicker basket, two Monroe University branded plastic cups and a portable speaker arranged near the university logo imprinted in the center of the grass.

I hated the gigantic smile on my face.

"A picnic?" I squealed.

"You like it? Is this what pretty sassy smart girls like for first dates?" He teased, licking those damn lips again.

I nodded, capturing the meatiness of my lip between my teeth.

Quinton removed his shoes, and I followed.

"Nice J's," he laughed.

"Why is that funny?" I frowned, carefully removing my retro Jordan's.

"I honestly didn't peg you as a Jordan's kinda girl. Shit, I didn't think you owned a pair of sneaks....definitely not J's."

"What kind of girl did you peg me as then, Quinton?" I questioned, gawking as he unpacked the basket. He poured soda from the two-liter Strawberry Vess into the cups before revealing two food boxes.

"Chinese food! Seriously?" I squealed again.

Quinton audibly chuckled, delighted by my excitement.

"I did a little research and discovered that the beautiful...and smart, Jemma Warren loves her home town Chinese food. Especially shrimp fried rice," he explained.

"How? When?" I stumbled over my words.

"My Pops is in town and I asked for a favor to impress this pretty ass girl. I mean, this smart, pretty ass girl." Quinton nudged the tip of my nose.

There was no use attempting to suppress my smile. The dimmed stadium lights coupled with the shimmery moon offered an impeccable backdrop for what was turning into the perfect first date. We sat in comfortable silence as we ate. Periodically stealing glimpses and sharing rosy-cheeked smiles.

"So you never answered my question." Quinton raised an eyebrow. "What kind of girl did you peg me as?"

He glared at me for a long minute, as he swallowed his food. Quinton was surveying every curve of my face, almost making me uncomfortable.

"The kind of girl who would prefer high heels over J's, and baked chicken over Chinese food," he chortled.

"So, prissy? That's what you thought... or think. You think I'm prissy."

I narrowed my eyes. "Can I be honest?" I asked and he nodded, taking a big gulp of soda. "You're not the first to think that and probably won't be the last. I guess I was raised to be a little prissy. Ballet since I could walk. Piano, linguistics studies, debutante balls and every leadership program my parents could find. My mother would probably pee in her ruffled skirt and platform heels if she saw me in these shoes. She hates them, while my daddy loves it. But I, on the other hand, just like what I like. Sometimes I want to be the prissy chick in high heels and a mini skirt and other times I prefer to kick it in my J's and a t-shirt. So, take it or leave it. Prissy is not an insult to me."

"Nah. I didn't mean it like that, sassy smart girl. I think you're perfect." Quinton winked.

We spent the next two hours talking about nothing and everything. Quinton even challenged me to a race on the track. I won after getting a significant head start and almost busted my ass trying to clear a hurdle. He picked me up, tossing me over his broad shoulder as I boisterously laughed. Quinton made me feel so carefree; comfortable in my prissy prim and proper skin.

It was a little after midnight when we reached the steps of Shabazz Hall. Quinton hadn't relinquished my hand since we left the athletic complex. He clasped both of my hands, fondling my fingers as he gleamed, closing the distance between us.

"Thank you for an amazing first date." My voice quivered.

"Was it amazing enough for you to meet me here at the same time next Saturday for a second date? Or do you have another wall for me to paint?" Quinton perched on the stoop pulling me into the center of his parted legs.

"Technically you didn't finish the job alone, so I may owe Jamar a date." I giggled, our hands still enclasped.

"Fuck that! Jamar don't need shit," he growled. Quinton released my hands, resting his fingers at my exposed waist. Unconsciously, he tickled his fingertips at the small of my slightly exposed back. It was a hot, steamy Missouri night but an invigorated chill coursed through my body. I visibly quaked. Quinton sexily smiled.

"Real talk. Can I see you again, Jemma?" His expression was serious.

"I think that's the first time you called me by name," I uttered shakily.

"Stop avoiding the question." He cupped my chin, encouraging me to look at him as he stood from the stoop. "Pretty sassy smart girl Jemma, can I see you again?" Quinton nestled me into his body, firmly wrapping me in both arms as he stared down at me.

I felt the cooling sensation of the peppermint in his mouth against my lips. So close, one miniature move, one slight exhale, and our lips would collide. I desperately desired the luscious collision.

"Yes," I breathily whimpered.

He revealed that glistening smile, and I was in love.

"Goodnight, Jemma Warren."

Quinton stroked a finger down the arc of my cheek then across my lips before he leaned in delivering the softest, sweetest, candy-coated kiss. I fisted his t-shirt drawing him nearer, eliminating the miniscule breach. He cradled my cheeks, willingly offering me his thick, pursy tongue. My pussy skipped a beat and a dewy dampness settled in my panties. Our tongues capered in a languid, yet ambitious dance.

Seven months into this thing called young love and Quinton and I were inseparable. People around campus considered us the perfect combination. I was the ying to his yang. A kindred connection. I had no doubt that we were madly in love. On Valentine's Day, my nineteenth birthday, I relinquished my virtuous sinless treasure to Quinton and it was glorious. Inch by salacious inch, Quinton gently and patiently inhabited every crevice of my saturated walls. Breathlessly whispering, "My pretty smart girl, you are perfect." Every moment making love to Quinton was like a brand new day. New discoveries of my body, what pleasured me and how to please him. He was the physical manifestation of an undreamed fantasy. The man attached to that dick was unequivocally labeled the love of my life at only nineteen years old.

The last week of my freshman year was exhausting but I successfully delivered a flawless final presentation in my psychology class. As quickly as I spoke the last words of the speech, I hurriedly sprinted to the ladies restroom, vomiting for the third time that morning. I leaned over the sink to rinse my mouth, then peered at my reflection in the mirror.

"No, no, no," I mumbled to no one but myself. "Please God no." I walked back to the classroom room to listen to my classmates' presentations while texting Quinton.

Me: Hey. Are you busy right now?

Q: Nah, bae. I just finished lifting weights. I have training in 30 minutes.

Me: I threw up again.

Q: Shit!

Me: Yeah. Shit. Q! What if I'm pregnant? My parents are going to kill me. My father is going to kill you.

Q. Baby calm down. We will deal with this together, ok? I love you.

Me: I love you more.

I walked four blocks to my friend Maxine's apartment. She lived off-campus with her half-sister who was a senior at Monroe. Quinton was planning to meet me there after his training. I stopped at Walgreens and purchased every brand of pregnancy test. I walked through the apartment door and Quinton was nervously pacing the floor waiting for me.

"Anything?" he asked.

"Q, I haven't taken the test yet. I stopped at the store on my way here." I pulled the brown paper bag out of my back pack. "I held my pee all the way here so let's do this. I'm ready to get it over with."

In the back of my mind, I knew I was pregnant. I'd been diligent about taking my birth control pills but one random weekend when Quinton and I drove to Kansas City, I forgot my pills. We used condoms but that shit didn't sustain the entire weekend.

I still prayed to the high heavens that I was wrong; that this was just a scare. Quinton leaned against the bathroom sink reading the instructions as I concentrated on aiming for the tip of the test stick. After cleaning myself, I laid the test on the counter and endured the longest ten minutes of my life. Quinton paced back and forth over the available space in the tiny bathroom with a balled fist to his mouth.

"Quinton!" I shouted. "Can you please stop pacing? You're making me nervous and pissing me off."

"Damn bae. I'm sorry but I'm nervous too." Quinton pulled me into his chest. "J, look at me. Baby, I love you. Whatever happens it's just J and Q, right?" Quinton sang to the rhythm of the popular Tony.Toni.Tone' song Just Me and You. We settled in that position and faintly swayed to the imaginary music in our heads.

He lifted his head and peered over my shoulder to get a view of the test results. Breathing labored, I glared into his emerald eyes as my lips quivered at the sight of his beautiful orbs growing misty and terrified. Quinton meshed his forehead against mine and whispered, "just J and Q, bae. I got you. I got us."

I quietly sobbed, uncertain of my life and our future.

1

JEMMA
PRESENT DAY, 2020

T he view from the patio off of our main level master bedroom was magical early in the morning. The simmering summer sun rationed beams of light across the aqua blue water in the oval shaped pool in the backyard. I lounged in the rocker with a steamy cup of coffee admiring the beauty of the strawberry hydrangeas and warm yellow marigolds in bloom. Inhaling deeply, I meditated on the power and goodness of Jesus as I whispered a word of prayer for my family, friends and every person I would encounter today.

All summer this patio had become my refuge, my sanctuary since I'd awakened most mornings to emptiness filling my king size bed. The vivid yellow painted walls with framed family portraits of happier times couldn't brighten the melancholy that held me hostage. The click of my bedroom door, faint footsteps, then the shower water didn't cause me to stir as I continued to sip my coffee while Mary Mary "Yesterday" resounded through the built-in speakers. *Quinton,* I mouthed then released a breathy exhale.

Just J and Q had substantially altered over the past twenty years. Our feverishly passionate young love had now morphed into a halfhearted, misaligned dissolution. The romanticized nostalgia of immature intellects with the cute baby girl could no longer sustain a marriage weakly built on lovesick friendship and situational necessity.

In a word, Quinton and I had become predictable and detached. Neither of us ever strayed too far from our daily routine. Breakfast on the patio for me and an early morning run, shower, get dressed, coffee - two sugars, no cream, avocado wheat toast and a banana in the kitchen for him. After the shower, he'd momentarily join me on the patio and say *good morning J* and kiss against my forehead or cheek before walking back into the bedroom to grab his phone from the nightstand and check the second phone he kept in his work bag that he didn't think I knew about.

"Good morning, J," he greeted me.

The *'pretty sassy smart girl'* salutation he'd lovingly utter in our younger years was long gone. Freshly showered with the scent of Irish Springs soap wafting through the air, he deeply inhaled. Quinton was a delectable sight covered in only basketball shorts that had no intentions of concealing his dick. The previous version of J and Q would've included me on my knees digesting every inch of his girth before straddling him on the outdoor sofa chair. But now, I just sipped my coffee.

"Good morning, Q," I retorted, eyes focused on a bumblebee bouncing across the tips of the marigolds instead of my damp rippled-chest husband.

"Jem, I have a track meet this weekend in St. Louis. We're leaving early tomorrow morning. I want the guys to get some practice before Saturday," he announced, staring absently into the backyard with his hands settled on his waist.

Quinton was the head track coach at our alma mater Monroe University. Medals with the name Quinton Holiday adorned the walls of the track and field building of the Lou Brock Athletic Complex. The former track star turned track coach trained a number of olympic worthly athletes making Monroe one of the most competitive college track programs in the country.

"I'm aware," I dryly responded. "It's on the calendar."

This had become our commonplace, our new normal. Share schedules, updates on our daughter, dress for work, return from work, eat dinner… me alone mostly, then goodnight. Repeat. I stood from the rocker joining him in the absent stare into nothingness.

"I have the provost finalist dinner tonight and Roni will be in town," I responded, padding across the patio door threshold to enter the bedroom.

"Dr. Jemma Holiday gets the final say for the new provost, huh?" Quinton teasingly probed as he followed me, grabbing his pants from the bed to begin getting dressed.

Similar to my husband, I returned to our alma mater as the Vice President and Dean of Student Affairs. My position required me to sit on the administrative board that was responsible for hiring executive level positions at the university.

"Unfortunately I got selected to have dinner with the two finalists. They are cutting into my girls weekend with Quaron and Maxine." I rolled my eyes, untying the belt of my white robe.

Ambling into the walk-in closet, I perused my meticulously organized clothes and shoes to identify something to wear today and pack for girls' night. Quinton's baritone caused me to turn around, eyeing him standing in the closet opening.

"My baby sister talks to you more than she talks to me. She's coming when I'm going." Quinton laughed. "That was probably intentional."

"Yep. Probably," I whispered to myself while shrugging my shoulders.

Quaron and Quinton were only fourteen months apart but like oil and water, unable to mix. Me and Quaron, on the other hand, were best friends, sisters. And she knew *everything* that had transpired over the years between me and him. Quaron often vocalized her love and disdain for her brother because of his behavior.

"It's just a girls weekend. Nothing against you." I said, attempting to stroke his ego. "It should be fun."

"You, Quaron and Maxi together? I'm glad I won't be here. The last time I had to pick y'all drunk asses up off the floor. You're on your own this time," Quinton chuckled.

Identifying a dress to wear, I disrobed to complete nakedness. Ass and titties on full display and Quinton did not flinch. Not even a gaze in my direction. It was our new normal that honestly wasn't so unique anymore. The mental detachment had been our *modus operandi* for the past three years or so, but the impassioned sexual intimacy dissipated at least a year ago. Now we sporadically fucked. Unfeeling, unexpressive, stoic sex only to relieve the agonizing pressure in my pussy. No intimate fulfillment required. And honestly that desire faded several months ago. So, yeah, predictable and detached.

"There's toast in the kitchen if you're hungry," Quinton said, pausing my internal ranting.

I nodded, eyeing him as he ambled into the kitchen.

Turning to the full-length mirror, I surveyed my body. Long neck, smooth skin, round perky breast that held a story, voluptuous childbearing hips and thighs. I wasn't the slim-thick homecoming queen of the past but at forty years old, I often reminded myself that I was a honey-hued curvaceous cutie. A goddamn tenderoni.

"Good morning, gorgeous," I sang, encouraging myself as I continued getting dressed.

Twenty minutes later, my stilettos clicked against the hardwood floors entering the kitchen. Quinton sat at the island typing into his phone as he finished the toast he started eating before he came into our bedroom.

"Did Shiloh tell you she's coming with me this weekend," he blurted, still focused on his phone.

"Oh she is, huh? She didn't tell me but I think I know why. That lil boy Jordan must be all healed if Shi is riding on the bus with the team," I laughed.

Shiloh Gianna Holiday was the absolute joy of our world. She was nineteen years old, beautiful and brilliant. Shi followed in her father's footsteps as a track star at Monroe University. She was running before she actually walked upright. Quinton and I welcomed Shiloh into our world at just twenty and nineteen years old respectively. Practically babies. The track star and university royalty getting pregnant out of wedlock was a true scandal. To say our parents were disappointed was an understatement. Our mothers cried, our fathers cursed for hours until we all agreed that an abortion was not an option.

While shame and embarrassment lived in my heart, I walked around that campus with my tummy bulging and my head held high. I was determined to successfully complete my sophomore year nine months pregnant, exhausted, but I did with a 3.7 GPA and made the Dean's List. I remember going into labor the night after my psychology final. Twelve hours later, a seven pound six ounce baby girl changed my life forever. Quinton cried like he was a newborn baby. He held Shiloh almost in the palm of his massive hands kissing against her forehead declaring his love for her.

Glaring at me with tears streaming down his face, Quinton blurted, "*Marry me, J,*" with our baby girl cradled in his tattooed arms. "*I want us to be a family, Jemma. I love the shit out of you, bae.*"

How could I say no to that romantic proposal from my first... everything, the love of my life? Quinton and I were married at the Monroe University chapel just weeks before the start of his senior year, my junior year.

The Holidays and my parent's, the Warrens, were a Godsend. They sacrificed their empty-nest phase to care for Shiloh. Even as parents and a married couple, Quinton and I were blessed to still have a traditional college experience. I pledged a sorority and he a fraternity, held student government positions and secured internships all while our baby girl alternated between our parents in St. Louis during the week, and then to me and Quinton every weekend. It was hard as hell, but some of the happiest days of my life.

"Yeah, I'm going to keep my eye on Jordan's yella ass." Quinton furrowed. "Shiloh can't make the same mistakes we -" he abruptly paused, realizing what he said. "I didn't mean it like that, Jemma. "

"I know." I interrupted, nodding my understanding. "I get what you're saying, Quinton. Shiloh is the best thing that happened to us but she doesn't need to be nineteen years old with a baby and a husband. She needs to live her young life carefree. We struggled so she wouldn't have to."

"Exactly, Sweetie. Just J and Q," he smiled. "I'm gone. Have a good day." He rested one last kiss against my cheek. I closed my eyes with a slight shake of my head.

We never kissed anymore - like really kissed. I thought, watching him amble away looking just as fine as he did twenty years ago. *Just J and Q, huh?* I mused, thinking about just how much me and Quinton had changed over the years. I recall when we would daydream about having the house to ourselves once Shiloh was an adult. Plotting all of the places in the house we could freely make love instead of sneaking in quickies while Shiloh napped. We have complete disposal to this big ass empty house and he doesn't touch me. Leaning against the white marble countertop in the kitchen, I blew the steam away from my second cup of coffee while leering at the vacant doorway he just exited. Quinton was once the love of my life, my everything, but now he was just a stranger in my house.

* * *

Despite the emotionless exchange with my husband this morning, I strutted into the university administration building feeling kinda cute in an eggplant-color fitted dress with a gold zipper up the back framing my booty perfectly. My summer Senegalese twists were pulled into a high bun and nude heels draped my feet. It was mid-June and while I should have been on vacation, I had the task of selecting a new provost since Dr. Milson departed the university after twelve years to move closer to his family in California.

The committee selected two final candidates and asked me to host them both for the final interview. I was scheduled to have lunch with Dr. Sheila Brewer this afternoon. Dr. Brewer was my first choice for obvious reasons. She had amazing credentials with almost twenty years administration experience at other historically black colleges and universities. And self-ishly, the university's executive level administration needed a bit more estrogen at the table, so she was my choice. Dinner with Dr. Ezekiel Green was scheduled for this evening. The meeting was really a formality in my opinion because I'd made my decision. He had great credentials as well, primarily in the corporate sector before transitioning into university administration. But what Monroe University did not need was another addition to the administrative team's *good old boys club*.

"Dr. Holiday, welcome back. How is your summer?" Sharon smiled. She was the administration office manager for the past ten years.

"It's wonderful, Sharon. How's yours? How are the grandbabies?" I asked.

"Bad as hell." She chuckled. "But those are my babies." Sharon stood to hug me. "Your meeting with Dr. Brewer is confirmed for lunch today at 1pm at Oasis. The dinner with Dr. Green is scheduled at 8pm at Trace in the W Hotel downtown. He will not arrive in the city until close to six o'clock so he requested a late dinner."

"Eight o'clock," I scoffed. "He has a lot of nerve." I rolled my eyes.

"That's why I made sure your hotel suite will be ready at three and booked a private booth for you, Dr. Dupont and Professor Holiday at five so you can get the girls' night started."

"You are the best Sharon." I was excited to hang with my girls tonight. Unfortunately the dinner with Dr. Green would interrupt our fun but we'd have a plethora of libations, food and gossip in the suite.

Although one school year just ended, I was already preparing for the start of a new school year. It was stressful with last minute admissions, withdrawals, summer programs, organizing the welcome event and managing helicopter parents who didn't want to allow their babies to grow up. I was heads down focused since the moment I walked into my office this morning.

"Knock. Knock. Hi Mommy." The prettiest emerald orbs peeked around the partially ajar door. Shiloh's sweet voice pulled me from my concentration.

"Hey baby love." I rose to pull her into a hug. "How are you? I wasn't expecting you today, looking all cute."

Shiloh was Quinton's clone. Her eyes were a darker shade of green than his, but the curly dark brown hair, athletic talents and height, practically towering over me with her 5'9" frame were identical. Although I carried her for nine months, she only carried my dimpled smile and honey brown skin tone - a few shades darker than her dad's.

"Thank you, Mommy." Shiloh curtsied then blushed. "I just came by to say hello before we leave for St. Louis since you, TT Q and Aunt Maxi are going to be getting white girl wasted tonight." Her boisterous laugh was way too loud for my liking.

"Excuse you little girl. We work hard so we can play hard." I teased, playfully pinching the tip of her nose. "And speaking of wasted, does this cute little sundress have anything to do with a certain track star frat boy named Jordan?" I questioned.

"Mommy! Really? Jordan is cool." Shiloh rested on the couch, rolling her eyes as teenage girls did. "Daddy talks too much. Me and Jordan are just friends. We had a lot of classes together last semester plus track so we just, you know, get along."

"Ok, Shi. You already know what I'm going to say." I lifted an eyebrow seeking her understanding.

"My treasure is precious and he must be worthy," she dragged her words annoyingly and rolled her eyes again. Those damn eyes were going to get stuck in the back of her head.

Shiloh was my baby girl, my sweetness and we'd always had an open and transparent relationship. I wasn't the type of mother who painted perfect pictures of life. I told the truth and nothing but the truth, sometimes embarrassing Shi with my openness. Shiloh was very aware of me and her dad's history. Both of us openly shared our journey of love, pain, appreciation and regret. Young love, naive parents, but by the grace of God we persevered. Quinton and I would be hypocrites if we forced unrealistic expectations of sex until marriage on our daughter. I simply wanted her to make the best decisions for her and stay protected.

"My girl." I smiled. "Walk with me. I have a lunch meeting at Oasis in a few."

The restaurant was across campus so I scheduled a golf cart to pick me up. I had no desire to walk in almost 100 degree weather for ten minutes across campus.

"Mommy, do I need to chaperone you Delta girls tonight?" she chuckled knowing all too well that me and my sorority sisters could get a little rowdy.

"No ma'am. No kids allowed this weekend." I nudged her shoulder. "You make sure you go see your grandparents while you're in St. Louis with your dad, ok?"

She nodded as the golf cart pulled in front of the administration building right on time.

"Be safe, Dr. Holiday." Shiloh teased while giving me a hug. "I love you three thousand."

"I love you three thousand and one." I laughed, watching my beautiful baby girl confidently saunter across campus.

Arriving at the restaurant about ten minutes prior to the scheduled meeting, I was seated just as Dr. Brewer was escorted to our table by the hostess. She was a pretty woman probably in her early fifties with a fly sandy brown bobbed haircut, dressed in a cute red and black pants suit. I rose, extending my hand to greet her.

"Dr. Brewer, it's a pleasure to meet you. I'm Dr. Jemma Holiday. Please join me." I motioned to the seat at the small table facing the window over-looking the stunning campus.

Dr. Brewer was a pleasure. We immediately connected on creating more opportunities for women in higher education executive administration roles. She clearly outlined her plan for Monroe University and I was sold. We exchanged LinkedIn and other social media information before we parted ways. I purposely didn't research any candidates beyond their resumes because I wanted to make an in-person first impression versus gathering intel from the internet. It was going to be difficult to be fully engaged during this dinner with Dr. Green after a perfect encounter with Dr. Brewer.

I returned to the office quickly plowing through the rest of my day. I took an Uber to campus since I was riding to the hotel with my peer, friend and linesister Dr. Maxine Dupont. Maxi was the Vice President and Dean of Financial Services. We'd been friends since pledging Delta Sigma Theta Sorority in college. Maxi was a gorgeous petite chocolate drop with a powerful presence. I always compared her to actor Tika Sumpter.

We arrived at the W, checked into the suite and then headed back to the hotel's restaurant, Trace, for drinks and appetizers before my 8pm dinner with the second candidate.

Quaron came sauntering into the restaurant looking like a brick house with her shapely figure and honey-blonde booty-length faux locs. If Shiloh was Quinton's clone, then Quaron could've been her mother instead of her aunt. They looked like twins - height, figure, skin-tone, everything. Quaron was a visiting professor teaching a marketing seminar this summer and a few classes in the fall. She'd made a name for herself as an inclusive marketing guru for brands like Nike and Louis Vuitton. Quaron recently vacated her corporate job and started a lucrative consulting firm while sharing her knowledge as a college professor.

"Hey loves," she greeted me and Maxi. "Don't let me forget my damn bag at the valet. You know my mind is bad." She dramatically feigned exhaustion.

"First round is on me, ladies," I squealed as the waitress approached our booth. "Hello. I'll have a lemon drop martini and the lobster stuffed mushrooms."

Maxi and Quaron proceeded to order cognac margaritas, sticky wings and crab cakes. A few men at the bar made no attempt to quell their attraction to us. Sternly staring attempting to gain our attention. I guess three black professional and visually appealing women were a hot item. Quaron's stallion-like frame and flirtatious ways guaranteed us free drinks for the rest of the night.

"Let's make a toast," Maxi said, lifting her glass, and we followed suit. "To sisterhood, lifelong friendship, revelations, and renewed hope."

"And *new* dick," Quaron squealed, interrupting the serene, meditative mood. We hollered, clinking our glasses together in agreement.

There was never a dull moment with these ladies. I laughed until tears streamed down my face. It was nice to have a reprieve from complaining about Quinton or silently questioning his whereabouts. Maxine and Quaron were very familiar with the issues between me and my husband. Well maybe I was the one with the issue since I was well aware of his extramarital affairs but somehow tucked away my hurt to ensure we remained the famed couple of Monroe University.

Quinton and I were campus royalty. The married track star and homecoming queen with a long lineage of Monroe University graduates, both graduating top of their class with a two year old child remained a headline. We were often the talk of the town. When I finished my doctorate at St. Louis University and published my first women empowerment book as a best seller while Quinton competed at the 2004 Summer Olympics in Athens, Greece, we were solicited for every event and fundraiser at Monroe. Ten years ago both Quinton and I were offered opportunities of a lifetime. I was Assistant Dean of Students and Q became the assistant track coach then head coach two years later. We had been living the elite life.

"Dr. Holiday, your guest has arrived." The waitress's words brought me back to the present moment.

I checked my watch, not realizing how time had slipped away from us.

"Thank you, can you clear the table then send him over please?" I asked, standing from the booth turning to Maxi and Quaron. "I should be done in an hour or so. Are y'all going to the room?" They nodded, but no words. Their collective eyes were focused over my shoulder.

"Dr. Jemma Holiday?" A sultry bass-filled timbre called out from behind me.

The power in his vocalization shook my core. I slowly turned on my four inch stilettos to visualize the object of their dreamy eyes. I am not sure what to expect based on my girls' response and his panty dropping, Will Downing-ish voice.

Well hello, Dr. Green. Damn! I was drooling. Like seriously drooling over this towering fudge-colored specimen standing before me. I swallowed hard, my vocal chords were in desperate need of lubrication.

"Yes. Yes, I'm Dr. Jemma Holiday." I cleared my throat and inhaled deeply.

My God he's fine and smells like heaven! I silently mused, but Maxi and Quaron gave my private thoughts sound as they echoed in a whisper, "*Damn he's fine.*" I slightly shuddered to get my thoughts together.

"You must be Dr. Ezekiel Green. It's a pleasure to meet you." I extended my hand.

"Please, call me Zeke. And the pleasure is all mine." His gleaming white teeth sparkled. I swear I saw a lucent light bling against a tooth like a damn Colgate commercial.

He was a slender, yet muscular tall build. Definitely taller than Quinton because I had to toss my head back a bit to fully digest him even in four inch heels. Dewy milk chocolate skin, cleanly shaven bald head, leading to a neatly trimmed lightly salted beard. Dr. Green gave me actor Aldis Hodge vibes. The navy blue suit fit his frame like a glove with blue and gray accents in his tie and pocket square. This man was a lovely specimen of handsomeness.

"Dr. Green." I refused to call him Zeke. "I would like to introduce you to Dr. Maxine Dupont, Vice President and Dean of Financial Services and Professor Quaron Holiday, a visiting professor teaching an intensive marketing seminar in our business program this semester."

"Dr. Dupont, Professor Holiday, ladies, it's a pleasure." Dr. Green nodded to both of these clowns who were literally ogling him from his silk scalp to the shiny designer shoes.

And, of course they lingered a second too long at the dick print in his fitted slacks.

"So, are you two sisters? Holiday is not a typical last name," he inquired, pointing a finger between me and Quaron, catching our matching last names.

"Yes. Sisters." Quaron quickly answered as I was about to add in-law.

"Will you ladies be joining us? I didn't realize this was a panel interview," he laughed, but continued to probe.

"No. Not this time. Dr. Holiday is in charge. You two have important business to discuss. Dr. Green, it was nice meeting you. Good luck... she's a tough cookie so I hope you're ready." Quaron goofily laughed.

"Yes, it was a pleasure, Dr. Green. Have a good night." Maxi continued, flashing a toothy grin before whispering to me, "Ok, bitch. This is it. The one night stand of our dreams. He ain't getting the job anyway so you might as well see what that D do."

I rolled my eyes but wasn't surprised. She knew everything so it made sense that Maxi would definitely be the first to condone me cheating on Quinton. But I was of the mindset that two wrongs don't make it right, but probably just produced more hurt.

"Good night ladies. I will see you all a little later," I sternly said, vainly attempting to keep my composure.

Quaron and Maxi sauntered across the restaurant, periodically peering back at us until we were out of their sight.

"Shall we be seated?" Dr. Green signaled for me to take a seat in the private booth. "Looks like you all already had the party started." He laughed, pointing to the empty martini glasses that hadn't been removed.

"Yes, well, girls night was already scheduled before I was asked to host this meeting. So I had to kill two birds with one stone," I countered.

"My apologies. I didn't intend to disrupt your night, Dr. Holiday." He sexily grinned and I needed him to stop. My pheromone levels were firing in ways that have laid dormant for several months.

"No worries. Duty calls," I nervously responded. "Should we order before we get started?"

He nodded, dallying a stare before observing the menu. I ordered the grilled salmon and he ordered the New York Strip steak. The sides were sharable so we agreed on the rice casserole and glazed sriracha brussel sprouts. The waitress arrived with a cognac for him and another lemon drop that I didn't order.

"Excuse me, I didn't order another drink," I said, brow furrowed.

"The ladies you were with asked me to um... keep the party going," the waitress chuckled.

I shook my head, embarrassed. Dr. Green nibbled the inside of his lip, flirtatiously smiling at me.

"I'm so sorry. My friends are just loud and wrong." I giggled, unconsciously pinching my cheek, a nervous tendency that I hadn't conquered.

"No worries. Seems to me that they want you to loosen up and have a good time." He flashed that sexy ass smile again. This man was deliciously lethal.

We talked about his experience and his motivation to enter higher education. Dr. Green had an intriguing story. From military school, to Syracuse wide receiver, undergraduate and MBA degrees to Wall Street then higher education. I was still sold on the first candidate but I understood why the committee was having difficulty making a decision. After an hour of dinner and interviewing, I was done with my interrogation.

"Well Dr. Green, those are all the questions I have. Do you have any questions for me?" I asked, tossing my napkin on the table.

"Yes, was the dean of students what you wanted to be when you grew up?" Dr. Green circled a finger around the rim of his cognac glass before taking a slow sip.

"Um, great question. Actually, no. I wanted to be a professional dancer."

His brow lifted in surprise. "What stopped you?" he probed.

Shiloh. I thought, my eyes transfixed on him and nothing at all. I pinched that same sensitive spot on my cheek.

"My apologies, Dr. Holiday. I'm making you nervous. It was inappropriate to pry," he said, noticing my discomfort, but I denied it.

"What makes you think I'm nervous?"

He was silent. Just surveying me. Why in the hell is he staring at me with that thick ass tongue peeking between plump perfect lips? He adjusted his tie before responding.

"You strike a finger down the curve of your face before gently pinching your cheek. You've done that every time I asked a personal question, anything about you." Dr. Green glided his teeth across his bottom lip before sexily smirking.

I extended a hand to my cheek and then quickly recoiled. We settled in an uncomfortable hush for an extended heartbeat.

"Join me for a drink in the lounge? I was told that a band would be playing tonight," he blurted.

"Um, Dr. Green - "

"Zeke," he interjected.

"Dr. Green," I stressed. "I don't think that's appropriate. We are here in a professional capacity only. And you do see this ring on my finger, correct?"

I glared between him and the three carat ring that Quinton gave me on our ten year wedding anniversary replacing the simple diamond-less gold band that I cherished and still wore. Simple meant good and uncompli- cated. I would kill for a glimpse of those times.

"Yes and it's beautiful. I promise you this is strictly professional and innocent."

Dr. Green raised his right hand with that Colgate smile. I narrowed my eyes suspiciously observing this luscious man. *Was he really trying to bull- shit me?* I thought as he continued.

"You shouldn't be making promises you can't keep, Dr. Green." The breathiness of my voice conflicted with my words.

"I have a pretty good track record with keeping promises, Dr. Holiday. Try me."

I narrowed my eyes, focused on the way he licked his lips and then smiled. Fuck, I swear my unruly kitty started pulsing and dripping. She hadn't done that in far too long. *My goodness! Doesn't he know I'm somebody's wife? Does he care? Shit... do I care?*

2

ZEKE

D r. Jemma Holiday was absolutely gorgeous and sexy as hell. The way that damn purple dress hugged her thick frame like it was tailored made for her beautiful body... I was momentarily speechless. But her voluptuous body paled in comparison to the double-dimpled wide smile and those golden eyes.

When I walked into the restaurant and spotted three of the most beautiful black women I'd ever seen, I was secretly hoping that the braided bombshell beauty with skin the color of maple syrup was my dinner companion for the evening. The heavens stayed answering my prayers when Jemma extended her hand to me in introduction. I low key wanted to pull her into me and beg her to be mine. *What the fuck is wrong with me?* I ruminated. You couldn't miss the rock on her left hand so she was clearly a married woman. But, shit, there was something magnetic about Jemma; a sad hopefulness resided in her eyes. And I was captivated.

"Can I be transparent, Jemma?" I murmured, breaking the lingering silence.

She nodded.

"I am aware that Dr. Sheila Brewer is the other candidate the committee is considering. I've met Dr. Brewer and believe that either of us would be a great choice for the future direction of the university. But I also understand that the university is seeking gender diversity on its lead administration bench. So while I am very optimistic about the prospective opportunity, I am confident that Dr. Brewer will likely be the final choice. So with that being the case, I've enjoyed our conversation and I honestly would hate for our time to end."

By the expression on her face, Jemma was speechless. I clearly didn't give a fuck. I put all my cards on the table... and won.

"Um, ok. Just one drink. I can't stay long. Girls night, remember?" A nervous nibble to the corner of her bottom lip was adding to the unconscious pinching of her cheek.

Joyful regret appeared to lace her face. Unlike her friends, I pegged Jemma as the play it safe type of woman who walked to the beat of someone else's drum. She had a sly innocence that was extremely attractive and intriguing.

"Excuse me for a moment, I need to call my husband first," she announced and I softly chuckled.

Her modesty was cute but I had a feeling she made that declaration more to remind herself that she was somebody's wife than for my benefit. I settled the check when Jemma excused herself to make the phone call. I took the opportunity to return my brother, Ezra's, text from earlier.

Me: I'm good bro. Yeah, I made it. Monroe City might be my new favorite place.

Brody: Oh shit. What's her name and did you fuck?

Me: Jemma.... Nah, it ain't like that this time. She's fine as fuck though.

Brody: Be careful with them midwest girls bro. They cornbread fed with a lil hood.

Me: Bro, you stupid. But that ain't a bad combination. I'll hit you when I'm back.

Brody: Yep.

Jemma was completing her call when I peered up at her. Tension and irritation dressed her pretty face. Her brows smacked together as she addressed the person on the other end... *her husband*. She returned to the table demeanor despondent with a faux smile that wasn't even close to brightening her gorgeous eyes.

"Is everything ok, Dr. Holiday?" I questioned, then stood from my seat slightly closing the space between us. Unconsciously, I reached out to cup her chin when her gaze disengaged from me.

Gently swatting my hand away, she shakily whispered, "Yeah. Yes. Um, everything is fine."

There was that fake ass smile again. Whoever was on the phone caused her mood to change instantaneously. I have no clue why I cared, but I didn't like that shit and I couldn't prevent the scowl on my face. The waitress approached with the receipt disrupting my frustrated private musing. I reached for the billfold to sign.

"No, Dr. Green. I got it," she said, reaching for the silver tray.

"It's already been taken care of, Dr. Holiday," I retorted as we played tug of war with the holder.

"No. Please allow me. This is university business," she insisted.

"My father would turn over in his grave if he knew a woman paid for my dinner," I said, then gently guided her hand away from the receipt.

I lingered against the softness of her skin a minute longer than necessary, but I felt no resistance when my thumb stroked the top of her hand.

"This is not a date, Dr. Green. This is business and the university pays for business," she soberly pronounced, withdrawing her hand. "And my condolences for the loss of your father." Her inflection shifted, now soft, compassionate.

"Thank you. Business or not, Ezekiel Daniel Green, Sr., would still call me a punk if he saw you pulling out your credit card." I laughed, hearing my father's voice scolding me and my brother the first time we told him a girl paid for our lunch at school.

She blushed before uttering, "Well, I guess we wouldn't want to disobey Mr. Green, so it'll be our little secret," Jemma quipped.

I could think of a lot of shit that could be our little secret. Her smile brightened as I escorted her out of the restaurant. That smile, those dimples, that ass - this shit was going to be my kryptonite.

Dr. Holiday and I transitioned to the W Lounge where there was a singer and pianist. The songtress's voice was beautiful, covering R&B songs from the eighties until present day. We perched in a dark corner illuminated by only candlelight. Jemma kept looking around the club as if she was going to be caught in the act of something. I got comfortable, loosening my tie and tossing my suit jacket across the chair. She ordered another lemon drop martini as I continued to sip cognac.

It didn't take long for Jemma to get loose, relaxed. We almost had too much fun together. She felt like an old familiar friend that I was getting reacquainted with. We laughed, talked, and swayed to the music, reminiscing on our whereabouts when certain songs were sung. I wanted to ask her to dance through all of my favorite songs but I knew she would refuse. When the melodious chords of Lauryn Hill and D'Angelo 'Nothing Even Matters' rumbled through the microphone, I couldn't contain myself.

"Dr. Holiday, may I have this dance?" I stood, refusing to take no for an answer.

"Um, I don't know. We've been here an hour longer than I anticipated. I should probably go," she peered around again to see that everyone was lost in the music, not paying attention to us.

"That means you're having a good time. This is my favorite song and it's just a dance. I promise I'll be a perfect gentleman." I raised my right hand giving her my scout's honor.

Reluctantly, she nodded.

I extended my hand, then escorted her to the dance floor. My hand rested against the small of her back right above that perfectly rotund ass. Jemma maintained a safe distance with her hands resting on my shoulders. Keeping my promise, I softly clutched her waist drawing her a little closer to me. I tried my best not to inhale but dammit I did it anyway. She smelled like vanilla, roses and a hint of spice. Shit! I tightly closed my eyes, lost in her heavenly aroma. *Z! Nigga! She's married,* I reminded myself. But the way Jemma's soft hands slowly crept to my nape, clasping her fingers against my skin, didn't signify any traces of a committed relationship to me.

"This *is* a great song," she uttered, shifting her head up to look at me. Those big golden eyes and her sweet tone pleasantly disrupted my reverie.

I glared down the bridge of her nose nodding my head in agreement. "Yes, it is. Anything Lauryn Hill, Jill Scott, Erykah Badu is like… " I paused, vainly endeavoring not to count the flecks of gold in her eyes. "Their music is like the summer sun on your shoulders, family reunions in the park," I declared.

"Sunday dinner at grandma's house, a hot bath and foot rub after a long day," she chimed in.

"A long nap on a rainy day. It's like..." I paused, unable to locate the words.

"Easy, free, familiar, safe. This music restores when you feel depleted," she breathed, as her beautiful orbs unhurriedly closed.

Jemma remained in a state of contemplation for a long minute. It was clear in her guise that she relied on this type of music to mend something that had been severely broken in her. We settled into a cushy position through two more songs before she excused herself to the restroom. Although she endeavored not to be transparent, I could see right through her. The dewiness coating her pretty eyes indicated an internal battle between behaving saintly or sinning. Wicked versus righteous. The good girl in her was beefing with the bad girl. It was written all over her face.

I returned to our table and took it upon myself to order another round of drinks. I didn't want Jemma to leave but I knew that she would likely end our night once she returned. I nodded my head and smiled at a group of women seated at a table across from us who'd been ogling me all night. Shaking my head, I chuckled, glancing around the space until I spotted Jemma. She too was the benefactor of attention from various men as she ambled across the room. I didn't blame those cats, this woman was stunning with no effort. I rose to pull out her chair, but leaned in to speak before she was seated.

"Are you ok?" I whispered against her ear. She nodded, flashing me a fraudulent smile. I narrowed my eyes but decided not to badger. "Another round?" I asked, encouraging her to be seated.

"You have me out of my element, Dr. Green," she smiled brightly. This time it reached her eyes as she sipped from the martini glass.

"What is your element, Dr. Holiday?" I leaned back in my chair, continuing to regard her. She had a little patch of freckles on each cheek that went unnoticed before. Her heart-shaped lips were covered with a fresh coat of lip gloss. I snickered mutely, noticing how her nose scrunched when she was contemplating a response.

"On a Friday night? I would probably be reading a good book with a bottle of wine or talking my daughter through random college girl drama," she chuckled, thwarting the pleasantness of my musing.

"Ah, so I have the privilege of giving you a night on the town in Monroe City? Lucky me." I laughed tauntingly.

"You are a lucky man indeed," she bantered, joining my guffaw before continuing. "Speaking of Monroe City. It's very different from New York. Why the desire to transition, Dr. Green?" she probed.

"Before I answer that question, can we get off of the clock please?" I inquired, further loosening my tie and rolling up my shirt sleeves. "Can you at least call me Ezekiel? And can I call you Jemma?" I lifted a brow seeking agreement. "Deal?" I extended my balled fist.

Jemma squinted her sparkling orbs for a heartbeat before she uttered, "deal."

Fist to fist, the connection dallied for a moment too long. My manhood was slowly thumping like a dying patient's heartbeat in dire need of resuscitation. I don't know what the hell was transpiring, but Jemma was fostering shit I hadn't felt for a woman in a long time. My dick's response to her was that of a normal man. She was a beautiful, sexy woman so constantly quelling my growing member would be expected. But my damn heart; it pounded uncontrollably every time she smiled like she wanted to be the woman of my dreams.

"Thank you." I smiled, fingering the rim of my cognac glass before answering her question. "I was born and raised in New York. Brooklyn. My career endeavors have afforded me the opportunity to live in a lot of amazing places, but I'm ready for a new challenge. Monroe University has been competing to be in the top five ranked HBCUs for years and I want to be a part of the journey to get it there." I shrugged. "And honestly, I've never lived in the midwest so here's my chance... especially now that I've made a new friend."

"Oh, really. Who?" Jemma teased, searching over her shoulders playfully.

"Hopefully you, Jemma Holiday." I winked.

Jemma audibly exhaled, then sipped more of her martini.

"I should go. I'm sure my friends are waiting for me. I've completely disrupted girls' night," she mumbled, clearing her throat nervously.

"My apologies. I didn't mean to intrude on girls' night. But I must admit, I'm having a good time. Thank you." I raised my glass to her and she coupled it with mine.

"It was my pleasure and thank you." She nodded, smiling before gulping down the rest of the alcohol.

"Let me walk you out," I said, standing to my full posture.

I settled the tab and we exited the lounge headed towards the lobby. The table of women extended a harmonious "goodnight" when we walked by. Jemma and I loudly laughed. The vodka and cognac had officially taken over.

"Dr. Green," she sang. "The ladies man I see."

"Nah. They could've been bidding you goodnight. You never know these days." I joked, nipping the tip of her nose.

I was too damn cozy with this woman that I'd only known for a few hours. I was clearly begging for trouble. We leisurely ambled through the hotel, aimlessly continuing our conversation about nothing and everything. Engaging with Jemma was easy, uncomplicated, but I had to let her go.

"Is your car in valet?" I asked.

"No. Um, we - my friends and I have a suite in the hotel."

"Oh. Y'all were having a serious girls' night. What floor? Let me walk you to your room," I requested, knowing she would decline.

"No, Ezekiel. That won't be necessary. I think I can find my way."

I grinned a little hearing something other than *Dr. Green* rolled off of her tongue for the first time. She outstretched her hand for a shake.

"Again, it was a pleasure meeting you, Dr. Ezekiel Green."

I shook my head and stared at her white painted nails with a furrowed brow scowl. Did she really think we were ending this night with a damn handshake? Extending my arms, I cradled her in a firm, yet respectful hug. She momentarily hesitated, but then rested her hands against my back. I was gluttonous - a greedy ass nigga, stealing every opportunity to inhale, shit, digest her for a moment longer.

"You are an experience, Dr. Jemma Holiday. Thank you for allowing me to partake," I whispered in her ear through an anxious snicker, reluctant to relinquish her as my hand remained resting on her forearm.

"It has been an experience indeed. It was great chatting with you as well. Good luck with everything," she voiced with a slight tremble.

Jemma nibbled that damn lip again and nervously tugged at her cheek while goosebumps invaded velvety smooth skin. The apparent attraction was mutual. I wanted to whisper in her ear, *I know your pussy is wet. Let me take care of that for you,* because my growing erection was about to disturb all of her peace and happiness.

I was confident that this would be the last time I would lay eyes on this woman since I was not going to be offered the job. My thinking was messed up, but I wanted her for just a little bit longer. I was already at no, so I said fuck it...

"If you desire to continue our chat at any time tonight, I'm in suite 2021." I slid my room key into the outside pocket of her dress, then leaned in and whispered, "Don't think. Don't hesitate. Just come."

3

JEMMA

D r. Green and I stood at the elevator waiting for it to arrive in the lobby. At the sound of the ding, we entered the car followed by a few additional hotel guests. I anxiously stood at one corner while he calmly settled in the other. An older gentleman eyed us both and said, "what floor for the beautiful pair?"

"Um, fifteen for me, please," I quickly blurted.

Dr. Green snickered before announcing, "twenty please. Thank you."

The gentleman smirked then shrugged as he pressed both numbers.

Ezekiel feigned busy on his phone, while he occasionally stole glimpses of me in the mirror. A blush painted my face because I had my own peep show going on too. When he lifted his head, I tried my best to avert my stare but I couldn't. Something in me needed to absorb a little bit more of his chocolate skin, gaze at the tip of the tattoo that peaked above the opening of his shirt, his beard with a speckle of gray and that damn bald head. Shit!

The unhurried ascend of the elevator allowed me to preserve our few hours of memories. Why did I want to apprehend him? Store him away in a time capsule for safe keeping, then gain access when my circumstances are different. I would happily make his acquaintance in another lifetime.

The older gentleman's tired eyes darted between me and Dr. Green's reflection in the mirror as he gawked at our apparent chemistry. I lowered my head to my phone and it suddenly dawned on me that Quinton hadn't responded to the call or text that I sent him earlier when I was in the lounge's restroom. The elevator chimed at the fifteenth floor.

"Ma'am. Fifteen?" the older gentleman questioned.

I slowly nodded. I lifted my head capturing Ezekiel's glare in the mirror one last time. Melancholy flooded my face as I delivered a woeful smile, muttering, "have a good night," never parting from our gaze.

"The night is young, Dr. Holiday. Enjoy," Dr. Green sexily expressed.

Exiting the elevator, I decided it was best if I didn't look back. The doors closed and he was gone. Unmuting the ringer on my phone, it chimed with multiple text notifications. Quaran and Maxi had replied to my text from earlier informing them that I was having a drink in the lounge with Dr. Green.

> Maxi: Yeeesss bitch. Have fun.
>
> Roni: Ok, sis! Have fun, boo.
>
> Roni: And you're not doing anything wrong, Jemma.
>
> Roni: Does that nigga have some brothers, friends?
>
> Maxi: Shit, an uncle, cousin? LOL
>
> Roni: Just checking in sis. You good?
>
> Maxi: Ok linesister! It's almost midnight. Gone get that good dick from the good doctor.
>
> Roni: Yes please. You need something new up in them walls.
>
> Roni: Ok, that was wrong. I should really have my brother's back but....
>
> Maxi: Fuck his punk ass. Do you bitch!

I boisterously laughed at their antics as I swiped the key to enter our suite. Quaron was perched in the lounge chair while Maxi was stretched out on the couch. The room service tray sat at the front door entrance with only remnants of fudge brownies, ice cream and pizza.

"Well, well, well. You look the same unfortunately. Hair and clothes are intact so I guess you didn't have the one night stand of our dreams," Maxi said, disappointment lacing her tone.

"And you look sober. So you didn't fuck, huh?" Roni asked. Her scowl was also filled with disappointment.

"What am I? Eighteen, with no responsibilities? No, my clothes are not disheveled. No, I am not drunk. And *no*, I did not sleep with that man." I rolled my eyes as I walked over to Maxi motioning for her to unzip my dress.

"I mean, I'm just saying. *I* definitely would've fucked," Roni mumbled, sticking her tongue out before sipping her dark liquor.

"Well, that's not how I roll. Sorry, sis," I bantered, then shuddered from the familiar tune blaring from my phone. *Quinton.* I huffed, rolling my eyes.

"Hello?" I answered, unable to minimize my angst.

"What's up, J. I can't talk for long. I saw that you called. We made it," Quinton blurted, his background too loud for me to fully understand him.

"I would hope so, Quinton, it's almost midnight. You couldn't call me earlier? I had to call our daughter to figure out where you were."

"I know. My bad. I figured y'all were on your third bottle of something by now," he laughed trying to lighten my mood but the shit wasn't funny.

"Excuses, Quinton. But continue to do you... as usual."

"Jemma, don't be like that, ok, Sweetie. Have fun tonight. Tell the girls I said what's up and send us some good luck for tomorrow." He paused, then I heard his assistant, Jamar's bass-filled voice, "Q, you ready to roll to the spot?"

"I gotta go, J. Goodnight." Quinton hung up.

My head jolted back, neck rolled as I stared at the phone. Wow! No, I love you, I miss you, nothing. But why the fuck was I surprised?

"What did he say?" Maxi irritably questioned. "Clearly some bullshit as usual because you walked in here floating on cloud nine then one phone call from his ass and your demeanor goes to shit."

Quaron just shook her head. She was always caught in the middle of me and Quinton's foolishness. I hated that she felt like she had to choose sides.

"Dammit, Quinton," she testily whispered. "I want my dumbass brother to win but he's an asshole."

"Yep," I agreed. "And he's with the other asshole." I smirked, brow furrowed as I turned in Quaron's direction.

"Jamar?" Quaron questioned, coughing as she almost choked on the french fry she was devouring.

I nodded. She shook her head.

Quaron and Jamar were hot and heavy though our college years and into graduate school until he rekindled a romance with his high school sweetheart during his ten year class reunion. Roni was heartbroken. He married and eventually cheated on and now divorced the woman. *Maybe I should call Veronica to see how her new man is treating her post divorce.* I thought, snickering at my internal musings.

"Two birds of a fucking feather." Quaron's throaty snarl snapped me back to the present. We simultaneously shook our heads as she unflinchingly gulped the cognac.

I finally stepped out of my dress and tossed it across the room onto the other lounge chair. The room key that Ezekiel gave me flew into the air, somewhat in drama-filled slow motion. It lingered for far too long, landing on the carpet in the middle of the three of us. I froze because I knew all eyes were on me. When I glanced at my friends, they were gawking at the thing like it was a pregnancy test.

"What is that, Jemma?" Maxi asked, pointing her black painted nail to the floor, smiling from ear to ear.

"And before you lie, please remember that you put the key to *this* room on the table over there." Roni lifted her brows and motioned to the white key card resting on the narrow sofa table.

"Ummm…" I squealed. "It's Ezekiel's. I mean, Dr. Green's." I clenched my teeth as I dramatically plopped on the couch.

"And?" Roni probed.

"And… he invited me to his room to continue our conversation," I said, nervously nibbling my white-tipped fingernail.

"Jemma!" Maxi and Roni shouted in unison.

"Bitch, go." Maxi pointed to the door.

I shook my head and mouthed, '*no, no, no.*" "I can't do that, y'all." I quickly walked into the bathroom to wash my face and brush my teeth. They swiftly followed me.

"Ok, aside from the whole husband thing… why not?" Maxi sarcastically probed.

"I mean… there's that. Duh!" I said, with a mouth full of toothpaste. "And I've only known that man for what… five hours?" I spit, leering at their reflections in the mirror. "He could be a rapist, a murderer, a pedophile," I deliriously ranted, aggressively spreading Oil of Olay cleanser on my face.

"Pedophile? Bitch, you're forty." Roni snarkily reminded me. I scowled, offering her my middle finger. "Real talk, Jemma, and be honest with us. Did you enjoy your time with Ezekiel?" she questioned.

I nodded, leaning against the bathroom counter in nothing but a bra and panties.

"Did you want the night to end?" Maxi probed.

I shook my head. Swiping the drying towel down my face, I softly whimpered, "No."

* * *

Two hours later, I was perched on the floor with my back against the couch eyeing three empty wine bottles, a mutilated cheesecake, Rose Nyland in the background telling another St. Olaf story and my two best friends passed out. About an hour into our girls' night, they'd introduced edibles to the party so they were fucked up. I declined.

My sober musings battled between destruction and desire. Destroyed images of Quinton doing only God knows what with only God knows who briefly had me on the brink of ruin. While Ezekiel's soothing anthracite orbs had me yearning, craving to be graced with his baritone voice one more time like an old, familiar friend.

I twirled the thin hotel room key card in my fingertips. Unconsciously circling it over and over again, I contemplated every rational and irrational reason to stay my ass in my room, or take a stroll on the wild side with the doctor. Good and evil were sparring in a knock down drag out brawl.

You're a good girl, Jemma?

Be bad now and ask for forgiveness later.
You look a mess… stay your ass put!
But did you see how smooth that man's bald head was?
You're somebody's wife.
But where is Quinton's ass right now, huh?

I irrationally debated for too damn long. I shook my head, hoping the motion would shake the demon from my psyche.

"You're in your head, Jemma Jule," I whispered, sticking the key card to my forehead like an idiot.

I laughed at my antics then momentarily pondered Ezekiel's words earlier, that made me smile. *"You're an experience, Jemma."* What did that mean? Was it a compliment? I wanted to probe further but our night had to end.

"Don't think. Don't hesitate. Just come," whispered in my subconscious. I shuddered, momentarily looking around the room to locate the voice that was clearly in my head. Ezekiel Green was driving me crazy and I knew nothing beyond the fact that he was fine. And funny, and smart, and kind, and…

"Fuck it!" I breathily uttered.

Quietly standing to my feet, I slipped on my Gucci slides and crept across the room to grab my phone and room key. For two seconds I thought about changing clothes but that action would just give me more time to change my mind. I hurriedly ambled down the hallway before I lost my nerve. One elevator bay stood already ajar as if the devil himself was summoning me to partake in ho-like behavior.

Catching my reflection in the mirror, I was horrified by my appearance - fresh-faced, no earrings, with my braids pulled into a messy bun and dressed in black biker shorts, a white t-shirt with *'Unapologetically Dope since 1913'* inscribed in red. *Maybe I should've changed clothes,* I thought.

"Ho much, Jemma?" I sneeringly asked myself facing the mirror while I quickly typed a text to Maxine and Quaron. ***Ok bitches. I'm going in!***

Shaking my head while rolling my eyes because I was getting on my own nerves, I pressed number twenty but the button didn't illuminate. I glanced at the gold-plate above the panel informing me that the elevator required a key to access other guest floors. *Ugh, I'm so stupid. What if the key doesn't work?* I deliriously deliberated swiping the key across the gold plate. Instantly, the number twenty brightened, staring at me as I glared back at it not even realizing the elevator was moving.

Ding! I quaked from the sound then deeply exhaled tip-toeing off of the elevator. The devil was truly busy because as soon as I made a left down the hallway, suite 2021 practically slapped me in my face. I halted for a second because I didn't fully think this through. It's late and here I was breaking into this man's hotel room at almost two o'clock in the morning. I didn't have his phone number to inform him of my late night creep. What if he's asleep? What if he changed his mind? What if he decides to file sexual harassment charges once he finds out he's not getting the job. I'd officially lost it.

I silenced my phone before swiping the key. The unlock sound and green light flashing meant that there was no turning back. Gingerly stepping into the suite that matched mine, Ezekiel's imposing body was sprawled out on the couch across the room.

The loveseat appeared miniature compared to his Herculean frame. Dressed in gray fleece Nike shorts, a plain white tank with one leg draped across the cushion and his arm resting behind his head, the other arm was holding a brown tattered book. Dark rimmed glasses settled on his broad nose enhancing his sexiness. The television was silent and offered the only visibility in the space. At the sound of the door opening, he peered up then leisurely rested the book against his chest as if he was awaiting my arrival.

The thunderous click of the heavy door closed behind me but didn't disrupt our focus on each other. My lungs plummeted into my stomach, my ass, then my toes. I could not speak. We idled in muted recklessness for what resembled eons, but mere minutes ticked by.

"Hi," he sexily uttered.

"Hi," I tensely croaked. I swallowed hard, praying my lungs would reappear. "I don't know what I'm doing," I whispered, lowering my eyes to watch my fingers fondle the key card.

"But yet here you are," Ezekiel throatily murmured, his gaze continuing to penetrate me. His smile was mellow and provocative; slowly diminishing my apprehension.

"Come," he requested, patting his hand against the loveseat cushion. He reached behind him flipping on the floor lamp to guide my path.

I obliged, desiring to run across the room but opted to casually narrow our distance instead. Perching on the edge of the couch, I laid his key on the table in front of me before glancing around the room. Another pair of Nike shorts and a matching t-shirt were draped across the chair with colorful Air Max's positioned beside it.

I slightly giggled at the thought of him laying his clothes out as if preparing for the first day of school. I directed my gaze to him, taking a gander at the intricacies of the arm tattoo that enticed me earlier. The mirage paying homage to New York was beautiful. *He* was beautiful. I had to immediately look away before I reached out and touched it... touched *him*, opting to eye the book still resting on his chest instead.

"The Fire Next Time by James Baldwin," I said, lifting a curious brow. "That's pretty heavy reading for a Friday night."

Ezekiel laughed, bending his muscular leg to sit upright. He stood, but didn't respond, closing the book then taking a few steps to secure it in his black Louis Vuitton backpack before walking towards the mini bar.

He motioned to the refrigerator, questioning, "would you like a drink?"

I shook my head.

"Those mini bar prices are ridiculous. And don't let the pretty display fool you. If you pick up the water bottle for more than thirty seconds they will charge you fifteen dollars." I jokingly warned.

"Well, this one *is* on the university's dime. Business... remember?" He winked.

Ezekiel retrieved a small bottle of Knob Creek and poured it over a few cubes of ice. His swag was so damn intriguing. It wasn't arrogance, just pure confidence. The bold bow-legged sway of his saunter was clearly making room for the length that was responsible for the impressive imprint against his shorts.

Don't inhale. Don't inhale. Don't inhale. I appealed to myself but my dumbass took a deep whiff of him anyway. Dial soap and Creed cologne infiltrated my senses and soaked my damn pussy.

"I co-teach a summer intensive critical race theory class at NYU." He motioned his head to his backpack referring to the book. "My lecture is tomorrow night so I was just making note of a few things."

"Huh?" I shuddered, his baritone disrupting my cologne-induced daze as his words registered.

"Oh. Ezekiel, I'm so sorry. I didn't mean to disturb your work. I shouldn't have come. I'll go." I quickly rose feeling like a foolish woman but was pulled back down to the couch just as briskly.

"No. Please stay," his tone was low, firm... pleading. He maintained a gentle hold on my wrist as his hypnotic gaze traveled down my body until I was seated. Those imposing hands held magic potions, casting a spell on me.

I audibly huffed, "what am I doing here, Dr. Green?"

"Continuing a perfect night, Dr. Holiday. Something that is or is not happening in your world brought you here," he conferred. A lustful smile dressed his face. "You're not doing anything wrong, Jemma," he confidently declared.

Why did everyone keep saying that when everything about this was so wrong but felt so damn right... and daring and uncharacteristic. I was pretty and perfect Jemma who had already bankrupted her allotment of mistakes years ago when I got pregnant. So irresponsible behavior was not acceptable, but nothing about this, whatever the hell it was, felt rash. Even after only hours in his presence.

Ezekiel glided the back of his hand down the side of my face then cupped my chin. "You did good, Jemma. You didn't think or hesitate. You followed your instinct."

His eyes. That gaze. His caress. That dick. Shit! I was convinced he was performing voodoo.

"I - I've never had a one night stand," I blurted like an airhead but my assertion was earnest.

"Neither have I." He nibbled at his plump bottom lip with those gleaming white teeth. "It sounds to me like Dr. Holiday thinks I'm a fuckboy in these streets or something." Ezekiel kissed the back of my hand as we boisterously guffawed and my momentary apprehension completely faded.

"Seriously, Jemma, I don't know why but I just enjoy you and I didn't want the shit to end. Good, bad or indifferent, it is what it is. And you being here tells me you've enjoyed me too." He lifted my chin again to focus on him, raising a brow seeking confirmation.

I nodded, sliding my teeth across my bottom lip. I had to do something with my damn lips before I kissed up the length of the curvy statue of liberty tattoo dressing his muscular arm.

"Let's just chill. I have an early flight and I would be honored if I could spend my last few hours in Monroe City with you." He shot me a closed mouth smile then winked. *Fucking sorcery,* I thought.

After ordering room service and popping a few miniature bottles of wine, Ezekiel encouraged me to get comfortable as he removed my slides and propped my feet up on the couch. His long hard limbs entangled with my thick soft ones as he rested against one end of the couch and I lounged at the other.

We were cozily crowded; enjoying each other's company and completely disregarding our reality outside of this suite. Why was I so carefree with this man? I probably should've been disturbed by how he absentmindedly stroked his fingertips up and down my leg. Better yet, I should have been concerned by how much I enjoyed it when he fingered the seam of my shorts drawing circles around the scar on my knee as he played twenty-one questions.

"What's your favorite ice cream?"

"Salted caramel," I said without hesitation.

"Which one is the best... Friday, Next Friday or Friday After Next?"

"Friday," I blurted like I had to beat the buzzer.

Ezekiel's brow furrowed. "Why?"

"The original is always the best." I shrugged.

"What's your favorite book?"

"The Bluest Eye by Toni Morrison." I excitedly said, really getting into this game.

"What book are you reading now?"

"Black by Joan Vassar." This time his brow creased in unfamiliarity. "Oh, you would love it. Trust me." I sternly proclaimed and he nodded.

"Who's your favorite poet?"

"Nikki Giovanni." For whatever reason he smiled at that answer but I decided not to probe.

Ezekiel actually asked me twenty-one questions and I readily answered them. I loudly chuckled when he gestured a drum roll with his fingers on my knee before asking the last question. That innocent action transmitted goosebumps up my leg; the sensation trailing its way to something else he could beat on between my thighs.

"And your favorite song is?"

"E-Money. The queen of neo-soul, Ms. Erykah Badu." I giddily pronounced, doing a slow body roll for emphasis.

"Not your favorite artist, goofy, your favorite song," he chuckled.

"Anything Erykah Badu is my favorite song, but if I had to choose..." I paused, pursing my lips while tapping my fingertip against my chin. "Next Lifetime," I uttered much more breathily than intended.

Our orbs frolicked in an inquisitive glare, synchronously processing the lyrics, but elected not to breathe life into the unspoken sentiments.

The tenderhearted queries volleyed between us all night. No subject was off limits - race, music, social justice issues, literary geniuses, you name it. Ezekiel's aimless strokes against my flesh became faint as I fought the heaviness of my eyelids. Everytime I endeavored to leave, he'd foster another conversation about everything and nothing, preventing my departure. I didn't want to fall asleep here. I *could not* fall asleep in this man's hotel suite.

6:07am I fucking fell asleep in Ezekiel's room. *Shit!* My last memory was glancing at the clock around four thirty in the morning, begging my body to stay awake. Covered in a blanket and a pillow propped behind my head, I observed my surroundings but something... someone was missing. The weightiness of his massive structure against my body was no more. The dark chocolate-hued God was gone.

Sitting up on the couch, I glanced at the chair that previously held his clothes. His backpack and suitcase were gone creating a hollow in the space. I audibly stretched, checking my phone for a message from him but quickly realized that he didn't have my number. Shiloh messaged me, but Quinton's name was nonexistent in my new call log. I shook my head, reading through the early morning messages from Maxine and Quaron.

> Maxi: Yeess bitch. I just woke up and you're not here. You betta, sis!

> Roni: OMG! Who are you? I like this fuck a nigga Friday Jemma. LOL

> Maxi: Are you done with that man? Is he feeding you this morning?

> Roni: Yep. That dick.

> Maxi. Well, hurry up and get your fill because a bitch is hungry. We're going to breakfast at 9.

I giggled, then loudly, dramatically exhaled, slapping my hands against my thighs motivating my limbs to get moving. My eyes perused the space one more time as if Ezekiel was going to hop out of the closet yelling surprise. I shook my head as my eyes connected with an object laying on the table. It was another book that almost appeared antique with a dark brown and gold cover. A piece of paper with 'For Jemma' scribbled on it peeked from the top seemingly acting as a bookmark.

"The Collected Poetry of Nikki Giovanni," I read aloud, swiping my finger across the foiled print. My eyes widened. How? Why? Where did this come from? Opening to the marked page, my lips curved into a small smile as I read the note.

Dr. Holiday, my apologies for sneaking out but I had a 7am flight. You were sleeping so soundly I didn't want to disturb you. Jemma, it has been a pleasure. If you never grace my presence again, please know that you have made a lasting impression. Maybe we'll meet again like butterflies in another lifetime. Keep shining, beautiful.

P.S. Nikki Giovanni is my favorite too. As well as Rocky Road ice cream, Next Friday, and Eric Roberson... I'm torn between two songs... Dealing and Borrow You.

Be good, Dr. Holiday.

- Zeke

I giggled, making a mental note to check the lyrics of both songs before I directed my attention to the book. The poem on the bookmarked page couldn't be a coincidence. It expressed the sentiments of a woman who had been stifled by a man. A woman that was made to believe that her growth, self-worth and identity were rooted in the perception of a man until she decides that it is not.

Could he see? Could he discern my malaise, feel my ambivalence? Was the downheartedness that apparent? Tears welled, clouding my vision as I blinked, permitting them to fall, absorbing the literary magnificence of Nikki Giovanni's 'Woman'.

"She tried to be a book, but he wouldn't read. She turned herself into a bulb, but he wouldn't let her grow. She decided to become a woman and though he still refused to be a man. She decided it was all right."

My teardrops stained the pages, leaving traces of a much needed cleansing release. In just one night, Ezekiel saw me - my good, my bad, hurt and distress. A perfect stranger validated my needs, recognized me for who I was; and even if for just a night, he adored it anyway.

Unexpectedly, I chortled through my tears catching a peep of myself in the full-length mirror. The gleam painting my face could not be denied. It was brilliant and joyous and carefree as I basked in the memory of the best one night stand ever.

4

ZEKE

"*C*an *I borrow you? Maybe he wouldn't mind. Just for a song or two, we can act like you're mine.*" The melodies of Eric Roberson blasted through the speakers in my home office. I ambled across the walnut hardwood floors to place a book on one of the floor to ceiling wooden bookcases matching the color of the floors. I'd been preparing the final lecture for the summer intensive course I was teaching.

Humming the neo-soul tune, I glided a finger across the spine of a James Baldwin book, thinking about *her*. It had been a few weeks since I'd returned from Monroe City and I could not get Jemma Holiday off of my mind. Visions of her honey orbs, dimpled crooked smile and beautiful face resided behind my closed lids daily. Shit, images of her curved bodacious body pirouetting across my mind rocked me to sleep almost nightly. Jemma was a goddamn wonder… and a fucking problem.

Visibly shuddering to shake her from my psyche, I sauntered to my desk to resume my work. Even if I didn't get the job at Monroe University, I was leaving my role at NYU and had some other opportunities in the works. I hadn't received any notification from the university about the status of the job yet.

I was certain that I wasn't going to be offered the role; however I did expect that the university President *or Jemma* would contact me directly since I hadn't received a snail mail rejection letter. Sifting through over two hundred emails, I had a few LinkedIn notifications that I typically ignored, but this time, two automated email notices caught my attention.

Hi, Dr. Ezekiel Green, Dr. Jemma Warren Holiday would like to join your network.

Dr. Jemma Warren Holiday has sent you a message.

Leaning back in my office chair, I settled my hands behind my head, criss-crossing my fingers at the nape. I rocked back and forth, gawking at the messages on the screen as if they were going to jump off the page and slap some sense into me. Why the hell didn't I just accept her request and open the message. *She's probably thanking me for my time during the interview. Maybe this is my rejection notice.* I dwelled, blankly staring at my ultra-wide dual monitor.

"Zeke. Aye, Lil. Where are you at, man?" My brother's dramatically clamorous tone blared throughout my brownstone. I shook my head as I reached for the remote control to lower the music volume.

"Why are you yelling? I'm in the office," I instructed, not disjoining from my previous musing.

I could hear the heavy footsteps of my brother, Ezra, coming down the hall. I was bracing myself for his thunderous roar. This nigga was always loud and often wrong in his approach.

"Damn, Lil. I've been calling your ass. What've you been doing in here?" His irritation was apparent but I was confused as to why.

"What do you want, Big? I'm working, man. What's the emergency?" I scowled right back at his ass.

My older brother was a pain in my ass and my best friend at the same time. We were exactly two years apart, ironically born on the same day, different years. As kids, our mother often dressed us alike and people thought we were twins. To this day, we were still called *twins* by some in our old neighborhood. Once we got in middle school, Ezra was annoyed with the twin reference and started calling me *Lil* to clearly identify me as his little brother. I, in turn, called him *Big* because he was my big brother but also because that nigga was huge.

We both stood at six feet, four inches; however where I was slender with defined arm and leg muscles, Ezra was husky with massive muscular mass. That dude stayed in the gym. I preferred a bald head, whereas he rocked short dreadlocks with tapered sides leading to a beard that garnered less gray hair than mine, although I was the youngest.

"It's not my emergency, it's your mother's emergency," he said, tossing his head back in frustration.

"I told *your* mother that I would bring her the cashew brittle when my schedule was clear," I explained.

"Well I guess your ass wasn't moving fast enough for Vesta Livingston Green," Ezra quipped as we collectively chuckled.

Our mother, Vesta, was a seventy year old retired high school principal who wanted what she wanted when she wanted it. I spotted some of her favorite candy at the See's Candies store in the airport in St. Louis and since then she'd been worrying me to death about bringing that damn cashew brittle to her house. So now she was sending my brother after me.

"She doesn't need that shit anyway," I chortled.

"But her baby boy bought it for her anyway," Ezra teased. "What are you working on, Dr. Green?" he asked, meandering around my desk. I abruptly sat up, vainly attempted to clear the LinkedIn notification from my screen but it was too late.

"Nah, nah, nigga. I see what you're doing. Are you stalking that woman, Lil? That *married woman*," Ezra emphasized.

"Man, get the fuck outta here. No, I am not stalking her. She sent me a LinkedIn message," I boasted.

"Then what's the problem? You can't get in too much trouble on LinkedIn." He lifted his brows in question.

I settled in an extended pause contemplating what exactly *was* the problem.

"This is how it starts, Big. First a professional connection on social media, then next thing you know I'm hopping in her DMs trying to fly her pretty ass to Brooklyn for black truffle pizza," I practically whined, rubbing a hand down my beard.

Ezra gave me a blank stare because he knew I didn't share my favorite food with just anybody. Wordless, he reached over my shoulder to click the message button on the touchscreen monitor. An icon of Jemma's picture popped on the screen. I'd only seen her with braids so to see the picture with her natural hair kissing her shoulders was gorgeous.

Dark brown wavy tresses with reddish-blonde accents framed her face adorned with tortoise wide-framed glasses and blazing red lipstick. Her arms were crossed over her chest dressed in a red blazer with a black shirt underneath. Simple diamond studs in her ears with a matching diamond necklace snuggled her neck. Damn, this woman was fine.

"Damn, she's fine. At least from the titties up anyway," Ezra nonchalantly stated. I glared at him like he was an idiot.

"Man, shut up." I shook my head, unable to focus on her message. "She *is* fine though… *everywhere*. And thick." I sing-songed for extra emphasis.

I'd told my brother everything about Jemma. Even how I hovered over her sleeping body in my hotel suite, beholding her beauty for so long I almost missed my damn flight. I had to capture every curve of her face, the slope of her nose, and those silky pouty lips because I truly didn't believe I would ever see her again. My dumb ass even mentioned to him how I wrote her a note that I left with the Nikki Giovanni book. It was sheer coincidence that I had a book of poems by *our* favorite poet with me on that trip.

"What does the message say?" Ezra was asking but he could see the message over my shoulder.

> Hello Dr. Green. It was a pleasure to meet you. I was very impressed with your background and have shared my input with the hiring committee. They are reviewing the final applicants and will be making a decision in the coming weeks. Good luck with your future endeavors. Dr. Jemma Holiday

There was a separate message sent just minutes after the first.

> P.S. Next Friday as your favorite… hmm, that's debatable. Never tried Rocky Road ice cream and your Eric Roberson selections… #messy. LOL Nikki Giovanni is GOAT… glad to see we have something in common. Thank you for the book. It's magnificent. I hope I'll have the opportunity to return the gesture. Be good, Dr. Green.~ Jemma

My entire face lit up and I didn't give a fuck as my fingertips eagerly danced across the keyboard to reply.

"Make sure your greeting includes Mrs. in the salutation since she's

Mrs. Holiday," my brother said, then rounded my desk dropping into the seat across from me. "She's beautiful, Lil, and I know y'all had a moment but..." Ezra's gruff tone trailed off, expression serious. My brother bull-shitted about a lot of things, except his baby brother. "Just be careful. I know you, Zeke."

"What do you know, Ez?" I pushed back from the keyboard, cocking my head to the side with narrowed eyes.

"There's no gray area with you. It's all black and white. You either feeling a woman physically to fuck, or you feeling her mentally... and fucking her is optional. The fact that you had this fine, smart, bootylicious ass woman in your hotel room in the middle of the night and y'all just *talked*. That's mental shit for you, bro." He said, shaking his head. "Yo' *Ralph Tresvant man with sensitivity ass* will be in love."

I flashed my middle finger as we howled in laughter.

Later that evening, my brother and I walked to a neighborhood bar where we met my cousin, Myron, to grab some drinks and wings. After several hours, multiple beers and the willpower not to take this big-booty red-bone waitress home with me to do exactly what my brother said was my M.O., I strolled back into my brownstone at close to eleven o'clock. I showered and collapsed in bed with a book and my iPad.

I tried reading, journaling, *shit,* my ass even played Words with Friends with some random people online but I couldn't keep my mind off of her LinkedIn. I accepted her connection invitation but didn't respond to the message. I wanted to respond. I needed to respond, even if it was just to say hello and thank you.

I blankly stared at a painting on my wall while my head rested on the headboard with one leg hanging off of the mattress. Jemma Holiday had me shook. Deciding to navigate away from LinkedIn and peruse my other social media pages, recommendations for who I should follow popped in my Instagram notifications. Among the list of miniature icons was a slightly familiar face with the name *JulesPen*. The image was a caricature of an image, so I squinted to ensure it was actually *her.* And it was. And she was stunning. *Jemma fucking Holiday.*

I clicked the page first to determine if the access was open or would I have to request to follow her. *This is some old eighth grade type of shit,* I mused, chuckling. I breathed a sigh of relief when the page had open access. Jemma Holiday was author, JulesPen. I had completely forgotten that she was a writer and lover of words. During my interview research I found that she was a published author of three best selling motivational books and often spoke at various women's events.

But *JulesPen* had a very different persona than the woman I met a few weeks ago. There was a blend of daily affirmations mixed with sensual inferences about self-love, body positivity and sexuality. Watermarked images of beautiful black womens' bodies with words layered on top like *Note to Self... You are Enough and Perfectly Imperfect.*

But one image in particular, her post from yesterday, caught my eye. A striking grayscale portrait of a woman practically naked, the only hint of color was a red silk scarf cloaking her breast and buttocks. The canvas was a portrait of *her* with the words of Nikki Giovanni's poem *Woman* layered on top. It was stunning... *she* was breathtaking. Thick thighs, curved hips, that damn arch in her back and the seductive way she touched her lips... shit, my dick pitched a damn tent in my boxers. I reluctantly snatched my eyes away from the picture to read the caption below.

Even beautiful strangers from another lifetime can remind you of your worth.

"Fuck! Goddamn, Jemma," I growled, clicking the follow button on Instagram and then responded to her LinkedIn message.

* * *

"Common and Tiffany Haddish over Serena? Blasphemy." I audibly chuckled reading Jemma's message as I quickly typed a response.

@InQUisitivE1: 100%! Common and Tiffany seemed easy. Uncomplicated.

@JulesPen: Common is GOAT and Serena is GOAT respectively. They would make a lyrical athletic genius. Little Common Williams. LOL

@InQUisitivE1: Common Williams?

@JulesPen: Yes. Serena is so boss she would demand that he take her last name.

@InQUisitivE1: Damn! LOL. Don't do Common Sense like that.

@InQUisitivE1: What about Angela Rye? No GOAT babies for them?

@JulesPen: Angela Rye? Boooo! No thank you and goodnight, sir.

I slapped a hand across my face, baying in laughter. Jemma and I had been going at it like this in our Instagram DMs for about a week now since I responded to her LinkedIn message and followed her on IG. She followed back immediately and liked a few of my pictures but didn't send a message. After a few days, I said fuck it and messaged her a picture of a mural painted on the side of the black-owned bookstore in my neighborhood that included Nikki Giovanni and other black literary greats. That one post opened the floodgates to almost daily communication.

Those goddamn dancing dots were going to kill me anticipating her next words. How the hell was I sprung on a woman I'd only met one time. A fucking married woman. Of course I was physically attracted, that fat ass alone was enough to make a nigga weak. But her beautiful mind captivated me. Intelligent, savvy and she kept me laughing with her sarcastically humorous wit. On some days we'd spend hours discussing music, politics, college experiences, to her trying to convince me to watch Bridgerton on Netflix. I was falling deeper and deeper into the unknown abyss with this woman and I hadn't heard her voice or seen her face in weeks aside from periodic pictures she'd post.

The casualness and fluency of our ability to communicate was easy. She was quiet in the midst of storms. A peace that I couldn't explain or comprehend. I feasted on her every word; a damn glutton for her literary prowess. She even extended me the trusted privilege of reading the first few chapters of her new book claiming she needed a man's perspective. Glancing at the clock, I finally realized it was after ten o'clock for me, so a little after nine for her.

@InQUisitivE1: LOL. You are wild. Sweet dreams and goodnight, Jemma.

I panted, breathing strained as I pushed through the last mile of my morning run. Crossing the imaginary finish line, I hunched over, placing my hands on my knees. Rapid inhales and exhales slowly began to calm as I stood to my full height, hands now rested on my waist watching my friend, Stella, round the track.

Stella Nolan was a tall, slim-thick woman that I'd met about five years ago through a Black entrepreneurs group in New York City. She was just an inch or two shorter than me with dark chocolate skin that reminded me of Lisa Leslie. A one night stand after a business event developed into a friends with benefits type of situation. At the time, we were both recently divorced and only interested in casual sex with no strings.

Last night, I had a craving for black truffle pizza from one of my favorite restaurants in the city and she had tickets to an off-Broadway show. Nights with Stella were guaranteed to end with my manhood knee deep in her pussy but last night that was the farthest thing on my mind.

I checked my phone navigating to Instagram to see if Jemma responded to my message. I sent her a picture of my black truffle pizza last night which was not uncommon. We'd swap food pics in the midst of our other stimulating conversations. But she hadn't responded which was uncommon. I shook my head because my ass had it bad. I couldn't help but wonder what she was doing that prevented her from answering my message. Yes, Jemma was married but the frequency of our correspondence was not that of a married woman. We talked morning, noon and night some days. Typically, the little dots would start bouncing before I could exit the direct message screen, but not today.

"You're moving slow today, Ms. Nolan." I peered up from my phone, teasing Stella as she finished her final lap. She tossed a dismissive hand my way while crouched to sit on the track with her long legs stretched in front of her.

"Whatever. I haven't run in two weeks," she panted.

"Excuses, excuses. Come on, I need to go if we're going to get coffee."

Extending my hands towards her, I helped her from the pavement. We walked less than a mile to the coffee shop and sat at a small bistro table outside. Stella didn't waste any time telling me about a woman she'd met at a conference a couple weeks ago and how she already wanted to visit her.

While some would consider this conversation awkward given that she begged me to let her swallow my dick just hours earlier, Stella was a woman who liked who and what she liked. And she liked sex... gender didn't matter. In her words, gender was a social construct. I can't say that I agreed but who was I to judge when Stella had no limits and gave zero fucks in the bedroom; often inviting a *friend* to join us.

I hadn't whispered a word to her about Jemma which was out of the ordinary. Women that crossed my mind only for a moment were fair game for our morning discussions, but Dr. Holiday was completely off limits.

A couple nights ago, I didn't fall asleep until well after two in the morning because I'd gone down a rabbit hole burrowing myself into Jemma's IG page. I read affirmation after affirmation, poem after poem, consumed, *shit,* obsessed with all things *her.* After spending time with the fascinating woman in my hotel suite, scouring her page and reading her books, in my opinion, *JulesPen* was the true authentic Jemma. Not the robotic, sometimes lifeless Dr. Jemma Holiday. She was perfectly imperfect and beautifully broken and this persona lived on the pages of her written commentary.

"Zeke. Darling. Your phone is ringing." Stella's raspy tenor woke me from my daze.

573 area code… that's Monroe City.

"Dr. Ezekiel Green speaking," I answered.

"Dr. Green. This is Dr. Dominic Whittaker, President of Monroe University."

"Yes, Dr. Whittaker, how are you sir?" I questioned, glaring at Stella with bright eyes.

"Is this a good time?" he asked.

"Yes, sir. I'm getting a cup of coffee after a morning run but this is a great time."

"Dr. Green, the committee was quite impressed with your candidacy and we would like to offer you the opportunity to take Monroe University to the next level by becoming the number one choice for historically Black colleges and universities in the country as our new Provost."

I stilled in my chair. I was undoubtedly in shock. Excited and… shocked. Did he really just offer me the provost role at an HBCU fulfilling my deferred dream? Back in high school, I desperately wanted to attend Howard University but my sports acumen afforded me a full-scholarship to a predominately white institution which was an opportunity I couldn't negate financially. I have no regrets, but I'd been determined to add the black college experience to my resume.

"That's amazing news, President Whittaker. Thank you, sir. I'm honestly speechless and honored, sir."

"Well, Dr. Green, with your business acumen, and commitment and advocacy of critical race theory in higher education, especially PWIs, will go a long way at Monroe. Our chief people resource officer will have an email out to you shortly detailing the offer. I believe that you will be pleased as we have exceeded your expectations." He assured me.

"Thank you again, President Whittaker. I greatly appreciate the opportunity. As I am sure you can relate, this is a major decision for me and my family. I would appreciate the luxury of a week or so to fully consider the offer. I understand your time constraints with the new school year starting soon so I will do my diligence to ensure I have an answer for you straightway, sir."

"Of course, take the time you need. You have my direct line so feel free to contact me at any time. If you decide to become a Monroe University Jaguar, which I believe you will, I would like to host a dinner with my senior administrative staff sooner than later to get them acclimated to the change. Our previous provost is beloved by many so the sensitive nature of the change management strategy is critical."

"I completely understand, President Whittaker. If I accept the opportunity, I am well aware of the shoes I will have to fill."

We ended the call with various salutations as I sat placid, awestricken.

"You got the job," Stella said with a hint of sadness lacing her voice.

"I got the job."

5

JEMMA

"He got the job," I breathlessly huffed, as I read the email President Whittaker distributed to the staff while I was on vacation.

"Who got a job?" Shiloh asked, perched next to me on the airplane.

We were returning from our annual family trip in Cabo where we owned a timeshare property. My parents, Mr. and Mrs. Holiday, Quaron, Shiloh, Quinton and I spent a week in paradise. It was the perfect opportunity for me to wind down before the start of another hectic school year. It also gave me an opportunity to work on my latest untitled book.

"Um, the new Provost was announced," I said, still distracted by my trance. I probably read the words twenty times. *I am happy to announce Dr. Ezekiel Green, Jr. as the new Provost of Monroe University.*

"Is it the woman you wanted? Dr. Brewer?" Quinton's baritone shook me from my reverie. I didn't even realize he was paying attention.

I shook my head. "No. Um, I guess they decided to go with Dr. Green."

"The NYU guy, right?" I nodded. "I heard he played professional football for a minute," Quinton continued but I wasn't sure if it was a question or a statement.

Ezekiel had played professional football for four years with the Tampa Bay Buccaneers. He shared stories of his time in the NFL with me that night at the W Lounge. A conversation that continued on the couch in his suite. I intently listened as he detailed his past endeavors, disclosing the non life-threatening lung condition that ended his football career. Of course I wasn't going to share that knowledge with Quinton, so I simply shrugged.

"Mommy, I thought you were fighting for the lady, Dr. Brewer, to get the job?" Shiloh questioned, never disjoining from her phone.

I shrugged again. I'd heard that Sheila Brewer was dealing with a medical issue that may have prevented her from committing to a new role but it hadn't been confirmed. Given this announcement, I prayed that she was in good health, making a mental note to send her a thinking of you card.

The sudden turbulence as we prepared for landing was no match for the heaviness in my stomach as the thought of having a real life in living color visual of Dr. Ezekiel Green every day slightly tormented me. It was one thing to communicate and occasionally flirt with him online, but now I would have to work with that tall dark chocolate God of a man... *every day.* This was bad... really bad.

"I guess the board decided to go in another direction. Dr. Green was a strong candidate too. He'll be good for the university," I confidently proclaimed because I believed it to be true.

"Well I'm going to immediately get on his calendar to ensure he's prioritizing the budget for the track team. I've brought too much money into Monroe University to beg for simple shit like new equipment," Quinton complained. I nodded, rolling my eyes because I'd heard this tirade before.

I stared out of the window observing the scenic view below me as the plane prepared to land in Myrtle Beach. It was the location of my father's annual family reunion that would close out my vacation before returning home. Shiloh and I committed to a social media free vacation so my phone rapidly chimed with notifications once I connected back to the world. The last time I communicated with Ezekiel was a week ago, the day before we left for vacation, when we bantered about Common's relationship issues.

Checking IG, he'd sent two messages; one was a picture of the black truffle pizza he raved about and the second simply read, *What's up, Jemma. You good?* I considered replying but closed down the app instead. What would I say? In my head, Ezekiel was a mythical man who lived in my dreams never to be seen again. Shit, he resided in my damn iPhone which provided the illusion of safety. But now, he was my leader, my boss. What the hell could I say?

Since the university released the official announcement, I was certain that it was all over LinkedIn as well. Waiting to depart the plane, I clicked the icon and there he was. The picture attached to the announcement should've been a sin. His cocoa-colored skin complimented the tan suit, crisp white dress shirt and purple and gold tie. Hundreds of congratulatory messages graced the post. *I should probably extend my congratulations.* I thought. It would probably appear a little weird if I was the only university administrator that didn't offer acknowledgement. Even Maxi's crazy ass commented on the post probably right after she sent me a text saying, **"Bitch... the one night stand of our dreams got the job. WTF."** Followed by the spiral eyes emoji.

I rolled my eyes then quickly typed, *Congratulations Dr. Green. We are looking forward to your leadership at Monroe University.* That response was just dumb... impassive and unemotional. But I felt quite the contrary. Fervent unexplained tenderness for the good doctor pestered my heart.

Ezekiel and I had been connected, practically entangled for weeks. I knew what this man ate for breakfast, lunch and dinner. Knew how far he ran every morning and when his sudden cravings for black truffle pizza hijacked our communication. I was even privy to when he took his mother to her doctors' visits. A week of no communication had been downright brutal. No matter how much I fought it, Ezekiel raided the intricacies of my mind and that feeling terrified me.

"J! We gotta move faster," Quinton annoyingly shouted as we hurriedly traversed through the crowded airport.

I darted a testy and equally annoyed eye at him. My ability to mask my disdain for Quinton was becoming increasingly more difficult the greater the tension grew between us. I often questioned if my attitude towards Quinton had anything to do with my growing connection with Ezekiel. But I had to quickly remind myself that this marriage was on sinking sand long before this thing, *whatever the hell it was*, with Dr. Green started.

I was thankful when we arrived at the rental house so that I could take a short reprieve from my family and more importantly Quinton. The four bedroom beachfront mini mansion was beautiful. I leaned against the sliding patio doors admiring the gloriously deep blue hue of the ocean. Seagulls aimlessly, freely soared so high they appeared to kiss the sun.

"Hey my baby girl," my mother sang entering my room. At sixty five years old, my mother was just plain beautiful. It was almost disgusting. Her honeyed bronzed skin and curvy physique that matched mine made her look more like my sister than my mother.

"Hey Ma. You and daddy get settled in your room?" I asked as she joined me on one of the many decks attached to the house.

"Yes. Your father is resting so that he can talk crazy all night with his brothers," she chuckled, rolling her eyes. "Where is my princess and Quinton?"

"Shi went for a run on the beach and I think Q joined her. You know them, they never miss a workout," I chuckled, glancing back towards the stunning view.

She nodded, joining me to peer out at the magnificent scenery. "Are you ready to talk about it?" she said, never parting her eyes from the ocean waves.

"Talk about what, Ma?" I asked but I already knew. I couldn't hide anything from Maureen Warren as a teenager and that remained true today. Her spidey sense was always on.

"Child, don't try to play me," she swiftly darted a scolding eye my way. "Are you ready to talk about why you and my son-in-law appear more like business partners than husband and wife?" My mother lifted her brow, silently questioning.

"The distance between you two has been apparent for a while, but this trip..." Her voice trailed off into a concerned hum. "You all have been like strangers. And baby girl, you are cloaked in heartache, sadness and irritation. I see it in those beautiful eyes your daddy gave you. Angst is all over you," she whimpered.

I didn't know what it was about a mother's touch that gave you permission to break but I completely broke when she tossed an arm over my shoulder to pull me in for a hug. The dam of tears speedily overwhelmed me. My mother was silent as she allowed me the space to simply let my heart break. After a few moments I regained my ability to speak.

"Ma, I'm so tired. Me and Quinton... it's not what it used to be. I don't know him anymore. The man you see now is like a stranger to me. My Q, the man I thought was the love of my life is no more. He's gone. We don't talk, we don't kiss, we just... don't. If I'm being honest, he doesn't want me. The passion we once had has expired." I vacantly shrugged.

"Things change, people change. The needs of a twenty year old are starkly different from the desires of a forty year old. So, the question is, do *you* want him, Jemma?" My mother pursed her lips with squinted eyes awaiting a response.

I glared at her for a long minute. She loved Quinton like a son she birthed so I had to navigate this situation carefully. I'd already mourned my severed relationship but this grief would be new for my mother, my entire family.

"Be honest, my love," she encouraged, squeezing my hand tight.

"No," I whispered. "I don't want him. I haven't had him, mentally or physically, in a very long time," I loudly huffed, collapsing my head against the back of the chair.

"Do you want somebody else?" She asked, meticulously arched eyebrows hiked to the clouds. I nervously nibbled my bottom lip as I pinched my cheek. I had no response for my mother but the answer prancing in my head and frolicking in my center was a resounding *yes, yes, yes.*

"Are you dipping your pretty toes in another body of water, little girl?" Her tone was forceful.

"What, mama?" My eyes narrowed in misunderstanding.

"Don't play coy with me, Jemma Jule," she sternly reprimanded then lowered her voice to a whisper. "Are you being unfaithful, Jemma? You are still somebody's wife you know."

"No, ma," I blurted.

"A new dick can feel good at the moment but two wrongs will never make anything right," she exclaimed.

"Ma!" I yelped, shaking my head at her potty mouth. But then I stilled, eyes wide. Did she say *two wrongs?* I questioned mutedly. Two wrongs means that she has knowledge of Quinton's extra-marital affairs. Oh my God, does the whole family know? I couldn't speak.

"I -" I throatily croaked. "I know, ma," crept from my lungs as I processed this conversation.

"Baby, there are only a few reasons for a woman to mentally check out of her marriage while physically existing in the bullshit," she smirked with a chuckle. "Abuse... and I know Quinton's ass ain't ready to die. Financial problems... and I taught you to have your own pot while managing his too. Or, he's laying his burdens down with another woman."

Women. I thought but wouldn't dare articulate that to her.

"If he's cheating then you have a pretty simple decision to make," she matter-of-factly stated.

"Simple?" I probed, willing myself not to cry.

She nodded.

"If Quinton is doing what I believe he's doing then he is showing you exactly who he is. So you have to make the choice to either believe him or don't. Some people say once a cheater always a cheater but I don't necessarily believe that. However, I do believe that you will never forget the indiscretion. But if you choose to forgive you have to release the anger for your sanity, not his." My mother sounded like she was speaking from experience but I wouldn't brave the ask. After forty three years of marriage I was certain she'd seen some shit.

My mother cupped my cheeks, swiping away tears as she continued, "So, beautiful love of my life, you have options. You either stay and tolerate or you leave and liberate. You hold all of the cards, sweetheart."

* * *

"Dr. Ray will see you now," the petite receptionist said in the squeakiest voice.

I nodded, checking my watch then glancing at the front door to the office. We'd been back in Monroe City for about two weeks and Quinton and I were having our first couples therapy appointment. I'd presented the idea of therapy to Quinton over a year ago but he refused, opting to attempt alternatives to an actual therapist. He planned a vacation that we had to reschedule due to his mother becoming ill. Rescheduling turned into cancellation because we never took the trip and Mrs. Holiday was doing just fine now. Quinton even went as far as purchasing the Five Love Languages book; he made it through chapter three and was done endeavoring to save his marriage.

Work and life got in the way and eventually we fell into our normal zombiesque routine. Last month, after a brutal tear-filled argument ending in me screaming, *"Fuck it. I'm done,"* and the same sentiments were echoed again just a couple weeks ago in Mexico, he agreed to attend therapy. At Quinton's virtually impossible request, I identified a therapist who was an HBCU educated Phd that was not in Monroe City. Dr. Ray's office was about twenty miles outside of the city; just far enough away to provide the illusion of discretion.

Ambling over to the midnight blue door, I lightly tapped as I opened it, greeted by the raspy, almost sultry voice of Dr. Morrison Ray. My eyes widened at the Barry White bass that slapped me in the face before I ever laid eyes on the doctor. Thankfully the face and physique did not match the voice. Dr. Ray was a brown-skinned stocky gentleman likely in his early fifties. And he had hips, like actual womanly-shaped hips. It was kinda weird. He was weird but highly recommended. Dr. Ray was a black male licensed family therapist who specialized in couples counseling for those of the melanated persuasion.

"Good morning, Dr. Holiday. I am Dr. Ray. It's a pleasure to meet you?" He said, standing to shake my hand. "Is Mr. Holiday joining us?" Dr. Ray motioned for me to be seated on the couch before peering behind me seeking my not so better half.

"Please call me Jemma and I honestly don't know if Mr. Holiday will be here. He hasn't responded to my calls." I shrugged, appearing defeated. Shit, I was just plain tired. If Quinton couldn't prioritize counseling, why would I expect him to work towards mending my broken heart.

Dr. Ray nodded, as I took a seat on the plush peanut butter leather sofa. He settled across from me on an identical sofa. Bottled water, a box of tissue, a pad of paper and a cup of writing pens sat on the table between us. The office was decorated with warm hues of variant browns, blues and ivory. Glancing around, I spotted multiple degrees on the wall, paintings and family portraits. Dr. Ray was pictured with a woman who I assumed was his wife, four other adults and three young children.

"Anita," he blurted.

Jolting, I turned to him and uttered, "Excuse me?"

"That is my wife of thirty years Anita," he proudly proclaimed pointing towards the picture. "My oldest son who carries my name, his wife Jessica, my daughters Alyssa and Alexandria, as well as my granddaughters Avery

and Raven, and that chunky baby boy is my newest grandbaby Malcolm."
He beamed with pride.

"You have a beautiful family. Thirty years of marriage... wow. That's
such a blessing. My parents have been married for over forty years," I
uttered with a brightened smile.

"I can say the same to you. Twenty years of marriage... wow," he
mockingly chuckled and I couldn't help my laugh. "Now, should we wait
for Mr. Holiday?" He lifted a brow.

I peered at my phone noticing we were already fifteen minutes into our
ninety minute session, but no texts or phone calls from Quinton. We drove
separately because he had an early training session with his track team in
preparation for an exhibition meet on Saturday. Blinking rapidly, I bit my
tongue before audibly exhaling to prevent the threatening tears.

I shook my head as an unruly tear rolled, then I mumbled, "No. No, we
shouldn't wait. I understand if you need to cancel this appointment. You
are a couples therapist and I am clearly not here as a couple today," I
sarcastically smirked, wiping the lone tear.

"I am a therapist, Jemma. One person, two people or a group of ten, I
will still do my job," Dr. Ray announced.

"And what exactly is that for me individually?" I probed.

"My job is to help you sort through the puzzle pieces of your life. Not
to solve the puzzle necessarily, but offer you potential methods to safely
cope with the disarray while *you* independently decide to either solve the
puzzle *or* elect to play another game." Dr. Ray leaned against the arm of
the couch with a fist resting under his chin and legs crossed in his khaki
chinos and brown loafers. "Does that sound like a plan?"

"And what if my husband decides to show up after all? What does that
mean for my *puzzle?*" I skeptically questioned.

"Mr. Holiday's actions shouldn't dictate how you navigate your puzzle
or your life, Jemma. He has his own to solve and you have yours."

Well damn! I thought. That simple analogy was loaded with so much
complexity my head was spinning not even an hour into the session.

"Now, tell me about Jemma," Dr. Ray requested as he intently concentrated on me.

"Ok. Um, I am the Vice President of Student Affairs at Monroe University, a writer and motivational speaker. A wife and mother to my nineteen

year old daughter. That's pretty much Jemma Jule Holiday in a nutshell," I sang, concealing my desire to cry with a faux expression of happiness.

"Ok. Thank you for the resume. Now tell me about the real Jemma."

"What do you mean?" I asked, feeling a bit uncomfortable, exposed.

"I want to know about the Jemma who is about ready to burst into tears right now." Dr. Ray uttered, never altering his stance on the couch. While I, on the other hand, absently bounced my right leg so fast my tip-toes were hurting in the stilettos.

"The real Jemma?" I whimpered, tone questioning. I leered at Dr. Ray, my emotions teetering between angst and anguish. I swallowed hard, momentarily darting my eyes towards his family portrait before focusing my attention back on him. "I don't know her... the real Jemma. Is she still that twenty year old who made a life-altering mishap or the forty year old who beat the odds and debunked the stereotypes? I don't know. So... I'm not sure who she is," I sighed, one tear streaking my face.

"Ok. Well how does Jemma of today feel?" He probed, remaining stoic.

I shrugged my shoulders like a little kid. I was so uncomfortable but I needed to talk to someone who wasn't vested in me. Who would not ridicule or judge. On the outside my life appeared perfect, but internally I was rotting; falling apart at the seams.

"I feel numb other than when I'm mad. Sometimes anger is the only emotion I have to let me know I'm breathing. That I'm alive," I breathily muttered, embarrassed to admit the truth. "Hate and disdain are a close second."

"Hate and disdain for who?" he queried.

I halted for an extended heartbeat, absently staring towards the doctor. "Me," I cried.

"Why?" Dr. Ray was placid but focused.

I sucked in my cheeks before releasing an exasperated sigh. "For not being enough. For not wanting to embarrass my family. Not feeling like I'm strong enough to... walk away and choose me," I admitted, licking salty tears from the corners of my lips.

"That's good, Jemma. That's a great start," he confirmed with a nod. "Now, let's work on introducing that twenty year old who lost her way because life required her to mature fast, to the forty year old who is plotting a new course and stronger than she thinks. How does that sound?"

I nodded, thumbing away the stray tears.

Hours later, I strolled into my house exhausted, but hopeful. I'd already settled my spirit to not argue with Quinton about his no show for the appointment today. I was a living breathing reflection of a woman fed up.

"Hey," I dryly greeted, walking in the side door from the garage carrying a grocery bag. Quinton was seated at the island typing on his computer.

"Hey, J. Any more bags in the car?" he asked, tone matching mine but mixed with additional agitation.

"No," I said while simultaneously shaking my head. "Are you ok?" I hesitantly asked because the simplest questions annoyed him lately.

He peered up at me, brow furrowed. "Yeah. Why'd you ask that?"

"You just seem upset about something. Distant." I carefully chose my words.

"Jemma, I'm fine. No need to talk or analyze anything. I don't need you to counsel me. I'm good," he scowled.

I cocked my head to the side. That *counsel me* reference shot heat through my flesh. "Nah, clearly no one can counsel you, Quinton. You don't need help because you clearly have it all figured out," I angrily snickered.

"What is that supposed to mean?" He said, appearing seriously confused.

"We had a therapy appointment today, Quinton. With the marriage counselor. The one I found with your specific criteria."

"Shit," he mumbled, rubbing his nape. "Jem, I'm sorry. Next time, I promise."

I scoffed, rolling my eyes. "Whatever Quinton. There won't be a next time," I blurted, ambling out of the kitchen. "We need to leave here by 5:30... fyi," I said, disappearing down the hall.

"For what?" His voice echoed. Quinton appeared in the bedroom doorway wearing a creased brow.

"The provost welcome dinner at the University Supper Club," I irritably spat, shuffling through the closet.

"Shit. I forgot about that." He shook his head while stretching.

"Go figure," I muttered, stripping out of my clothes, heading to the shower. "Why do you have an assistant if you aren't going to adhere to your calendar?"

Quinton released a deep breath while heavily plodding across the bedroom to sit on the bed.

"Are you able to go, Quinton?" I couldn't prevent the attitude dancing in my vocal chords. I honestly couldn't care less if Quinton attended this dinner but I needed him to go as a distraction from *him*.

"Yes, Jemma, damn. I'm going, I have a lot of shit going on but I'm going," he barked then rolled his eyes. "We need to drive separately, though."

I slammed the closet door then bitterly spat, "Really, Q? Why? Where do you have to be? Can you just give *me* one night?" I shouted, standing before him completely naked.

"Don't start this shit, Jemma." He began stripping out of a plain white t-shirt and Nike basketball shorts. He was a magnificently attractive man so I completely understood why women flocked to him. Sometimes I wished that the goosebumps of the past would find their way to my flesh again. That the throb between my thighs would rekindle for him. But the flame, the attraction, was snuffed out so fast I couldn't even recall all of the events that created this new dynamic between us. This business traction we masked as a relationship.

"Start what, hmm?" I lifted an eyebrow before continuing, "Start wondering where the hell my husband has to be tonight?"

"Here you go, questioning me," he sighed, now naked too. We argued as if we were fully clothed. Nakedness meant nothing... did nothing for either of us.

"Quinton you can't keep planting seeds of doubt and watering them bitches with betrayal and then tell me I'm imagining the fucking weeds growing in my yard," I shouted. "God Quinton, can't you see that you weigh on me. Your urgency becomes my urgency. Your challenge is mine, but where's the reciprocity? When do I get the chance to forget? When can I make a mistake? When do you ever accommodate what I need? You say I'm your princess but where is my knight in shining armor?"

"Give me a fucking break, Jemma. Here you go with the fancy soliloquies. Save that shit for your books," he spat, rolling his eyes. "I said I'm going and then I'm bringing my ass home. You know you like to run your mouth and socialize and I ain't in the mood for that shit tonight. Excuse me," he said and walked right by me into the bathroom.

Wow. He didn't hear not one word I said. I scrutinized him with narrowed, angry eyes for an extended minute. If I was a different type of woman some random object would've been hurled at his damn head. But I stood in the threshold, opting for a frightening calm.

"You're clearly not in the mood for a lot of shit these days, Q. I don't know what the hell is your problem, but it ain't me. So I suggest you correct whatever the fuck is wrong with you and stop talking to me like you're crazy. If anybody should be upset it should be me. But you can stay or go, Quinton, I really don't care. Do you, like always, and I'm gonna start doing me." I secured my headphones on my ears and then walked by him, stepping into the bathtub.

"And what the fuck is that supposed to mean, J?" Quinton probed, dick slanging and his face getting on my damn nerves.

I didn't utter a response but I silently deliberated, *I can show you better than I can tell you.*

6

JEMMA

Quinton followed behind my Mercedes in his pearl white Escalade as we pulled into the valet at the University Supper Club. The venue's vibe was upscale cabaret with some of the best steaks in town. I dressed in a black and white pencil dress that accentuated my curves and red patent Louboutins that had my calves popping. My summer braids were replaced by my natural curly chin-length coils styled in a wild, yet tamed bob-cut.

Quinton approached my door before the valet representative could. He opened the door and extended a hand to assist me out of the car. Given his position, our bodies collided and he glared down at me with an apology in his eyes that never transferred to his lips. Instead, he kissed my forehead, lingering longer than I expected... than I wanted. Quinton extended his elbow and whispered, "shall we." My plump red lips pinched in a thin line to quell my vexation. I nodded, accepting his arm.

Entering the private room, we momentarily paused to identify who had already arrived. Peering around the dimly lit space, I spotted Maxine first, then my eyes immediately gravitated to *him*. Dr. Green wore an all black tailored suit, white dress shirt with no tie, and a red pocket square. His beard was meticulously edged leading to his shiny bald head. He laughed at something Maxi said before taking a sip of whatever was in his glass. That damn Colgate smile was unforgettable.

"Coach and Dr. Holiday, I'm glad you could make it," President Whittaker greeted us.

"We wouldn't miss it, President Whittaker," Quinton happily retorted. I deeply inhaled, feigning a smile to prevent from rolling my eyes at him. He was a pro at this fake shit.

"Dr. Holiday, you've met Dr. Green already, but let me introduce Coach." President Whittaker motioned to the bar where Ezekiel was standing.

"You both go ahead. I'm going to run to the ladies room," I said, needing another minute before engaging with him face to face.

They nodded. I quickly darted down the hallway to the restroom. Maxi caught my departure in her peripheral and followed me. I closed myself in a stall next to another person before I heard the bathroom door creak.

"Dr. Holiday," Maxi sang. "Are we having a meeting in the ladies room?" She boisterously chuckled.

A familiar voice echoed from the stall next to me. "Why are both of you in the bathroom? What's going on?" Quaron rasped.

"Your line sister probably has to change her panties after laying eyes on the fine ass good doctor," Maxi laughed. "That nigga walked in here like double-O-seven."

I shook my head and then sat down since now I actually had to pee. Flushing the toilet and cleaning myself, I fixed my dress and walked out of the stall greeted by two sets of prying eyes.

"Aww, look Maxi. They are dressed alike in their black, red and white," Quaron jeered, cupping her mouth with her hands.

I swatted her away and dryly mumbled, "I really hate y'all." I avoided eye contact with these two fools while I washed my hands.

"What's wrong, Jemma?" Maxi huffed, curling the corners of her nude-painted lips.

I leaned against the wall, eyes focused on the popcorn ceiling, then audibly exhaled. "I didn't think I would ever see him again. Why do I feel so guilty?"

"Guilty about what? Instagram messages?" Maxi questioned.

"Yes! I would be pissed at Quinton for chatting morning, noon and night with somebody on social media. I figured we would just keep sliding in each other's DMs and everything would be fine... all in fun. Because I was not planning on *e-v-e-r* seeing him again." I sternly declared.

"Sliding in DMs? What are you... a twenty year old rapper?" Roni's stale sense of humor was usually funny, but now it was just plain aggravating since the joke was directed at me.

"No, but I've never done anything like this before. He's not supposed to be here. I don't know how to pretend like -"

"Like you're not attracted to him." Maxi finished.

I nodded.

"Sis, you said if it was Quinton you'd be pissed. Well, news flash, it's been Quinton. He is the only reason you're even entertaining conversations with this man. My brother ain't no fucking saint, Jem," Roni whisper-yelled.

"Yeah but two wrongs - " I said, parroting my mother's sentiments.

"Jem, you haven't done anything wrong," Maxi interrupted. "You haven't slept with the man. It's just chatting... friendly conversations. Chats that make you happy, might I add."

Maxine was right, I hadn't crossed an inappropriate line with Ezekiel in reality. We never engaged in sexual conversations or eluded to seeing each other in the future. Our dialogue was easygoing, genuine, stimulated - a total mind fuck. But in Jemmaland, he frolicked in my fantasies, tongue kissed my pussy and fucked me unconscious.

Just this morning I awakened with him on the brain. Private episodes in the shower with my rose vibrator had become a regular occurrence since I didn't want Quinton's nasty ass anywhere near me. In months past, the images of my favorite sex-symbol actors made the moments that much better. But this morning, Ezekiel had become the star of the show. With the steamy overhead downpour and the multiple jets massaging my body, I perched on the warm shower bench and closed my eyes to initiate the movie of *him* that played in my head daily. Thankfully I had free admission because sometimes I would allow the reel to run on repeat. The neo-soul sounds of the *The Good Doctor* playlist danced through the room.

Stroking a finger across the slight plumpness of my scars, I fondled my breast before trailing my hand to the bare smoothness of my kitty. I circled there for several delightful minutes. I had been so damn wet as his glistening smile teased in my imagination. I licked my lips, caressing my clit to the pace of the music. I momentarily ignored the vibrator because I wanted this to last awhile and that thing would have me prime for take off in seconds. Tossing my head back, I allowed the water to offer lubrication but I required none. My kitty was drenched, fucking drowning in the sea of *him*.

The moans grew louder as intensity bubbled in my belly. Biting my lip, I would hear him faintly whisper, *you're a fucking experience, Jemma*. I had no clue what that meant and thought I would never have the opportunity to ask because those words resided in my illusions. But whatever his answer would be in actuality, I was certain the response would make my pussy drizzle. I clicked the rose three times to my favorite setting. *Slow, quick, quick, slow,* the red beast hummed. That thing was small but it packed a punch as I pressed it to my clit.

"Oh shit, Ezekiel!" I moaned in the shower alone with imagery of the onyx God burdening my body.

I actually moaned his fucking name boorishly and with no apologies or regrets. While he was a mirage, that damn orgasm was savagely real. So yeah, I hadn't done anything wrong persay, but with him occupying my professional space, restraint would be a grueling challenge. How was I supposed to walk into this dinner and welcome him as my colleague when I'd envisioned the curve, thickness and veining of his dick pounding my pussy.

"Jem." Maxi snapped her fingers. I shuddered as if I was being pulled from hypnosis.

"Um, yeah. Yes. You're right. I'm being silly." Needing to get my shit together, I turned to the mirror, checking my hair and makeup. I sucked in a deep breath and exhaled in a whisper, "I'm Dr. Jemma damn Holiday. I got this."

The three of us sauntered out of that bathroom like Charlie's Angels. But probably looked more like the Three Stooges. The dinner bell chimed just as we entered the private room. Two beautifully decorated ten-person dining tables were positioned at the opposite end of the room. I spotted Quinton in a corner with his phone lodged between his ear and shoulder as he talked between the phone and Jamar who stood in front of him. Ignoring them, I ambled to the bar before taking my seat but was intercepted by the aroma of Creed cologne. He wore Bois Du Portugal, the signature scent of Frank Sinatra. The citrusy yet woody blend was pure perfection on him.

"Dr. Jemma Holiday. It's good to see you again," Ezekiel said, extending his hand to shake mine. He clutched my left hand with his right then concealed the connection with his other hand providing him the freedom to delicately tickle my palm. Goosebumps. Real ass plump ass goosebumps crept up my arm.

"Dr. Ezekiel Green. It's good to see you too. Congratulations and welcome to Monroe. We are excited to see your vision for the university," I voiced, almost sounding rehearsed.

Our hands continued to entwine for a heartbeat longer than necessary. He took one step closer and I should've stepped back but I didn't. Ezekiel studied me. Just like the night in his suite, his stare made me feel exposed, like he was peeling back the layers to reveal my truth. But at the same time the stare was alluring and secure.

"Long time no talk to. My IG is not the same without you," he muttered, leaning in to whisper, "You don't have to run from me, Jemma."

"I know and I'm not," I breathily responded. The dinner bell chimed again and I endeavored to sever our tie but Ezekiel had more to say.

"Check your phone," he instructed before releasing me and joined the dinner party.

Leaning against the bar, I turned away, not needing the visual of his confident saunter. "What can I get for you to drink, ma'am," the bartender asked.

"A double shot of Clase Azul, chilled with a lime," I blurted, needing a little liquid courage to make it through the night. The bartender nodded then walked away to prepare my order. I took advantage of the moment alone to check my phone.

InQUisitivE1: I was hoping we would've had a moment to chat before dinner but I understand that this may be awkward for you. You don't have to run from me. Our chats, our communication is private, sacred. Just between me and you. It's been a safe space for me and I hope it can continue but I understand if you need to back away. The ball is in your court.

Taking my seat next to Quinton with half of my drink already devoured, I restlessly stared at my table setting waiting for something to save me. Either this dinner needed to end expeditiously or the tequila needed to hurry the hell up and get me good and tipsy. I glanced up and immediately observed Ezekiel looking my way. He nodded before biting his lip then smiled as he turned to continue his conversation. My goodness, I was in so much trouble. Fuck that, a bitch was in danger.

7

ZEKE

A wkward. That was the only word I could use to describe tonight's *encounter* with Jemma. Or maybe... funny as shit as I watch her play a game of hide and seek all night. She couldn't be in my presence for more than a few minutes and definitely not alone. If I went left, she went right. If others engaged her in the conversation she refused to make eye contact with me unless it was absolutely necessary. Jemma was running but what she didn't know is that I was the type of man who appreciated the chase.

I observed the dynamic between her and Coach Holiday, and if I was being honest, there was none. At least no interaction that would indicate his attachment to that fine ass woman who was wearing the hell out of that black and white dress.

Periodically, I would glance down towards the end of the table and the tension between the two of them was thick enough to cut with a knife; two strangers barely able to hold a mutual gaze. The historical connection was evident based upon the memories of the homecoming king and queen that volleyed around the table. A faux slight smile curved the edges of their mouths in response.

I observed the Coach more than Jemma because I wondered if he saw her. Like truly recognized the fucking beautiful wonder next to him? *Nah, his dumb ass blind ass fuck.* I silently mused, tossing back my cognac.

"Dr. Green, unfortunately I can't stay but it was a pleasure meeting you and welcome to Monroe," Coach Holiday said then hastily departed.

He tossed a glance at Jemma but she did not appear to be the least bit concerned, momentarily cutting her eyes over to him then resumed her conversation. *This fool ain't leaving nothing but space and opportunity,* the hood nigga in me thought. But I wasn't the only man who noticed. I saw the wandering eyes of several men appreciating her beauty.

Jemma pranced around full of tequila when her man left, like she'd been uncaged. The social butterfly was ready to spread her wings. She rocked her hips to the music piping throughout the supper club, still sipping. When she tossed her head back in a guttural chuckle and then bit her plump bottom lip, I knew it was time for me to bid the welcome event farewell. I was almost out of the door until I heard an unfamiliar voice speak my name.

"Dr. Green, are you leaving already? A few of us are heading to a local bar, Henley's, for another drink. It's for the grown and sexy crowd so no concerns about potentially mingling with students. Would you like to join us?" The pretty slim-thick tawny colored woman with light hazel eyes said.

"My apologies, tell me your name again," I asked, flashing a slight smile.

"Christina. Christina Hall. I am the university's Chief of Staff so we'll be working together quite a bit," she squealed, nibbling the gloss from her lips.

Christina was a fine redbone with a fat ass; normally the type I would solicit as my companion for the evening. But my dealings with the opposite sex as of late was one hundred percent abnormal.

"No, thank you, I appreciate the invitation, Mrs. Hall-"

"*Miss* Hall," she quickly interrupted, correcting me.

"Miss Hall, thank you for the invitation but I should probably call it a night." I said, eyeing Jemma over the bare right shoulder of the pretty woman in front of me.

All I saw was *her* and I desperately needed to rid myself of this veiled control. She had no clue the dominance she had over me.

"Jem, you are absolutely not driving. You can ride with me. I'll meet you at the car." I heard Jemma's friend, Maxine, call out as she headed towards the restroom. Jemma nodded, avoiding my gaze.

I shook my head because I was about to go out like a punk. "Actually, I will join you all. I should start getting acquainted with the Monroe City scene since I plan on being here for a while." I smiled, extending my arm motioning Miss Hall towards the exit.

Henley's was definitely a grown and sexy vibe. It reminded me of New York making me feel at home. Bright linen couches flanked the rustic wooden walls while tall bistro tables lined the dance floor and a small stage with a live band. At the entrance, they verified my identification then informed me that a VIP section was always available to me as the university's provost.

Miss Hall mentioned that this was one of the few establishments in the college town that offered privacy for university administrators with its thirty year old age minimum. No risk of engaging with traditional undergraduate students. This woman talked and talked and after about twenty minutes her words jumbled and voice sounded like a Charlie Brown character.

As she yammered, I shot Jemma a message as I sipped another cognac.

> @InQUisitivE1: Still hiding I see. You can come out to play. I promise I won't bite. [Wink Emoji]

> @JulesPen: I absolutely believe that you will bite. [grimacing emoji]

> @InQUisitivE1: You damn right. LMAO [tongue out emoji]

I'd been introduced to a handful of other university employees who were enjoying themselves at the club. So far one woman offered to prepare my meals until I found a permanent house and another openly admitted to semi-stalking my social media pages and asked to join me on a morning run. The women in Monroe were lovely and definitely cornbread fed, but my eyes searched for only one midwest dazzler.

I peered around the club bobbing to the music and noticed that Maxine and Quaron were on the dance floor leaving Jemma alone in one of the VIP booths. Miss Hall had finally excused herself to the bathroom so I took the opportunity to approach *her*.

I sauntered towards the booth, smiling, while uttering in a trill tone, "Dr. Holiday. I thought we were friends." She peered around seemingly attempting to find an escape but there was none.

I stealthily slid into the seat but maintained a safe distance between us.

"Or maybe I am just friends with JulesPen," I said, raising a questioning eyebrow. "Is that it? I can't talk to Dr. Holiday but I can communicate with Jules."

Jemma shook her head. "You're not supposed to be here," she whispered, almost inaudibly. "I wasn't supposed to see you ever again," she sighed, shaking her head.

"So, I take it I didn't get your vote for the job," I teased.

"Ezekiel. I mean, Dr. Green," she loudly huffed. "This feels so strange... wrong."

"What exactly have we done wrong, Jemma," I probed, propping my elbows up on the table signaling the waitress for another round of drinks.

"Our conversations were harmless through the phone. Just sliding in your DMs. Now here you are... in the flesh," she whispered with gritted teeth as her pretty eyes widened for emphasis.

I could not stop the hearty laugh that spilled from me.

"Sliding in my DMs. Really? What are we, twenty years old Jemma? That's what our kids do."

"No, that's what we've *been* doing," she yelped, while her eyes darted around the room.

"You hold all of the controls. If you say stop, we stop." I discreetly slid a finger across the top of her hand and she didn't recoil. "Do you want to stop, Jemma?"

The air between us thickened as I awaited her response. If I were a better man I would want her to say that we should stop. But because I'm an *ain't shit nigga* who desired a woman who was currently unavailable to me, I hoped for a different outcome. I couldn't do anything but respect her position either way.

Jemma closed her eyes and deeply inhaled for just a moment, her fingers still tangling with mine in the shadows of the booth. She shook her head.

"The wordsmith has no words," I quipped, tossing a flirtatious wink. She chuckled, resting her head on the seat. "No. I don't want to stop."

8

JEMMA

The Monroe University fundraiser was the premier kickoff event welcoming in a new group of scholars and their parents' money to the school. Quinton and I were expected, practically required to show our faces. The former olympian and record breaking track coach and his award winning, best selling author, Ph.D. wife were guaranteed to bring in over a million dollars for the university. So staying in bed eating cookies & cream ice cream like I desired, wasn't an option.

I did not have the energy to pretend today but duty called, so I schlepped out of the bed and footed across the master bedroom into the bathroom. I loved this place. The crisp gray and white tile floor cooled my freshly manicured toes. I peeked out of the bathroom at the clock on the nightstand to determine if I had enough time to take a bath and I did.

The bright September sun peeked through the skylight in our enormous master bathroom. Streaks of sun rays beamed across the jacuzzi tub centered in the room and connected to a massive shower. I turned on the hot water because I needed this bath to be steamy. Adding my favorite mango and shea butter bath bomb, I tested the water with my fingertips. Perfect. Bath time for me was a whole mood. Bubbles, wine, music, and dimmed lighting from the overhead chandelier. It was my time to rest, relax and relieve the stress of living a falsified life. A guise, pretending to be happy when it was all a charade to protect the Holiday name and my reputation.

I disrobed in front of the full length mirror hanging on the wall. My natural shoulder-length auburn hair was freshly silk-pressed and pin curled. Manicured brows, lengthy lashes, golden brown eyes and full lips. "Shit, I'm cute," I giggled, encouraging myself to get in a better mood.

I definitely wasn't a fashion model size; a solid 200 pounds of thickness but I loved every contour of my full-figured curvaceous silhouette. Smooth chestnut skin, shapely hips, and even my round graceful breast marked with surgical scars were beautiful. Stepping into the steamy bath, I heard rumbling in the bedroom. Quinton was home. "Here we go," I mumbled.

"What's up, J?" Quinton said, walking into the bathroom with a scowl. "Are you going to be ready on time?"

I lightly shook my head. Here I am butt ass naked and the only question my husband can ask me is if I would be ready. Five years ago he would've had me bent over the sink filling my kitty with his countless inches. But why was I surprised? He doesn't even attempt to be attracted to me anymore.

"I know when we need to leave, Quinton." I huffed. "I really don't need you to coach or manage me. I know my role." I rolled my eyes. "Hey Google, volume one hundred percent." I shouted, stepping into the bathtub. I really didn't want to hear a damn thing he had to say.

"Hey Google. Pause," Quinton shouted back. "I suggest you get your attitude adjusted before the fundraiser. This has the potential to be big for the university and the track program."

"Really Q. I suggest you stop talking to me like I'm one of your students. I am the damn Vice President and Dean of Student Affairs. I know better than anybody the amount of money we can bring in tonight," I barked. "Don't worry. My pretty, perfect, happily married Dr. Jemma Holiday facade is hanging in the closet. I'll definitely be wearing it tonight."

"Whatever, J. Just be ready." He walked out of the bathroom.

"Yeah, whatever." My lips quivered, fighting to prevent the tears. I was done crying over what Quinton and I once had. I couldn't deny that I loved Q. We had too much history for me not to hold a place for him in my heart but I did not like Quinton Holiday at all. Borderline hated him.

Thirty minutes later I finished my bath and perched at the vanity to apply the vanilla rose-scented oil to my skin and start on my makeup. Quinton was standing in the shower leaning against the warmed tile allowing the water to rain over his head. I know he was anticipating a stressful start to his track season but he appeared exhausted, anguished. Over the past few weeks he had been more aggravated and irritable than usual. Although we no longer had much of a marriage, we actually had moments of friendliness, tolerance. Something was going on with him but he wouldn't talk about it.

Quinton stepped out of the shower and it couldn't be contested; twenty years later and he was still sexy as hell. Those green eyes used to be magical, instantly soaking my panties and making me bow to his every command. Now those eyes held so much hurt and harm, I found myself not staring too deeply anymore.

Quinton exited the shower in all his naked glory. That dick was a work of art too. Deliciously girthy, lengthy with plump veins. I would be the first to admit, I'd been dickmatized by him since the first time he glided his glorious mass in my unsullied vagina. The only man to ever grace these sodden walls. Sexual satisfaction from Quinton was never an issue. After years of marriage, I never wondered what I was missing in other men because he salaciously delivered good dick to me regularly. But things can change in an instant - relationships, people, circumstances. So the countless inches that previously made my mouth water and render me comatose nightly, was now just another object connected to a man that I no longer desired.

He sauntered behind me wrapped in a towel glaring at my reflection in the vanity mirror. I paused applying my foundation as we held that stare for what seemed like a lifetime but only seconds diminished. It was an uncomfortable stillness that had become our new normal. Neither of us were willing to relinquish what had already vanished. Quinton placed his hands on my bare shoulders and gently kissed against my pin-curled hair.

"I'm sorry, Jem," he whispered, peering a second longer before he walked away.

I swallowed hard, blinking rapidly, my skin flushed with goosebumps. Not because I felt a sexual attraction, but because the intense, depressed timbre of his voice felt strange. That apology flowed deeper than just resolve for the earlier argument. Something was terribly wrong.

Quinton and I journeyed to the Martin Luther King Jr. Events Center on Monroe University's campus. The ballroom was beautifully decorated with the school colors maroon and gold. Fresh bouquets of yellow roses and fine china adorned every table. Scholars dressed in their best after five attire meandered throughout the ballroom soliciting silent auction donations. Various student groups promoted their initiatives while the university's jazz band entertained the five hundred guests. Even at ten thousand dollars per table the event was sold out.

"Coach and Dr. Holiday. You both look amazing as always," President Dominic Whittaker said, before sipping his champagne. President Whittaker was in his late fifties and had a history with the university as a former football player and now the university leader for the past ten years.

"Thank you, President Whittaker," Quinton said, resting his hand on the small of my back. "Where is your beautiful wife tonight?" he asked.

"She's around here schmoozing and being great as usual," President Whittaker guffawed much louder than necessary.

We chatted for a few moments when I spotted other administrators I wanted to chat with. "If you gentlemen will excuse me. I see a few of my students," I said. Quinton kissed my cheek and I obliged, putting on a great performance.

I ambled across the ballroom greeting donors, connecting with students and finally finding my way to Maxine.

"Damn, Dr. Holiday," Maxi squealed. "You look beautiful, sis." We hugged.

I was kinda feeling myself in a maroon sequin and satin one-shoulder knee-length cocktail dress that hugged my curves in the most professional way. I strutted in my favorite Christian Louboutin metallic gold pumps as my curls bounced over my right shoulder with a sparkling gold comb and dangling earrings.

"Thank you, sis!" I smiled. "You're looking pretty sexy yourself." Maxi spun around showing off her strapless black dress.

"I see you're wearing your mask well tonight. When I talked to you earlier you were one second away from not showing up to this thing," she quipped.

Maxi had been my marital sounding board on one too many occasions. If it were up to her, I would've left Quinton two years ago.

"Girl, I'm exhausted already and we just arrived. But as much as I hate this stuff, you know I had no other option." I rolled my eyes. "Not for the Holiday's of Monroe University," I scoffed.

Maxi and I chatted and gossiped about folks as we sporadically shook hands and greeted passersby. The chime of the bell interrupted our conversation. The university president and others were about to give greetings, starting with a welcome from Quinton. I adjusted my fake mask because I knew he would put on a good show, and I needed to fall in line as the leading lady.

"Ladies and gentlemen. Thank you so much for coming out to the 10th Annual President's Fundraiser. Once again we are the hottest ticket in Monroe City," Quinton fakely guffawed. "For those that don't know me, I am Quinton Holiday, head coach of the record breaking Monroe University men's track team." The crowd loudly applauded, especially students from the team.

"Thank you. Thank you," he chimed, motioning his arms to calm the crowd before he continued. "Monroe University has a special place in my heart. It has been a second home for me since I was eighteen years old. First as a student and a member of the track team, then assistant coach and now as the head coach. Monroe is where I made lifelong friendships, but more importantly, it's where I met and fell in love with the homecoming queen, my beautiful wife, Dr. Jemma Holiday." He motioned for me to join him on the stage. "Sweetheart, come say hello to the people."

My counterfeit smile and pageant wave were in full effect.

Quinton continued his speech with his hand resting on my back. I inhaled deeply in an effort to maintain my composure and continue this fake ass dog and pony show. After a few minutes on stage, I immediately felt a spark of heat move through my body, a familiar sensation. Anthracite eyes were staring at me as his sexy gaze observed my every move. I avoided his watchful eye, vainly endeavoring not to blush, but it was too late.

I had successfully avoided him over the past few weeks since our offices were in different buildings. Clearly given my position, I would have to encounter him at various meetings but I wanted to circumvent the accidental meet-ups in the hallway or the awkward moments in the staff lounge. This thing with us, whatever it was, needed to remain strictly professional on the campus of Monroe University. But after hours, I delighted in the IG dialogue that continued as if he still resided in New York. Quinton concluded his speech and we exited down the stage steps walking right into *him*.

"Dr. Holiday. It's great to see you again." Dr. Ezekiel Green stood in our path holding a cognac glass looking sexy as hell. His black on black custom attire gloriously embraced his tall muscular frame. *Damn!*

"Dr. Green. It is good to see you as well." I paused. "You remember Coach Quinton Holiday," I nervously re-introduced. But why was I nervous when the two of them filled the same space? Regretfully, I hadn't done a thing with this man.

"Nice to see you again, Coach Holiday. I am looking forward to catching a track meet soon." Ezekiel's glistening smile produced a slight tingle between my thighs.

"You as well, Dr. Green. Again, welcome to Monroe University. We'd love to have you at our next race. Don't hesitate to reach out if you need anything," Quinton declared. "Excuse me for a moment. Sweetheart, I'll be right back," He said, distracted as he hurriedly departed.

Ezekiel's narrowed eyes ogled me as they journeyed from the crown of my curly hair to the point of my four inch red bottoms.

"You are absolutely stunning, Jules. Pardon me, I should say Dr. Holiday in this environment." He sexily smiled. "But seriously, you look beautiful." Ezekiel referred to me as Jules during our online chats, but hearing his bold baritone saying it aloud caused a blissful caper in my center.

"Thank you. You are quite dapper yourself." I blushed. *You look good enough to lick,* I thought, clearing my throat. "How are you enjoying your first major Monroe University event?"

He nodded, glancing around the room before he said, "This is a wonderful sight. All of these brilliant black minds gathered in one place. If this is what I have to look forward to the rest of the school year then I'm ecstatic. "

"Yeah, it is pretty spectacular. And your transition? How is Monroe City compared to the big apple? " I chuckled, taking a sip of my drink as I unsuccessfully attempted not to stare into his chocolate eyes.

"Quiet. Clean," he chortled. "But you were right, it's different but so far so good. My neighborhood in Brooklyn felt like a small town so Monroe feels homey. I'm thankful I finally found a place because I definitely couldn't stay in a hotel another night." Ezekiel laughed exposing the cutest dimple in the oddest place below his right eye.

"Oh, that's great. What part of town are you in?" I inquired because that wasn't a subject we discussed in our safety net known as IG DMs.

"I'm in the Diamond Crest neighborhood. I guess that's considered the north side of town. I'm still learning about the city. Are you familiar?" He probed.

"Um, yeah. I know exactly where you are. You must remember I've lived in Monroe most of my adult life." I nervously responded because he was too close for comfort once again. I too lived in the Diamond Crest community.

We seamlessly engaged in conversation just as we did that night in the hotel. I couldn't understand why it was so effortless to communicate with this man, when talking to the man I'd committed the past twenty years to was like pulling teeth. Scratch that – communicating with Quinton was like surgically removing wisdom teeth with no anesthesia.

Everything was a debate. In this environment, Ezekiel and I were able to freely chortle. We were colleagues, right? People expected for us to engage but I maintained a safe distance. I grabbed a glass of wine from the server as he told me about his experience at the local grocery store when he requested ingredients for Jamaican food.

"Oh my goodness," I chuckled. "You definitely won't find that here. But -"

"Excuse me. Are you Jemma Holiday?" A woman approached out of nowhere interrupting my laughter. She wore a royal blue strapless dress with a silky straight bobbed haircut. The woman appeared anxious and bothered as she frequently peered over her shoulder. Oddly, she also was vaguely familiar.

"Yes. I'm Dr. Holiday. What can I do for you?" I smiled, turning from Dr. Green to focus my attention on her.

"Um, I'm Bethany. Bethany Williamson," she blurted.

I froze. Speechless. Unmovable. I knew exactly who Bethany Williamson was. She worked at the university's hospital and was Quinton's mistress. According to the phone records, Williamson was the last name of the person attached to the phone number that frequently called and texted Quinton. When I approached him about it, of course he lied and blamed it on a student with a crush. Although he'd had a student stalker in the past, I knew this was not the same situation. Bethany was a grown woman with a husband.

"By the look on your face I have a feeling you know who I am," she arrogantly continued as if she was proud to be the side bitch.

Ezekiel kept squinted eyes on me, noticing the crimson fire darkening my golden orbs. Tensely biting my lips as I continually flexed my fingers, banging a fist against my thigh. I didn't hear a word she said. All I knew is that I was on the precipice of a dangerously violent outburst.

"Quin is no longer accepting my calls and I just thought that you should know-"

Quinton quickly stepped between us, his wife and his mistress, interrupting her looming confession. Those beautiful green eyes of his were practically bulging from the sockets.

"Bethany, don't do this. Not here, not now," Quinton desperately requested, words slowly discharged through clenched teeth.

"Then when, Quinton? You blocked my number and we have some decisions to make," she declared, vainly attempting to lower her voice.

Quinton grabbed her wrist as she jerked, leering back at me.

"Quin and I have been seeing each other for over a year. He said he was leaving you. He said we were going to be together but now that I'm pregnant he wants to ignore me," she huffed as a stream of tears escaped down her coffee-colored face.

She continued to struggle with Quinton's firm grasp on her wrist.

"You don't get to do that, Quinton. You can't ignore this. He expects me to raise this baby alone," Bethany shrieked, directing her wrath back and forth between me and Quinton.

Passersby began to slow their pace to observe the scene that was quickly escalating. I gasped, words lodged in my throat, unable to speak.

The air evacuated from my lungs, depleting my oxygen supply. I couldn't breathe.

"What the fuck, Bethany," Quinton gritted through his teeth, trying not to create a bigger scene. "Why would you do this here? Go to your car. I'll be there in a minute," he angrily instructed.

Bethany flinched as he slightly shoved her to expedite her exit. Her tear-filled glare darted to me before she rushed away.

"Jemma, sweetheart, please don't leave. Let me fix this before she causes problems. I know we need to talk. I'll be right back. Promise me you won't leave," he repeated. "Dr. Green, can you watch her for me please?" He asked Ezekiel but didn't wait for a response before irately fleeing to the scene of his crime.

I was paralyzed. My limbs would not operate, eyes stuck on stupid as I replayed her quick commentary in my head. *Did I hear her correctly? Did she just say baby? Is this woman having my husband's baby?* The room darkened, the walls were spinning as if I was disoriented in a maze. I was going to faint as the wine glass began to slip from my hold. Ezekiel's massive frame broke my fall as he retrieved the glass from my hand, placing it on a tray as a server passed by again. I blankly stared at him, temporarily forgetting that he was standing next to me. My agonized face was flushed in embarrassment.

I wanted to scream, holler out my angst, but the only word I was able to enunciate was, "Zee."

The desperation and torment in my tone could not be neglected. Ezekiel's menacing grimace marked wrath and redeemer simultaneously. Two seconds off of beating Quinton's ass, while desiring to rescue me. He chose the latter.

"Jules, let me get you out of here," he whispered against my ear as he leaned into my shivering body concealing me from the onlookers.

Thankfully only a small crowd formed but that fact didn't quell the humiliation bubbling in my stomach. I was going to be sick. My wide eyes glared at him, nodding furiously, still hushed - speechless. Zombiesque, I aimlessly followed him as he placed a hand on that small of my back and discreetly held my hand directing me towards the back of the building. I could hear Maxi's voice in the background whisper-yelling my name but I couldn't speak. I was literally in a state of shock, dumbfounded. I had knowledge of Quinton's indiscretions, but his carelessness was a whole other subject. *A fucking baby,* I pondered.

"Jem. Jemma, wait." I paused, turning around to see Maxi but never released from Ezekiel's hold. "What is going on? I just saw Quinton outside arguing with a woman," she gruffly whispered, glancing over her shoulder to ensure no one was listening.

"Bethany. Pregnant," I muttered through an audible, exacerbated exhale. Maxi's eyes bulged. She required no additional details, immediately recognizing the name and the situation.

Bethany's disclosure of their relationship wasn't a surprise. I knew Quinton had been having an affair with her and I also knew that she was married to a university employee, Gavin Williamson. He was a landscaping manager for as long as I'd been in my role. Somehow I'd convinced myself that she would never be an issue because she had just as much to lose as Quinton. But clearly I was dead ass wrong.

"She needs to get out of here. Right now," Ezekiel demanded, directing his attention to Maxi.

"Ok, um, can you take her somewhere and I handle things here?" Maxi asked, brow creased with worry. "I'll cover for you both. Dr. Green, please make sure she calls me later."

He nodded. "I'll take care of her. You have my word."

9

ZEKE

J emma hadn't uttered a word since I placed her in my black Mercedes G-Class. She vacantly peered out of the window as we navigated the streets of Monroe. I asked her multiple times if she was hungry, if she wanted to go home but she simply shook her head no. I didn't know what else to do so I took her to my house. Approaching the black iron fence of the gated community, I entered my code. I moved into the two story colonial home just a week ago so she would have to navigate a few boxes but otherwise the place was pretty much put together. I hit the button to open the garage. She was still muted.

Her phone had been ringing non-stop since we left campus. That bum ass nigga Quinton kept calling and Jemma kept declining his calls. I really wondered what the hell he thought he was going to say to fix this. His mistress is pregnant and approached his wife with that shit at her place of business. That was beyond foul. It wasn't my place to step in but when I saw a murderous fire in Jemma 's eyes, I had to get her out of there immediately. That Bethany chick wasn't worth her reputation.

"Jemma," I uttered, trying to get her attention. "Do you want to come in or should I take you home?"

"This is fine." She finally spoke, reaching for the door handle.

"No. Wait. I got it." I exited the truck, rounding to the passenger side to retrieve her.

That beautiful face was still numb and stained with tears. I unlocked the door to my house and motioned for her to enter. This was not an appropriate time for me to be looking at her ass but damn. This woman was fine as hell. The first time I met Jemma, there was no denying my attraction. I wanted her. I *want* her. But she's married - unhappily - but married nonetheless.

That pretty ass smile, perfect maple syrup colored eyes, thick thighs, and shapely hips couldn't be ignored, but her beautiful mind is what had me completely intoxicated. That night at the hotel our conversation was natural, unforced from the time I sat down with her. I hadn't experienced that feeling in a long time. I literally could not stop thinking about Jemma, but I had to get her out of my head since I figured I would never see her again.

When President Whittaker called saying he was offering me the position, I was shocked to say the least. I later learned that the other candidate, Dr. Brewer was diagnosed with breast cancer. I prayed that she made a complete recovery, but I selfishly was thankful for the opportunity of a lifetime and to see *her*. Dr. Jemma Holiday had infiltrated every nerve in my brain. And now here she was, in my home because her dumb ass husband fucked up. *Damn. I'm in trouble.*

"You have a nice place," her melodic whisper broke my daze.

"Thank you. I still have a lot to do but I'm pleased with my decision." I peered around the four bedroom three and a half bath floor plan. "Can I get you something to drink? Water, coffee, tea -"

"Vodka," she interjected. "If you have it." She blessed me with her pretty smile.

Yeah, man. I'm in so much damn trouble, I mused, shaking my head.

"I got you." I paused, footing across the great room into the kitchen. "Please, have a seat. Get comfortable. Make yourself at home."

Jemma's phone rang again and she answered this time.

"Hey Shi. What's going on, baby girl." Jemma immediately perked up even if it was an act. It had to be her daughter on the other end. "Ok. Be careful Shiloh. Text me when you make it in, ok? I love you."

Jemma sat on the edge of the charcoal gray sectional and removed her shoes. She deeply exhaled, as her phone rang again. This time she didn't answer so that let me know it was Quinton. The expression on her face every time his name illuminated her screen was pure rage.

"Stop fucking calling me." I heard her whisper as she hit a button on her cell phone.

"Here you go." I handed her a glass half-filled with Tito's, a lime and one ice ball. I perched on the opposite end of the couch treading lightly. "How old is your daughter?" I asked.

"Nineteen going on thirty-nine," she chuckled. "Shiloh thinks she's the mother. Always checking on me," Jemma beamed. It was obvious that her daughter was her pride and joy.

"I completely understand. My daughter Eriya just turned eighteen. She calls me to make sure I take my vitamins and get enough rest," I cackled, the thought of my daughter bringing a similar joy. "Yaya will be starting Monroe in January."

"Oh, that's awesome. Congratulations." Jemma's elation was momentary when her phone vibrated against the cocktail table. She angrily read the text message. Whatever Quinton wrote in the text pissed her off. Jemma didn't even excuse herself, she called him right in front of me.

The Zeke from back in the day would've been all to pleased to let that nigga know that his woman was with me and I could most definitely take care of her how she deserved. But I chilled and silently watched the exchange, sipping on a glass of Angel's Envy.

"Quinton, do not call Shiloh. She's out with her friends so do not involve her in our shit. Correction...your bullshit," Jemma shouted. I could hear his bitch ass howling through the phone asking where she was.

"Why do you need to know where I am, Quinton? I'm safe. That's all you need to know." She paused. This time tears welled in the corners of her eyes as she listened. "Oh now you want to talk about us. It's a little too late don't you think? I can't fuckin believe you, Q."

It's crazy that he was yelling in the phone when he was the one who fucked up. Requesting her location again, she gritted through clenched teeth, "You don't want to see me right now because I could kill you. Fuckin strangle you for this shit."

Jemma dropped her head into the palm of her hand. "I can't do this right now. Just give me one night, Quinton. Please. Just one night to process this shit." Jemma ended the call then tossed the vodka back emptying the glass.

"May I use your restroom?" She quivered, trying her best not to cry and scream.

"Of course," I assured, guiding her down the hall to the guest bathroom.

I waited outside the door to ensure she was okay. Leaning against the opposite wall, I could hear the vehement sobs. That shit pissed me off. How dumb was this dude to jeopardize a relationship with a woman like Jemma. I'd done my fair share of bullshit in my past but never disrespect at this level. A few minutes later she exited, surprised to see me standing there. Her alluring velvety smooth skin was blemished with tears.

"Jemma, what can I do?" I asked, retrieving the tissue from her hand to gently dab away the tears.

But more were released as quickly as I captured them. Shit, I wanted to lay her in my arms because I was certain I could take her pain away. Caress her, shit, possess her, make Jemma mine. I wanted to… I shook my head, emptying the outlandish thought of love from my head.

Rage, dejection and heartbreak intertwined in the fiery flames blazing in her eyes. I was all too familiar with this emotion. Jemma leaned against the wall in the dusky hallway across from me and simply slid to the floor, her knees pressed into her chest, hands covering her face, fruitlessly concealing the pain. She released a wail that echoed through the vaulted ceilings and completely destroyed my fucking heart.

Instinctively, I carefully scooped her up and she cradled her face in the crook of my neck. Meandering into my bedroom, I rested Jemma on the bed, removing the cell phone that was still tightly clutched in her hand placing it on the nightstand. I didn't say a word, I just let her cry. I perched in the lounge chair across the room unable to convince myself to leave her alone. Silence invaded the space other than voiceless, simmering sobs. She laid motionless for at least half an hour staring out of the sliding doors.

"When I found out I was pregnant I thought my life was over. Quinton and I were so young and naive. We convinced ourselves that we could do anything. Prove all the doubters wrong. I've been somebody's wife and mother since I was twenty years old. I haven't known anything else but them... him. My marriage has been rocky for a few years now. A business relationship to maintain the honor of our family's name at Monroe. My tears are not for Quinton. I mourned the demise of my marriage a long time ago." She spoke at a whisper, disrupting my hushed inspection of her glorious frame. I walked towards her, resting at the foot of the bed as she continued.

"But I thought Quinton and I had an agreement. An unspoken arrangement but an agreement that he wouldn't hurt me like this. Destroy our friendship. But what Quinton has done to me, to our family? We can never be friends again. We'll never fully recover from this," Jemma sighed, pushing a breath through her reddened cheeks. "And crazy as it sounds, that's what hurts the most. Not the cheating, not even... a baby. But when your best friend is also your life partner and they betray you? Who do you run to for support, respite? It feels like my axis is spinning out of control with no one to balance me. Like I'm desperately trying to breathe but there's..."

"No air," I added.

Jemma peered at me for what seemed like a lifetime. I wanted desperately to kiss her but blanketed her with the cover instead.

"Get some rest, Jules. I'll be in the living room if you need anything." I had to get the fuck out of that room.

Observing Jemma's grief unleashed memories of my own that I preferred to remain deeply buried in the cavernous depths of my heart. My ex-wife Michelle and I have a similar narrative of young love and seasoned heartbreak. We met in high school and she was the smart, pretty cheerleader. I was the smart, thuggish, talented football player. Running the streets at seventeen with my grown ass cousins landed me in front of a judge for being an accessory to auto theft.

Thankfully the judge had mercy on my black ass because he and my football coach were fraternity brothers. The deal was that I would either finish high school in a military camp or go to jail. At the same time, Michelle found out that she was pregnant with my son. That shit made me straighten up real quick. We were married and the parents of a one year old all at the tender age of nineteen.

Life was a struggle but Michelle and I were a team until we weren't.

After almost seventeen years of marriage and two kids she decided she wanted to explore things she'd never had. Namely dick she'd never had since I was her first and only... until I wasn't. I'd done my shit before and during the marriage so I couldn't be too pissed until her extra shit began to impact our family. Late nights, forgetting the kids' events, missing work. She even started smoking weed which she'd never done. I begged to save my marriage more for my kids than me so we tried therapy. I still remember the rage I felt when I heard my wife, my best friend, tell me that she was in love with somebody else.

It was after midnight. Two hours passed and Jemma was still in my bedroom. I'd hoped she finally fell asleep until the silhouette of a gorgeous curvy figure appeared from the dark depths of the hallway.

"Hey," she whispered.

"Hey," I retorted. "Did you get some sleep?"

"Not really." Jemma halted, listlessly looking around the room. "I should probably get an Uber. Head home, or a hotel, or Maxi's. I don't know," she sighed, fidgeting anxiously and pinching her puffy cheek. "I don't know what to do," she inaudibly whined and that shit shot straight to my dick.

I rose from my position on the couch. The house was pitch-dark other than the glare from the TV. I stood inches away from her beautiful frame. The scent of vanilla and roses ignited my senses. Damn I wanted to cuddle her face and kiss the salted tear stains from her glowing cheeks, but I resisted.

"Jemma, it's almost one o'clock in the morning. What kind of man would I be if I let you get in an Uber at this hour? You're staying here tonight and I will take you wherever you need to go in the morning." I wasn't taking no for an answer. It was non-negotiable.

"I guess you're right. Um, can I have a t-shirt or something? This dress was not meant to sleep in," she softly chortled, but the smile didn't reach her eyes.

"Yeah. Um, I'm sure I can find something." I unconsciously clutched her hand in mine as we sauntered back into my bedroom. I searched through a couple boxes finding a NYU t-shirt and a pair of basketball shorts.

"Is this ok? It's the best I can do." The smirk on my face was a bit too lustful for the moment.

"It's fine. Thank you, Ezekiel. I really appreciate you. And I'm sorry about tonight. Getting you involved in my mess. I'm so sorry."

Tears threatened to fall again, this time it appeared more from embarrassment. Jemma's hands trembled, audibly irritated as she huffed in frustration struggling to release the side zipper on her dress.

"No need to apologize." I shook my head preparing to walk away to give her some privacy but her trembling limbs paused my retreat. "Do you mind if I help you?" I asked.

She nodded her consent.

Although I'd only known her a short time, I was acutely aware that while she was a strong and powerful woman, she was delicate, fragile. I unhurriedly ambled across the room and stood behind her as she lifted her shaky arm giving me access to the zipper. It was tiny so my massive hands made it difficult to maneuver, as did the aromatic savory scent of her perfume.

I released the zipper, causing the one strap to fall from her shoulder as the dress loosened from her frame. My God I wanted to kiss her smooth nutmeg-colored shoulder when she peeked over to look at me. But I discarded my desire.

Jemma turned around clutching the front of the dress so it wouldn't fall to reveal what I was certain was perfection.

"Thank you," she whispered.

Big beautiful mystified eyes gazing lustfully. I couldn't resist thumbing away the remnants of tears. The tussle between good and evil, right and wrong frolicked in my head. Common sense screamed for me to back away, while her dewy glistening orbs rendered me weak. My long legs took one more stride forward, depleting the gap between us.

Holding the t-shirt in one hand, I trailed a finger down the curve of her face, against her neck and her goosebump covered chest. I encouraged Jemma to release the dress still tightly clenched in her hands so I could help her get changed. Her breathing was shallow. The rhythmic rise and fall of her chest was hypnotizing.

Beautiful curves delighted my eyes. Jemma was thick with an hourglass figure and undeniably sexy. She partially released the dress revealing the black satin and lace strapless one piece bodysuit. The bra was sheer exposing her diamond hard nipples that distended against the delicate fabric.

I kissed against her forehead, nose, her right cheek then the left. We exchanged inhales and exhales, our lips threatened to become acquaintances. She leaned forward and closed her eyes, exhaling a sigh of relief. Our temples coupled before I placed the sweetest gentle kiss against her tear stained lips. Our first kiss.

"Jules," I breathily murmured, sounding like a bitch but I didn't care.

One innocent kiss became a bouquet of tiny kisses. My hands caressed the small of her back as she extended her arms, fingertips massaging my nape. When our tongues connected I was fulfilling a desire that simmered in me for months. The opportunity to taste the sweet lips I'd yearned for daily. I crowded her mouth with my tongue, languidly swiping and stroking to the progression of her moans. The sequin fabric of the dress quickly dissipated, pooling at her feet unveiling a voluptuousness that I desperately wanted to explore. Waist beads decorated her waist leading to the most ample, plump, perfect ass.

"Jemma, you need to walk away... right the fuck now." My voice was throaty, intense as I firmly fisted her hair with both hands.

I licked then kissed her neck as I deeply inhaled, my eyes lazily lowered with passion. I reluctantly withdrew from her succulent flesh, stuffing my hands into my pockets. She stood still, muted, beautifully exposed as I took several steps back trying to avoid dropping to my knees to lick her pussy. The shit I wanted to do to Jemma's body would be unruly, unnatural, and just plain nasty.

"The shit I want to do to you, Jules... my God." I shook my head, not realizing my inner ponderings were given sound. "You keep giving me a reason," I said, whispering gruffly.

She closed the gap I had created for her safety.

"A reason to what?" Jemma whispered, clasping the seam of my shirt preventing my intended escape.

I wrapped four fingers around her neck as my thumb stroked her bottom lip.

"To snatch you from that nigga and demonstrate to you how your mind and body should be worshipped. Satisfied. Fucked." I halted, thirsting to delicately choke the shit out of her while spreading her wide to taste heaven. "Don't let the suit and degrees fool you. I will fuck you Jemma. But... we shouldn't."

10

ZEKE

I forced those words from my lungs because I absolutely thought we *should* but didn't want to be the reason for her regrets. Jemma recoiled, abruptly opening the space between us as she slightly jerked away from me. Rejection. Her downcast expression reeked abandonment, misuse... neglect. She needed something and I desperately wanted to be her donor; to give her life, grant her every desire. I already had a mental connection to Jemma, but if she gifted me her body, I would never give that shit back.

My hands landed on three colorful waist beads as my fingertips cascaded down to her hips, drawing her closer to me.

"Jules, look at me. Please believe, I want you. *Terribly.*" I rested my temple against the side of her face, whispering against her lips. "But we shouldn't." I faintly spoke while shifting my head side to side, trying to convince myself more than her.

"Ezekiel, we should," Jemma hushly blurted with confidence. "Have you ever dreamed about me?" she asked.

I nodded, my temple still glued to her satiny skin.

"Because you *stay* fucking shit up in my dreams. So we should, because in my mind we already have,"she concluded breathily. "I just want to be reckless and unruly. Just one time in my life, so Zeke, we absolutely should," she whispered, stroking the arc of my face. "We can," she raspily moaned.

This woman shocked the shit out of me as she gazed directly into my eyes then greeted my lips with sprinkles of soft, wet kisses. I licked my lips, yearning, shit, greedy for a taste of Dr. Holiday when I reciprocated the groan, uttering, "And we will."

The bulge against my gray sweatpants grew steadily. My dick was aching, throbbing for Jemma. But I would be satisfied with just a taste of her creamy goodness. I was not a gambling man but I would've bet a million dollars that her pussy was candy-coated sugary sweet.

Jemma was breathless, panting with every kiss and touch. I caressed her neck with one hand while kneading her beautiful ass with the other. Her moans grew louder as she tightly embraced my neck. Silent tears still stained her face. Pleasured while still pained by the tumultuous day. Her body tensed. Jemma was in her head. Overthinking. But she continually drew me in closer. She wanted this... she desired this. I just prayed she craved me as much as I thirsted for her.

In an effort to dismantle her internal conflict, I nibbled her cheek, then against her ear and whispered, "let me take care of you. Let me make those dreams a reality. Just for tonight. Please."

I wasn't too proud to beg even if I knew that it was temporarily fulfilling her needs.

"Yes," she breathly affirmed.

"You are so fucking pretty. Since the first day I met you... your beauty is unmatched. Jemma Jule was the perfect name for you because you are a jewel, a fucking precious gemstone. This face, those eyes, your lips... damn, woman." I captured her mouth, biting into her bottom lip before continuing the salacious tongue lashing.

I slowly, happily unwrapped her from the body-smoother as if it was my birthday. Shit, she was the prize, the ultimate gift and I had to be careful with her. I gently rested her on the king-size bed. Her hands were coyly folded across her body, concealing her breast. She was exquisite and I wanted access to all of her. Trailing kisses up her inner thighs, I reached the crown of her jewel. Deeply inhaling, I glided my nose against her smooth bare center, delighting in its sugary aroma. I journeyed up her stomach sprinkling kisses against every inch of her bodacious frame.

Music was always playing through the surround sound speakers wired throughout my home. Alicia Keys 'Like You'll Never See Me Again' blared throughout the room. The lyrics were appropriate for this moment because I was absolutely going to hold and kiss Jemma like it was the last time because it probably was. I recollected the moment I had to leave her in my hotel suite. I hovered for long minutes regarding her beauty, studying her face while she was asleep because I truly thought it would be our first and last time together. The memory caused me to kiss her often and deeply.

Jemma was nervous but begged me not to stop every time I asked if this is what she wanted. Her trembling hands still sheathed her breast. I tried nudging her hands away but her grip was tight. I needed to see her, all of her.

"I - I have scars. On my breasts," she stammered her words at a whisper. "They are big and dark and ugly." Embarrassment and self-consciousness invaded her glorious face, refusing to release the clutched arms crossing her body.

"Jules, baby, I want to see every inch of you because I know it's sheer perfection. But we can stop if this makes you uncomfortable. " I nibbled against her chin then settled one kiss on her neck.

She shook her head as I delicately peeled back her fingertips, loosening the grip on her breast.

"Let me see you, beautiful " I lowly mumbled, almost inaudibly.

"No one has ever seen me like this. No man other than him. I - I've only been with Quinton," she confessed, almost in a shameful manner.

Shit. I was now playing the role those men played for my ex-wife. Offering Jemma a new experience. Acquainting her with dick she'd never had.

"I'm not going to hurt you, Jemma. I promise. I told you I don't make promises I can't keep." And I meant that shit.

I didn't understand why but I had become completely enamored with this woman. I knew I was in an unwinnable predicament, but I didn't care. I simply wanted to take her mind off her worries. Even if it was only for one night.

Jemma fully released her hands allowing me to do what I said I would - take care of her. I unclasped her hands displaying her gloriously round breasts. Scars and all - she was simply stunning.

"Damn, I was right, you *are* perfect," I whimpered, licking against one nipple before inhaling the full of her breast.

"Aahh!" Jemma noisily moaned, her back arching off of the stark white sheets. I continued my relentless pursuit, giving equal attention to the other breast. Nibbling against her neck before planting another kiss. The greediness of her kisses and strident outcry of her moans made it apparent that she hadn't been touched or satisfied in awhile. My hand navigated to her pussy, resting my thumb against her swollen bulb. She was so damn sensitive and soaking wet.

"Aaahh sssss," Jemma hissed.

We kissed like familiar lovers. Our tongues intertwined like kindred spirits, dancing to the rhythm of our harmonious moans. I played at her clit before gliding my fingers against her sodden folds, tenderly dipping one then two fingers into her glory. Jemma's insides were tight, soft and saturated. Her gooey molasses warmed my fingers as I pleasingly plunged into her depth tickling against the g-spot.

"Mmmm, Dr. Green," she sang.

Shit, I pressed her to call me Zeke, but I kinda liked the sound of her calling me doctor under these intimate conditions. I chuckled, mercilessly driving my fingers in and out and in and out of her ocean.

"What is it going to take to get you to call me Zeke?" I whispered against her lips.

Jemma was hushed. She licked along the seam of my lips before biting her own, fisting the sheets appearing to bask in the salacious thrust. Her essence contracted around my fingers, she was about to come, but I had other plans.

In an instant, I removed my fingers, greedily licking to ensure I left no trace of her honeyed nectar. I swiftly transitioned my lips to be face to face with her blossoming opening. It was the prettiest pussy I'd seen. Her juices glistened against her smooth, plump, sweltering flesh. I gradually tongue kissed along the folds of her private lips at a slow meticulous pace. Licking, sucking, slurping, drinking more of her saccharine juices.

"You are so damn sweet." I continued to have no mercy.

Recklessness was the name of my pursuit. Jemma was at the verge of break; loud moans, hard fist pounds against the mattress, grabbing and reaching for imaginary shit, anything that would save her. She vainly tried to escape but my deathgrip on her thighs made it virtually impossible.

"Please," she begged.

"Please what, Jules?"

"Please, Dr. Green," she whined.

"Tell me what you want," I demanded.

"Ezekiel. I want... shit. Please," she cried, bucking and gyrating against the bed unable to complete a sentence.

"Please what?" I mumbled against her saturated folds. With long, slow swipes, I repeatedly licked her entire fat ass pussy like a cat feasting on milk.

"If you tell me, I promise I'll make it happen for you." I continued to delight in the flavor of her treasure. "Tell me, Jemma," I commanded.

"Ezekiel! I want to come. I want you," Jemma screamed, as tears welled in her eyes.

"You sure you're ready for me, beautiful?" I teased, as lustfully tantalizing expressions of torture and satisfaction laced her face.

"Say it. Tell me, baby." I shifted my fingers, allowing my ring finger to pierce her ass while the pointer and middle fingers fondled against her g-spot but I never relinquished her clit from my sweltering lips. She became unhinged, momentarily insane.

"Yes! Oh shit. Oh shit. Oh shit. ZEKE!" Jemma reached a brutal climax, her mapled juices glistening against my face. I couldn't get enough of her delightsome flavor, moaning as I licked my fingers clean again. Fucking insatiable and my greedy ass still craved her.

Her breathing was labored as she released the sexiest melodious moan. Her back arched from the mattress still squirming from the aftershock.

"Jules, baby, you good?" I questioned, kissing up her forearm, massaging her dewy skin as I rested next to her quivering body.

"Oh my God, oh my God," she whispered repeatedly, fisting handfuls of her hair.

I smiled, dick swollen as I admired her beautiful pleasure. She was about to bite her damn lip off.

"Mmhmm. I'm good," she breathlessly chuckled. Completely satiated.

"Do you want me to stop?" I paused, cupping her chin forcing her to look at me. "Do you want me, Jules?"

She nodded.

"Yes or no, baby?" I demanded.

"Yes," Jemma whispered, running her fingers through my beard that was sheened by her wetness. She kissed me, licking her lips with a devilish grin as she tasted her personal essence on my lips.

A slight curve graced the corner of my mouth as I muttered, "you're such a good fucking girl."

I rose from the bed, removing my sweatpants as I grabbed a condom from the nightstand drawer. Jemma shyly, sneakingly, surveyed me, eyeing my tattoo covered chest and abdomen. Her eyes discreetly bulged as she watched me sheith my dick with the latex.

"You like what you see, good doctor?" I bantered.

She nodded, cradling that bottom lip between her teeth.

I kissed up the length of her sexy frame disrupting her daydream. I enjoyed kissing the oddest places; the top of her foot, her calf, the scar on her right knee. I explored her flesh - blemished and unblemished, no area was neglected.

Jemma was self conscious about her scars, unconsciously pulling the covers to hide them. I softly kissed and licked against the curvy plump scar under her right breast and the anchor-shaped marring on her left. Jemma was perfectly imperfectly and fucking beautiful to me. I didn't give a damn about those scars. She cradled the back of my head as her body began to meld into me, dismissing everything that attempted to cloud her judgment.

My pursuit was steady and purposeful. The mushroomed head of my dick loitered at the edge of her pussy lips before I progressively, patiently occupied every square inch of her treasure. My hardness slouthfully crept through the soft curves and plump ridges of her apex.

I desperately wanted to devour her but the way her tight walls clenched my manhood, I kept my strokes unhurried, deliberate, and methodical. I slid inside her dripping dams, resting a minute, allowing her jewel to adjust to my girth. Jemma was so snug and toasty. Shit! Now my ass was unhinged and insane. Fuck! This woman is going to be my undoing - my demise.

"Shit, Jules. You are so tight. My God gorgeous, feel so damn good," I groaned, still moving at a snail's pace, relishing in the warmth of her exhil-arating core. I nestled in the creases of her neck like a newborn baby.

"Ezekiel. What the fu- shit." Jemma incoherently covered her face with both hands. Shaking her head as she mouthed, *Oh My God*. Then whim-pered, "so good, so good. Ssss, so fucking good."

I covertly smiled against her neck. Jemma had a potty mouth and that shit turned me on. It pleased me to render this highly educated wordsmith wordless. Then there were tears, but I couldn't discern if they were tears of pleasure or regret?

I thumbed away the lone droplet, momentarily pausing my pursuit. I dreaded her response but I had to inquire.

"Why are you crying? Do you want me to stop?"

"No. No. Please don't stop. I just… it's just - " her moan trailed into a whine when she cradled her face into the crook of my arm.

Reluctantly, I slowly pulled my dick from the tranquility of *her* and nuzzled tightly against her dampened skin.

"What, Jules?" I asked, slithering a finger under her chin desperate for a shared gaze. I lifted my brows further encouraging an answer.

"I just didn't imagine it would be like this. That you would feel this good," she crooned, practically singing the words.

She seductively brushed the curves of my face, journeying her finger-tips down the length of my body, she whimpered, "I'm fine. I'm ok, Zeke. I promise."

Grabbing my ass, Jemma guided my monstrous frame back to its previous position. Even with the unexpected intermission, my rigid dick stayed at attention. I didn't conceal my smile this time when the sound of her sweet melodic voice called me Zeke. Jemma's little hand manipulated my sensitive manhood causing a guttural groan before she escorted my dick into the softest place. That shit was like a venus flytrap. Her fat outer lips slowly encased me as I steadily slipped in and out, then the kitty-cat snapped shut, trapping my girth powerfully in her snare.

"Shit, Dr. Holiday," I hissed.

Jemma locked her legs at the ankles around my waist, rocking her hips to the soundless rhythm our bodies produced. Her upstroke greeted my downstroke as she caressed my neck, encouraging me closer, deeper.

Picking up the pace, I adjusted one of her thighs over my shoulder, kissed her ankle, calf, then slithered my tongue between the bend in her knee. I desired to touch her everywhere as I salaciously pounded and thrusted against her treasure. Our moist bodies entangled in the most heavenly rapture.

"Zee. Zee," she hummed, painfully, yet pleasingly digging her nails into my flesh.

Zee, not Zeke. Shit! That made my dick twitch. She may as well have called that stupid nigga to say farewell because it was a wrap. Jemma wasn't going anywhere if I could help it.

"Jules, baby, shit. Oh my God. You are delectable," I groaned, energetically bracing her cheeks between my fingertips commanding her to look at me.

Our eyes tarried in a wanton flutter as I heavily murmured, "That mutherfucker is crazy to let go of this juicy, sweet, tight ass pussy."

That statement sparked something in Jemma. It was like she had some shit to prove. She lifted her other leg, practically forcing me to place both thighs on my shoulders. Grabbing the NYU t-shirt from the bed, she cloaked the fabric taut around my ass welcoming my heftiness into the cavernous depths of her ocean. The rhythmic dance of her bodacious hips caused her puss to constringe and grip my dick tighter and tighter.

"Damn, baby. Don't stop that. Whatever the fuck it is don't stop," I crooned. Like I said, I wasn't ever too proud to beg for some good shit.

Jemma's body language let me know she was reaching her pinnacle as well. Lips trapped between her teeth and eyes rolled to the back of her head, she was coming... hard and fast. And I was willingly following.

"Zeke!"

"Jules!"

"Shit, Zee, I'm-"

"Fuck, Jem I'm-"

"COMING!" The orgasm violently ripped through us as we lusciously announced our synchronous pleasure accompanied by a few other select curse words.

Jemma dug her nails into the back of my bald head. Bated breathing, the rise and fall of her chest steadily slowing. I briefly collapsed my six foot plus frame against her thickly petite body snuggled in her neck but she didn't seem to care, tautly wrapping thick legs around preventing my escape.

"Let me get up for a second," I said, planting tiny kisses on her dewy flesh. She released my neck and I lifted from the bed to discard the condom. Running the hot water while using the bathroom, I washed my hands then wet a towel until it was steaming.

Shit, my damn legs were wobbly as I padded into the bedroom collapsing next to her shimmery cinnamon skin. She appeared relaxed, anxiety momentarily paused. I gently laid the hot towel against her skin. She jerked and moaned as I caressed and cleaned the evidence of our enrapture from her. Lost in the afterglow, I planted a soft kiss at the crown of her jewel before disappearing back into the bathroom.

I admittingly ogled her, staring from the bathroom threshold. Jemma was so fucking pretty, especially when emblazoned by a streak of moonlight peeping through the blinds. She curled in the fetal position completely naked and completely satisfied, momentarily dozing until the heat from my massive hands embraced her.

"Can I ask you a question?" I asked, tone at a whisper.

"Mmm-hmm," she sang.

"Why did you become a writer? Jules seems to have a different persona than Jemma." I stroked my fingers through her curls as she nestled into me so close I couldn't distinguish my inhale from her exhale.

"I was born Jemma Jules Warren. I am named after both of my grandmothers. My maternal grandmother was Jemma Mae, a school teacher and my paternal grandma Jules or, JuJu as we called her, was a journalist. The first black woman to host her own radio show here in Monroe. I was close to them both so I guess my professions are my way of continuing to honor them." She smiled, trailing her fingernail across the hairs on my chest. This shit felt real close. Awfully familiar.

"That's beautiful," I uttered, getting lost in this proximity with her. "Can I call you JuJu?" I chuckled, pinching the crown of her cheek as she laughed.

"Um, no sir." Our banter lingered off into momentary silence until she breathily muttered, "But I like it when you call me Jules."

I could feel the corners of her face lift into a smile against my skin as she snuggled deeper into my neck. I returned the sentiment because she found calmness, respite... in me. Our closeness felt good. Too damn good for her to be somebody's wife. My ass was in so much trouble. Goddammit! Dr. Jemma mutherfucking Holiday.

11

JEMMA

He said he was leaving you. I'm not taking care of this baby by myself!
I was roused, awakened by the echo of the most God awful words spewing from a woman who's been sleeping with my husband for who knows how long.. and she's pregnant... with my husband's baby. I wiped my eyes because I had to be dreaming, well more like experiencing a terrifyingly heinous nightmare. My bedroom was dusky. The early morning sun was no match for the blackout curtains.

"Hmmm. Since when do I have blackout curtains?" I mumbled.

Peering at the clock on the black nightstand, the blaring white numbers read 6:42 am. Wait a minute, this wasn't my clock nor my nightstand.

"Maybe I'm still dreaming," I whimpered softly as I slightly shifted positions.

Shit! The ache between my thighs was very real though, as were the muscular, fraternity-hooks branded, dark chocolate arm that engulfed me. I was nowhere near my damn bedroom.

"Good morning, gorgeous. Are you ok?" The raspy sexy morning voice thundered against my ear.

My eyes bulged, desperate and afraid to connect the face with the lustful timbre. My damn kitty was clearly familiar with the cocoa-colored stranger because she instantly soaked in response to the bass-filled tone.

"Um, yeah. Yes. I'm good," I nervously responded, still facing the window refusing to confront my reality.

The lips attached to the voice kissed against my shoulder. I shuddered, quivering because the sinful recollection of those lips were downright delicious.

"Jemma. Look at me," he demanded, cupping two fingers under my chin encouraging me closer. I turned, gazing into the sexiest most soothing anthracite eyes.

"You're not trying to run out on me are you?" He smiled. "I promised I would take you wherever you needed to go today."

"I'm not running." I paused, admiring that damn Colgate smile. "And besides, how are you going to take me home? What would I tell Quinton if I pulled up with you as my driver?" I smirked.

"You would tell Coach Holiday that you had a good time last night. That somebody took care of you like you deserve." Ezekiel's chiseled face was stern. No jokes.

I glared at him. My honeyed orbs began to burn. I'm not sure why, but that statement catapulted through my core, brewing mixed emotions. Zeke was right. He did take care of me last night, making my body reach new plateaus that I'd never experienced. It had been a long time since I felt sexy, physically satisfied…shit, desired.

It had been months, at least six, since me and Quinton had sex. My body no longer responded to him. As deliciously gorgeous as he was, my kitty felt absolutely nothing the times he attempted. So he just… stopped trying. But what the hell was going on with kitty and Dr. Ezekiel Green? She was purring, gnawing, crying to get another taste of him. My body screamed and shouted its acceptance, speaking loud and clear in response to Ezekiel's touch and countless inches last night.

"Do you need anything from the kitchen? He asked, slightly hovering over me.

Shit, more vodka. A mimosa, I thought. "Water, please," I croaked.

He kissed against my forehead, then my shoulder and my knee before exiting the bed. I never knew how much I could enjoy a kiss on the knee.

Zeke stood with all his manly glory on display. That man's dick was a timeless precious artifact sculpted by the hands of Michelangelo himself.

Ezekiel being only the second dick I'd seen up close and personal, it was, in a word, magnificent. Long and thick like a king size Snickers. I wanted to taste the sweet and salty monster. But the head - shit! I'd never seen anything like that before. Not on Quinton, not even on the nastiest, grimiest porn sites. As Zeke became more erect, the head joyfully blossomed like a blooming rose. It was magical, growing bigger and thicker right before my eyes last night.

Zeke ambled across the room and out of the door not bothering to cloak himself and I wasn't mad. I took a moment to observe my surroundings since I didn't recall much of the space from last night. High vaulted ceilings similar to the living room, charcoal gray accent wall partially covered by a contrasting light gray tufted headboard. He clearly loved to read because the office I passed last night was filled with boxes marked books. Similar boxes were stacked against the wall in his bedroom. A picture of a handsome young man with Ezekiel's height and cocoa skin and a gorgeous young woman who stole her daddy's whole face was positioned on his nightstand.

"Eriya and EJ." The gruff bass-filled voice startled me from my reverie. "Ezekiel Jr., he's twenty two and driving me insane right along with my Yaya," he chuckled. The sparkle in his eyes at the mention of his kids was cute… and sexy.

He sauntered towards me holding a tray while I was still perched on the bed. Ezekiel noticed my confusion as I furrowed at the tray.

"You didn't eat much last night. I figured you may be hungry."

A toasted bagel, a wedge of cream cheese, strawberries, a banana and grapes were arranged on a plate with a bottle of water on a wooden tray.

"Thank you." I blushed, wondering why he was so attentive. *He did just knock every one of the cobwebs off of your kitty.* I mused. "Do you mind if I use your restroom?" I dropped my forehead into the palm of my hand because that was *the* dumbest question.

"Of course, Jemma," he chuckled, still naked and still fine as fuck.

I tightly clutched the blanket to cover my body. My modesty was a little delayed after he had already been inches deep in my softest place. Slowly sliding off the high-rise bed frame, my feet barely touched the ground. I spun around unhurriedly, continuing to wrap myself in the thick white blanket. He leaned against the headboard, laughing at my antics as he watched me tip-toe across the room with the blanket dragging behind me like the train of a wedding gown.

Closing the door, I allowed the blanket to fall to the floor. Gazing into the massive mirror, I appeared different. Shit, I felt different. The scars didn't seem as ugly today and I felt satisfied; surprisingly not an ounce of guilt invaded my psyche.

I sat on the toilet, again digesting my surroundings. He had a beautiful home. I desperately wanted to take a swim in his bathtub but that would just be too much. I was a bit too cozy in his house. *You need to take your ass home… or somewhere,* I pondered.

I grabbed the tissue to clean myself and my kitty was still just as juicy and sensitive as she was last night. I was shocked, unable to remember the last time my puss responded to Quinton in that way. At one point, I was beginning to think something was medically wrong with me, but clearly kitty just didn't like trifling ass Quinton anymore.

I exhaled, closing my eyes reminiscing about last night. *Jules.* He was so sweet and insatiable when he called me Jules. The way Ezekiel licked against my clit, driving his thick tongue deeper into my saturated hole… my Lord. But when he did that Edward Scissorhands thing with his thumb massaging my swollen clit, fingers in my pussy *and* my ass, I think I coded for a second. Like straight up flatlined. I was about to die. This man was committing murder. My autopsy report would read, *demise caused by intense, salacious intrusion by a massive dick.* Dr. Green is a nasty mutherfucker and I think I like it. Shit! I'm in trouble.

I mummified myself again, swaddled in the blanket as I ambled out of the bathroom. Ezekiel was focused on his phone before looking up at me with a suggestive smile. I reddened, nervously pinching my cheek, as he crooked his finger requesting my presence near him. Why the hell did I obey?

"Don't be nervous, beautiful." He sexily grinned. I quietly treaded towards him reaching his side of the bed where he sat upright on the edge… still butt ass naked. *My goodness!* He tugged at the blanket loosening the fabric from my flesh as he drew me closer to settle between his legs. The warmth of his caress felt delightful, relaxing… safe.

"Good morning, Dr. Holiday. How did you sleep?" he asked, tucking curly tresses behind my ear.

"Good morning, Dr. Green. I slept pretty good." I blushed, goosebumps crawling up my spine.

Zeke kissed the tip of my nose, each cheek, then sensually licked along the crease of my lips. My breathing labored and my pussy throbbed. He parted my lips slowly, suckling my tongue, twisting in the most salacious caper. One firm hand embraced the curve of my face while the other disrobed me from the blanket. Instinctively, I hastily moved my hands to cover my breasts but the attempt was in vain. He gently grasped my hands, shaking his head lustfully forbidding me.

"You are perfect, Jemma. You never have to mask anything for me," he confidently uttered those words as if there was going to be a next time.

He beheld my curvy physique, admiration laced within his comforting eyes. Zeke trailed a hand down the length of my body, paying special attention to my swollen mahogany areolas, nipples rock-solid. I gasped, "Ezekiel."

"Do you want me to stop?" he probed. I appreciated that he always verified my consent but my silly hot-to-trot ass hadn't denied him.

I should say yes, please stop. I needed to press pause but I desired, shit craved a fourth release. I willingly, eagerly granted him permission to my body. And if this fine ass, chocolate ass, blossoming dick ass man was ready to give, I was absolutely ready to receive.

"No," I breathily consented.

Zeke slid off of the bed standing directly into my personal space. Our bodies collided; the swell of his dick pressed against my stomach. The beat of our hearts drummed in kindred unity. I tossed my head back between my shoulders wondrously gazing at this beautiful man that confused and mesmerized my sensibilities.

Zeke tenderly thrusted me against the wall mellowly kissing every inch of my quivering flesh. He kneeled before me playing against my navel before licking the crown of my jewel. Draping my right leg over his shoulder, Ezekiel flattened his tongue to play and fondle against my private folds. Shit! Thank God for these Peloton legs because I was standing firm on that one leg welcoming all of him inside me. He cupped my ass as his tongue entered my throne. Sucking my pussy while squeezing my ass driving me bat-shit crazy.

"Zeke, shit. Zee, please." I pleaded, with my hands braced against his head. Unsure if I was begging for him to continue or for someone to save me from this deliciously lustful attack.

I quivered, tears welling in the corners of my eyes. This shit felt so good he had me ready to wail. I was coming undone, reaching the crescendo. I wanted to tell him how he made me feel, release a boisterous scream to the heavens but I acquiesced. Withholding my shouts of joy because this man should not be my delight. He should not be lifting me to the loftiest heights. I was somebody's wife, dammit.

"Oh my goodness. Oh shit." I softly panted.

Ezekiel rose to his feet taking me with him to the bed. I nestled in the comforts of his aromatic neck trying to conceal my tears as he cradled me like a baby. I couldn't even recall if he grabbed a condom but I suddenly felt the immense heaviness embedded into the depths of my treasure.

"Aaah!" I moaned, still hiding my face.

I couldn't believe that someone other than Quinton was becoming acquainted with my body. This wasn't just a one night stand kinda fuck. At least it didn't feel that way to me. Our bodies were sensually attracted like moths to a flame. Like bees to honey. Zeke wantonly embraced and caressed my body with a desirous stroke. Whispering adoring sentiments of my beauty and perfection.

"Jules, you are so damn beautiful."

But there was something about the way he called me *Jules,* it just hit different, causing a flood in my puss. His enticement was slow, steady, yet fated, assured… and sadly temporary.

I shivered at the thought of Ezekiel disjoining from my flesh, privately praying that this captivating climax would never end. I cried silent tears overwhelmed with emotions and this glorious dick.

* * *

The sun screamed for me to awaken. I stretched with one eye open, this time immediately recognizing my surroundings. I was still at Ezekiel's house. Still in his bed but he wasn't there. *11:21 am.* I desperately needed to leave but avoidance was holding me hostage. I didn't want to face my reality.

The bagel breakfast from earlier was still on the nightstand. I was starving since he decided to satisfy my appetite in other ways this morning. I popped a grape in my mouth before grabbing my phone. Quinton had been calling and texting all morning begging me to call him.

It's funny how he was suddenly so attentive when his ass was in jeopardy. Quinton wasn't stupid. He knew that we could never rebound given his current situation. Honestly, I'd been praying for the strength to leave the marriage; hoping for a sign. I guess God figured since another woman wasn't a big enough sign he would knock me right upside the head with a woman and a baby. My phone vibrated against the nightstand disrupting my haze.

"Hey Maxi," I whispered.

"Heffa, are you still with Dr. Green? Quinton has called me at least twenty times this morning because he thinks you're here," she whispered, but I didn't understand why.

"I know. I know. I'm about to call him. Can you pick me up in an hour?" I requested.

"Of course I can. But you're not slick. Answer my question. Are you still with that man?" Maxi probed.

"Yes," I coyly whimpered.

"Aww shit! Bitch I'm on my way and I need all the nasty details." She laughed.

"Why do you think there are any nasty details to share, Max?" I rolled my eyes as if she could see me.

"Because your ass sounds all tranquil and shit. Like you've been dicked down properly, ma'am," Maxi cackled.

Just as the words left her foul mouth, Ezekiel walked into the bedroom slanging said dick that pressed against his white basketball shorts. Smooth, cocoa-colored bare chest shining with lucent beads of sweat. Good Lord.

"Maxi I gotta go. I'll text you the address. An hour Maxi. Don't be late." I demanded then turned my focus to him.

"Hey. Why didn't you wake me up?" I sexily grinned. *Stop it Jemma before this man has you pinned against the wall again.*

"Why would I wake sleeping beauty?" He smiled. "You were resting so peacefully I didn't want to disturb you. So I went for a quick run."

"I'll be out of your hair soon. I'm sure you have better things to do today other than take care of me," I blurted and immediately regretted the statement.

Ezekiel eyed me dangerously. "It's been my pleasure, Jemma. You can stay as long as you want."

My phone buzzed again. This time it was Quinton. I sighed, irritated but I had to answer the call.

"Quinton, calling and texting me a thousand times is not going to change anything. I told you I was safe. I'll let you know when I'm headed to the house," I calmly stated. My demeanor had him confused and pissed.

"Jemma, where the hell are you?" Quinton barked, causing me to momentarily pull the phone away from my ear. I remained placid. "I've texted and called you all night. And I will keep calling when I don't know where my wife is or how she got there?" The agitation and desperation was loud. "Are you at Maxi's, Jemma?" He was eerily calm.

"Oh now you're concerned about your wife?" I laughed but shit wasn't funny. "You have alot of fucking nerve questioning me." I didn't answer the question. Ezekiel meandered from the closet to the bathroom feigning disregard.

"When you come home, are you staying home, J?" Quinton probed.

"I honestly don't know, Quinton. I'll be there in an hour or so. We'll talk then. Don't call me anymore." I hung up, wishing I had an old-school house phone to slam in his face.

Ezekiel walked out of the bathroom but didn't look my way. "Everything you need is in the bathroom whenever you're ready. No rush," he said with his back to me quickly ambling out of the room before I could say anything.

I texted Maxi the address and a request for clothes. I definitely couldn't go home in my cocktail dress. After several minutes, Ezekiel hadn't returned to the bedroom. I padded across the plush carpet into the bathroom, noticing a set of towels and a new bar of Dove soap. I rinsed my mouth and made a makeshift toothbrush with my finger and a towel. Scrubbing my thong in some hot soapy water, I shook my head whispering, "this is some hoe shit."

I took a quick shower, then lotioned and dressed in the t-shirt and shorts he offered last night. Slowly footing down the hall, I noticed Ezekiel lounged on the couch typing on his iPad.

"Um, can I put this in the dryer?" I asked, embarrassed as I dangled the wet thong from my fingertips."

"Or you could just leave it here?" he chuckled.

"I'm serious, Dr. Green." My blush completely conflicted with my words. "Dr. Dupont will be picking me up soon. She's bringing me some clothes," I muttered nervously.

"So we're back to the formalities I see. Ok." He pursed his lips while nodding, then placed the iPad on the end table. Crossed hands over his abdomen, he gawked at me then pointed to the laundry room next to the kitchen. I tossed the garment in the dryer and walked back to the living room.

"Ezekiel, I -"

"No need to provide an explanation, Jemma," he interrupted. "We knew - I knew what this was so it would be silly of me to have any expectations."

Ezekiel stood in response to the doorbell, coming to me first before answering. He cupped my cheeks. "I hope you had a good time last night. All I want is for you to be okay, Dr. Holiday." He swiped the stray tendrils of my hair while tenderly kissing my lips. "Ok?" he hummed, raising an eyebrow. I nodded. Reluctantly, he sauntered away to answer the door.

"Hello, Dr. Dupont. Would you like to come in?" Maxi peeked around his Herculean frame to look at me. I slightly shook my head signaling Maxi to take her ass back to the car. I needed a minute alone with him.

"Well, hello, Dr. Green. No. No thank you. I'll wait in the car," she sang while grinning way too big. "These are for Dr. Holiday." Maxi handed him a bag and turned to walk away.

I retrieved my thong from the dryer then dressed in a black t-shirt dress and flip flops, hoop earrings and lathered with Philosophy Amazing Grace lotion. I hurried back to the living room to find him settled on the arm of the couch with an exasperated expression on his chiseled face.

"Ezekiel-"

"Jemma, don't," he interrupted.

"No. Please let me say this." I closed the distance and clasped my hands in his. "I want to be clear. I don't regret anything that happened between us… that has been happening. I was fully aware and consenting. Honestly, after the crazy baby reveal last night I selfishly needed to feel wanted." I shrugged, more nonchalantly than I intended.

"That's it? Is that all you needed, Jemma? To feel wanted. You could've got that anywhere," he resounded, glaring at me.

Ezekiel withdrew from my hold, clearly irritated. I didn't mean to appear dismissive because that was a far cry from what I was really feeling. Shit, if I were being honest, he'd made me feel wanted and desired since the first day we met.

"Zeke. Please stop." I clutched his muscular corded arm inhaling his natural vanilla aroma. "I wanted you. I needed you, Zee." I tearfully admitted. Shit, I didn't want to desire this man but I did - desperately.

"I didn't mean to complicate things for you, Jules. But I won't deny that I wanted you the first night I laid eyes on you. Since that night in my hotel suite and every night since we started communicating. But - " He halted his words, exhaling as he ran a hand down the back of his head.

"I'm married," I whispered.

"Yes, and maybe a bit vulnerable. I don't want your desire for me to be inspired by a wounded heart. I'm fully aware that I was the rebound, shit, maybe even revenge. But that is not a position I'm willing to play again," he sternly declared.

"Zeke you make it sound so -"

"Accurate? Final?" He finished.

I bit the corner of my lip, rapidly blinking to quell the tears. This was too intense. Why did my heart break a little at the thought of this being it for me and Ezekiel?

"Jemma, please don't cry. Go take care of your business. Better yet, go settle your heart." He clutched my hand, pulling me to the door.

Ezekiel leaned his back against the front door, drawing my body into him. He embraced me so tight, so sweet, inhaling my scent before kissing against my neck. His hands journeyed down the center of my back then cupped my butt. Gentle kneads and squeezes coupled with delicate kisses brought more tears to my eyes. The moment was so intimate, so caring, so... reckless. I traced a finger across the intricacies of his handsome face. He kissed my fingertips with his eyes sealed tight when I grazed his lips. I'd lost my damn mind. I didn't want to let this man go. He whimpered, "Jules," causing our eyes to slowly open. We gazed at each other for a moment too long because my kitty wanted to stay for round five.

"Jemma, whatever you decide about your marriage, let it be your decision. Not based on what he wants, what your family wants or what has happened between us. Do what's best for you. Ok? Can you make me that promise?"

I nodded.

"Use your words, Dr. Holiday," he teased, blushing.

Kissing against the tip of my nose, he continued, "If you ever need to talk, need a friend, just drop your location and I'll be there."

"I'm clearly a whole ho because after all of this I don't even have your number," I giggled.

"Nah, that's definitely not what this is. Check your phone. I got you."

I nodded. "Ok. Enjoy the rest of your day, Dr. Green." I smiled, reluctant to leave but I had to go.

"That's highly unlikely without your pretty ass in my bed," he said, then stroked the tip of my nose followed by a wink. "See you later, Dr. Holiday."

12

JEMMA

"**B** iittcchh! You have ten minutes to tell me everything before we get to your house. I can't believe you practically live around the corner from that man," Maxi squealed as she pulled out of Ezekiel's driveway. "Jemma what happened?"

"It's a long complicated story," I huffed.

"Well uncomplicate and condense the shit then," she demanded.

"Zeke, um, Ezekiel, I mean, Dr. Green drove around the city and then brought me to his house because I didn't know where else to go. I was in a daze." I peered out of the window hearing Bethany's voice echoing in my head. "He let me scream, let me cry and simply rest. He was just there for me, Max."

"And that turned into y'all having sex?" Maxi's brow furrowed.

"Judgey much?" I rolled my eyes. "And didn't you say he was the one night stand of our dreams."

"I'm the last person to judge you, Jemma. I guess I thought your scary behind was going to punk out," Maxi giggled.

"Then stop looking at me like that. I was completely lucid. I knew exactly what I was doing." I confidently declared, because I was. "Did I go to his house with the intention of sleeping with him? No. Do I regret it? Absolutely not."

"Revenge maybe?" Maxi questioned.

"No." I paused for a long minute. "Renewal. Shit, release." I shuddered at the memory of Ezekiel's hands, tongue... his everything. "He was exactly what I didn't know I needed."

"That good, huh?" She laughed.

"Girl!" My head jolted from the headrest to look at her. "That damn good." I tossed my head back, snickering. "I feel like Nina from Love Jones. His dick just... talked to me."

"Girl, what did it say?" Me and Maxi loudly hollered, pondering the classic black romance movie.

"Do you have any regrets?" Maxi probed.

"No. None." I said, shaking my head with no hesitation.

"Damn! I knew the good doctor had good dick," she announced. "Was it the first and last time, because the way that man was gawking at you... my gawd! That wasn't a one night stand kinda stare."

"Then what kind was it, Max," I smirked.

"A *he wants him some of you* type of gaze," she cackled, sticking her tongue out.

I shook my head as we heartily laughed. Our merriment quickly dissipated as we pulled into the driveway of my house. Quinton was sitting on the porch since I texted him that I was on my way home. Head resting against his fists, he nervously bounced his legs. I leered at him sitting in the very swing that I'd hoped we would rock our grandchildren in.

"You need me to stay?" Maxi whispered, scrutinizing him, disdain piercing her eyes.

"No. I'm good. I'll be at your house tonight though. Well maybe a few nights until I figure this shit out. Is that ok?" We looked at each other, tears welled in my eyes. "I can't stay here."

Maxi nodded. "You can stay with me as long as you want. You know that." We shared a smile as she clutched my hand before I stepped out of the car and to my surprise she exited the car too.

Quinton bounced, rising from the swing, yelling, "really Maxi? She don't need a chaperone." Quinton fussed, stomping down the three steps towards us. "What, you think I'm going to hurt her? Like she needs protection?"

"Your monkey ass has hurt her enough, Quinton. Keep fucking with her and *you* are the one who might need protection." Maxi shouted over my shoulder as I held her back.

"Max. Stop. I'm good. I'll let you know when I'm on my way," I assured.

She leaned in to give me a tight hug and whispered, "call me if you need me."

I nodded.

I ambled up the steps not ready to have this conversation when my phone rang. It was Quaron.

"What's up sissy?" My tone was somber, exhausted.

"Sis, I didn't know. I swear to you I didn't know. I can't believe that stupid negro got a bitch pregnant," Quaron shouted.

"I know. I trust that you would've told me. Who called you? Maxi?" I probed.

"No. Q's dumb ass," she uttered. "He called last night crying like a bitch thinking he was going to get some sympathy from me. I threatened to call mommy and daddy on his trifling ass. Quinton knows he wasn't raised like that."

"Wow," I chuckled, shaking my head. "I guess desperation will do that to a man."

"Right! With his dumb ass. I'm on the road headed back to Monroe. I should be there in an hour."

"Ok. I'll probably be at Maxi's. Drive safe." I hung up before she could continue.

I walked in the house ahead of Quinton. He'd been drinking. An empty bottle of Hennessy sat on the kitchen island. *Oh, he's definitely desperate,* I thought because he rarely drank and definitely not Hennessy. I leaned against the island with my arms crossed. I'm certain Quinton was prepared for me to curse, scream and tear shit up like I would normally do when I was faced with one of his infractions. But I remained placid, silent, fed the fuck up, yet calm.

The tension in the room was so weighty, deafening awkward silence bounced around the vaulted ceilings. I don't know how long I stood there observing Quinton as he frantically paced the floor. Images of our family portraits over the years flashing in his background.

"J, I fucked up," he blurted. "I didn't mean for this shit to happen. Jemma, you have to believe that I never wanted to hurt you. It's always been just me and you... just J and Q remember? No other woman could ever take your place. You and Shiloh are my world. J, baby, I love you." His dramatics were almost convincing, yet comical.

I tossed my head back staring at the ceiling, and for the life of me I couldn't contain the boisterous laugh that escaped my lungs at Quinton's confession of love. My life could literally be written in the words of every nineties black romance movie. In my head I was dramatically shouting the classic Halle Berry line from Boomerang. *"Love. What do you men know about love? Love should've brought your ass home last night."* But I relented, deciding not to take the melodramatic route.

"Then what exactly did you mean to happen, Quinton?" I was eerily still as I sauntered towards him with my hands clasped behind my back. "When you sleep with women unprotected, a baby is one of many possibilities. So I guess you should consider yourself lucky, huh, unless there's an STD you need to disclose as well?" My smile was haunting. Shit, it scared me. Why the hell was I so impassive?

"But to say you love me, that I am your world. It's an insult, Quinton. Because if you truly loved me you would've walked away from her... and all of the others." His gasp made me pause. "Yeah, Q. I know Bethany is not the only one. But if it was really just J and Q like it used to be, you would not have been fucking that bitch raw in the first place. Correction. You wouldn't have fucked random bitches period."

Muted tears blemished my face as I continued to close the gap between us.

"Let us use this time to be honest with each other. I do believe you love me... *nostalgia*. You are holding on to love from the past, but you haven't been *in* love with me in quite awhile."

He vigorously shook his head. "Jemma, that's not true." Quinton embraced me, kissing against my neck, repeating at a whisper, "that's not true. I'm so in love with you."

I emotionlessly uncoupled from his hold, noticing the glaze covering his beautiful green eyes. He was crying.

"For at least four years this has been a business partnership, not a relationship. We've been the perfect Holiday family of Monroe University. A falsification. A spectacle. Things between us were already distant, but worsened when I got sick."

Quinton was silent. He couldn't look at me. "Do you remember the first time I asked you to make love to me after my first breast surgery, Quinton?" I paused, not really waiting for a response but it was a vain attempt not to cry harder. "You looked at me like I was a mutant. My scars disgusted you. No longer your perfect, pretty, angelic Jemma. I believe that's when it all started. The late nights out, the private conversations in your mancave, the second phone."

Quinton finally peered at me, eyes wide. He knew everything I said was true. Two years ago I was diagnosed with Fibrocystic Breast Disease. It literally seemed to have happened over night. One day while in the shower I noticed a small bump on my right breast. A week later, the one bump became three large lumps rousing me from my sleep in excruciating pain. After weeks of painful drainage tubes, various tests and multiple mammograms, thank God the lumps were not cancerous. But they had to be surgically removed leaving three significant scars and sporadic sensation in my right breast.

Six months later, two more cysts appeared in my left breast, requiring me to undergo the same procedures. Quinton was supportive throughout the doctor's appointments, surgery and my recovery, but when I was healed and ready to have an intimate connection with my husband again, he didn't want me.

"I lost every bit of my confidence. Daily insecurities plagued me; self-conscious about my appearance, my ability to satisfy you sexually." I shook my head as tears streamed, salting the corners of my mouth. "Everyday I blamed myself." I stared right into his beautiful eyes. They were still the most mesmerizing shade of green but no longer carried the sparkle I adored.

"J, I am so sorry. You have always been the most beautiful woman I have ever seen. Flawless. I knew I wanted you the first day I saw you in that dorm room. I would've painted all of Betty Shabazz Hall to ensure you were mine. You were the perfect combination - my best friend, homie, ride or die, and my lover. When you got sick, when the doctors didn't know if you had cancer or not, if you'd lose your breast, that shit scared me. I just lost control, lost sight of what I had right in front of me. Please tell me how to make this right. Let me fix this, Jemma." Quinton pleaded with tears in his eyes. He reached for me but I recoiled, repulsed by the thought of his touch.

"Quinton, you have a fucking baby on the way. A baby, Q!" I screamed, the first sign of any emotions.

He grabbed me and I momentarily broke. Hands that once rendered me weak stroked my nape. The sensation made me nauseous. I aggressively jerked away, pushing him off of me.

"I hate you right now! You have broken things in me that I may never be able to repair. You've stolen so many of my firsts. So many moments that I will never get back. I have loved you unconditionally since I was nineteen years old and I wanted to love you until death parted us. I've never been one to be curious about what I missed out on at such a young age because I had everything I needed in you. I thought you would always love me freely, relentlessly and without conditions. But I was wrong, Q."

His head drooped in shame. I forcefully lifted his chin demanding him to look at me as I stood steadfast in his face so he could visualize every shattered piece of me he'd caused.

"So shame on me for trusting you with my heart, Quinton. Shame on me for assuming the best of you not only as my husband, but my friend. Shame on me for always kissing you with my eyes closed so tight until I was breathless. Shame on me for losing Jemma while I feverishly worked to elevate you." The vehement wail soared from my lungs filling the space with the screeching sounds of wretched heartache.

"So to answer your question. This..." I motioned between me and Quinton. "Is unrepairable, incurable, hopeless. Just J and Q...is over."

13

JEMMA

I released the breath I didn't realize I was holding as I eyeballed him. Anguish, regret and fear coated his pale face. While grief, optimism and deliverance brightened mine as I slowly ambled to our bedroom. I needed to disappear. Quickly retreat because I could not stomach his presence any longer. When I entered my bedroom, thoughts of Ezekiel's room invaded my brain. Flashes of his tongue and hands lustfully commandeering my body ignited an uncontrolled shudder.

"Jemma." Quinton's pained baritone caused me to scramble to pack a bag. Guilt suddenly entered my psyche. Was I a hypocrite? Incriminating Quinton for his behavior, but pardoning myself for mine.

"Jemma, baby, you don't have to leave. I'll move to another room," Quinton said as he caught my arm to pause my pursuit.

Baby. I mused, dryly chuckling. "You know Quinton, I can't remember the last time you called me *baby*. Now here you are, the word rolling off your tongue with ease... or maybe it's just guilt."

"J! Come on. Please, bab-" He begged but I abruptly interrupted him.

"No. No, thank you. I can't be here. I need to think... breathe, and I can't do that here. Our home is no longer a safe haven for me." I scurried across the room into the bathroom packing my toiletries as he settled on the lounge chair watching me.

We lingered in awkward silence for at least thirty minutes. My pounding heartbeat was the only indication of life in the room.

"Mommy. Daddy. Where are you guys?" Shiloh's voice called out from the living room. My brows lifted in panic as I leered at Quinton, pissed that we had to share this bullshit with our daughter right now. I never lied to Shiloh and I wasn't about to start now.

"Knock, knock," she sang, nudging open the cracked bedroom door.

"Hey, hey. What are y'all doing in here?" Shiloh plopped down at the end of the bed just like she did as a little girl. "Ma, are you going on a trip?" she questioned, observing my luggage then looking between me and Quinton. Her beautifully innocent eyes, identical to her father's, broke my heart. "Daddy? What's wrong? Have you been crying?" She continued to nervously probe.

I stood stationary at the bathroom threshold holding my toiletry case, staring at Quinton waiting for him to speak. He was wordless, but I refused to rescue him this time. The minutes of silence felt like a lifetime passed us by.

"Shi, baby girl." He cleared the heaviness from his throat. "Um, me and Mommy are going to take a little break. We have some grown up things to work through," Quinton said, padding across the room to join her on the bed.

"A break? Why? What does that mean?" Her brows crashed together in confusion.

"Your mom needs to clear her head about a few things, sweetie. It's just a break." He unsuccessfully endeavored to sound convincing but my expression divulged the truth.

"Mommy, you're leaving daddy? Why would you do that?" Shiloh spat. Her green eyes glazed with tears.

"Quinton!" I fussed, brows furrowed in anger. "Either you tell her the whole truth or I will." Hot tears escaped from the fire burning in my eyes.

"Daddy! What is going on?" Shiloh shouted.

Quinton peered up at me and lifted his brow, seeking an ally. He had none. Not in me. I deeply exhaled, crossing my arms and remained completely hushed.

"Shi. Princess," his voice quivered. "Daddy messed up, baby girl. I, um. I have not been faithful to your mother. And - " Shiloh began to speak but he held up his hand. "Please let me finish," he sighed. "And the woman I was dealing with is pregnant and the child may be mine."

Hearing the words spill from his filthy mouth made me sick to my stomach. I desperately wanted to vanish, run to my car and just keep driving, but I had to be strong for my Shi.

"What? This is a joke right? Are you kidding me?" she questioned, dewy eyes wide, glancing between me and Quinton seeking clarity. "Daddy, why would you do this? To Mommy? To me? TO US!" Shiloh sobbed, yanking away from her dad's attempt to console her.

I couldn't breathe. The pain riddling my daughter broke my entire heart. We, this family, was Shiloh's world just as much as she was our world. How could Quinton not consider her? How could he be so selfish? So careless. But I couldn't ponder those thoughts any longer. I had to do what every Black woman, every Black mother, had to do for the sake of her partner and children. I put my angst on the backburner to temporarily become Quinton's ally and console my baby girl.

If he and I didn't agree on anything else in life, we agreed that we would love and protect our daughter at all cost. Although she was nineteen and entering adulthood, we were still going to need to effectively co-parent through this ordeal. We all would need guidance through this reckoning, but especially Shiloh. I joined them on the bed and she fell into my bosom as I caressed her tresses.

"Shi, people make mistakes all the time. I'm not perfect. Daddy is not perfect. But he's still your dad and loves you very much. My relationship with him doesn't dictate yours. Ok?" I assured her, stroking the loose curls that sprang from her ponytail.

"Do you have any idea how embarrassing this is? How irresponsible?" She shook her head in disbelief.

"Shi, babygirl, I am so sorry. We will fix this. *I* will fix this." Quinton held her hand preventing her departure. Shiloh glared at her dad, then turned to me.

"Are you guys getting a divorce?" Shiloh questioned.

"Yes," I said with certainty.

"No," Quinton declared.

Our voices rang in unison but our words discorded conflict.

"Nothing has been decided, Shiloh. Mommy and I have a lot to discuss. It's going to take some time." Quinton kissed her cheek.

He spoke as if he was the decision maker. My mind was made up. The Coach and Dr. Holiday's reign had expired. I didn't give a shit what the people would say. Would I be embarrassed? Yes. But did I care? No. My self-care and self-worth were the most valuable commodities to me. I couldn't keep functioning in this falsified bubble. I wanted my freedom, liberation… my damn peace.

"I can't do this right now. I'm going back to my dorm. Daddy, please don't call me a thousand times. I promise you we will talk, but not right now. I can't even look at you right now." Shiloh stood from the bed wiping away tears.

"Mommy, where are you going? Are you going to be ok?" She kneeled in front of me, tenderly placing her head in my lap.

Quinton paced the room, watching me and Shiloh. The imagery of his two favorite girls heartsick, killed Quinton; dejection was written all over his face.

"I'm going to Aunt Maxi's. I'll be there until me and daddy figure everything out, ok?" I kissed the top of her head. "Shiloh, look at me. We are going to be fine. I promise." I croaked, my voice quivering because this may have been the first time I lied to my daughter. I honestly didn't know how we were going to get through this.

* * *

Quinton begged me to stay as he put my suitcase in the trunk of my car. He was crying, like sobbing real tears. I had only seen this man cry twice and that was when Shiloh was born and when he tore his Achilles tendon in a race. I guess when you see your world crumbling right before your eyes, and you are the instigator, tears are inevitable.

When I said goodbye to Quinton, I was saying farewell to the past twenty years of my life. I knew I'd never dance in the sunroom with him on a rainy night again, watch him run drills in the backyard with Shiloh, snuggle with Shi in her princess bed when she couldn't sleep, cook in the kitchen I designed, or write another book in my den. That broke my heart. I cried muted tears because the ache of making a sound was excruciating.

I pulled into Maxi's driveway a little after seven o'clock. Quaron's car was already parked there. Pulling my suitcase out of the trunk, I heard the front door creak open of the refurbished eighty-year-old home. She and Quaron were standing in the doorway with their arms outstretched. My lips quivered as I approached them. Reaching the threshold, I dropped my bags and deafeningly bewailed, completely broke down as they slowly ushered me into the house. We perched on the couch side by side with me leaning against Quaron's shoulder.

My girls really came through for me as I observed boxes of tissue, bottles of my favorite red wine, strawberry cheesecake and Golden Girls playing on the television. We were prepared for a long night.

"Jemma, it's going to be ok. You'll figure everything out." Quaron caressed my shoulder.

"Will I, Roni? I just lost my best friend. My identity as a wife is gone. I've been somebody's wife since I was twenty years old. What am I supposed to do now?" I looked between my sister-friends for answers.

"You're supposed to put one foot in front of the other and just live, Jemma," Maxi said. "Find out who you are. Be free, spontaneous. Whatever the hell you want," she squealed with a tearful smile.

"Sis, you prayed for a sign, so here it is. Now, what are you gonna do about it? Sulk, be depressed, and despondent? No ma'am. You are mutherfucking Dr. Jemma Warren Holiday. The world is yours for the taking, boo," Quaron expressively jeered.

We boisterously guffawed because they knew I was a sucker for a good melodramatic moment. Maxi poured three glasses of red wine as we snuggled on the couch. They perched with me in silence until my crying ceased. I blew air through my lips, releasing a resounding exhale.

"Thank you. I love y'all," I sighed.

"We love you too, babe," Maxi said, while they both gave me one final firm squeeze.

"Now that you've cried for a couple hours and we have that out of the way," Quaron giddily interjected. "Tell me how did you get so lucky for the good doctor to whisk you away like captain save-a-hoe and dick you down pro-per-ly." She snapped her fingers three times.

"What I want to know is, how is it that you've only had two dicks in ya life and they have both been the best dicks in ya life." Maxi was serious about her inquiry.

"Ew! One of those dicks is my dumb ass brother. Can we not talk about that?" We cackled at Quaron's apparent disgust.

"Seriously, Jemma, you don't have to share details, but did he do you right?" Maxi asked.

"Nah, bitch. I want all the nasty details," Roni screeched.

I shook my head, unable to control my laughter. "Let's just say, the good doctor had all hell breaking loose in my body. He triggered sensations in me that have been dormant for months." I visibly shivered recollecting *him*.

"And the scars? How did you... did he?" Maxi nervously asked, knowing my self-consciousness about my breasts.

I paused, considering his words. *You're beautiful, Jules.* "He thought they were... perfect," I said breathlessly as a small smile curved the corners of my mouth.

"Okay! So did you schedule another appointment or will the good doctor be making house calls?" Maxi squealed. I shook my head at her exaggerated tone.

"Yeah, because Dr. Green is like a can of Pringles," Quaron confidently blurted. Me and Maxi scowled with confusion, then she continued. "Once you *pop,* the fun don't *stop.*"

I fell out over Maxi's lap. Happy tears streamed down my blushed cheeks. I laughed so hard at her crazy ass.

Once I caught my breath, I said, "Nah. Dr. Ezekiel Green is a drug. Shit, the worst kind. My ass would be completely addicted. Waking up insane every morning searching for my next hit. I gotta focus on me. I can't go there with him. Not again."

I squinted my eyes, nibbling the corner of my lip as a smidgeon of sadness overcame me, reflecting on my first and last time with Ezekiel.

Chime. I glanced down at my phone, furrowing at the name attached to the text message. I laughed at how he saved his number in my phone.

The Good Dr. Z.: I hope you made it safely to your destination. Anytime you need a friend. A release. Restoration. Drop your location. Anytime, any place... day or night and I'll be there. Goodnight Jules.

Shit! I am in so much fucking trouble.

14

ZEKE

The blazing summer heat vanished to make room for the beauty of the colorful hues of autumn. I'd attended my first homecoming at an HBCU and survived unscathed... barely. The sea of black people stretched for miles across Monroe University as I navigated the campus journeying from one speaking engagement to the next.

Women of every color of the melanated spectrum crossed my path but I only craved one. I hadn't touched or tasted Jemma since that fateful night *and morning* after the fundraiser gala over two months ago. Keeping a professional distance from her had become increasingly more difficult the more we communicated. Our IG exchanges quickly elevated to text messaging, then phone calls and now occasionally video chats. Selfishly, I was thankful that Jemma was still staying with Maxine. She had not returned home, but her marriage was never a discussion. It didn't need to be.

Although a cloud of complexity circled us, our seamless, uncomplicated ability to connect maintained even after we fucked. Jemma willingly graced me with the most superb pussy I'd ever had and a nigga was sprung. Even with the tumultuous night she had, she slept so peacefully and I hoped I had a little something to do with that.

The significant planning and logistics leading into homecoming weekend honestly didn't allow any room for things to be awkward between us. We had a university to manage and Dr. Holiday did not play when it came to her students, especially their experiences and safety during homecoming weekend. She knew every detail down to the minute and I was impressed. I wasn't Zee and she wasn't Jules at those moments, we were two university leaders who believed failure was not an option. But when the speeches and meetings with sponsors were complete, she transformed into the past homecoming queen, sorority girl of Monroe University. Jemma gyrated her fat ass during a Greek stroll at the grown folks day party and sexily puffed a cigar at the sip and smoke bonfire hosted by my fraternity.

I'd been discreetly observing her all night. Fitted distressed jeans, red shirt that dipped low in the back and red patent stiletto heels accentuated every curve on her body. Her naked lips were plump and glorious, but the fire engine red lipstick she wore had me ready to lick and suck that shit right off of her face. Her boisterous laugh and bright gleam had me ambling around mesmerized, erection on ten. When Coach Holiday arrived at the venue the bullshit immediately ensued. From a short distance, it was clear to me that she was attempting to avoid a scene, mouthing *no Q, we can talk later,* as he firmly clutched her arm, aggressively whispering in her ear. His sister Quaron even tried to make him stand down but Quinton wasn't having it. He appeared drunk and ready to fuck shit up. I'm sure my bass-filled interruption wasn't helpful but I didn't give a shit because I too was prepared to fuck shit up if necessary.

"Coach," my voice thundered behind him but was hushed enough for his ears only. "Not here, man. You have eyes on you," I said, sliding my phone into my pocket before crossing my arms.

He momentarily cut his eyes away from me to see the attention he was drawing. "I am speaking to my wife, Provost," Quinton slurred. "Not your concern. We're good, man," he said with a taut hold on her forearm and his hand fisted against her ass for emphasis.

"I beg to differ. It's my job to be concerned about anything that goes on at this university, including her," I declared, my tone unintentionally possessive. "My entire staff and student community are my concern."

Quinton's brows furrowed. "She's off the clock and don't have shit to do with you," he whisper-yelled, pointing a stern finger towards Jemma.

"You've been at Monroe for like two seconds so you still gotta earn your stripes around here, son. This is *my* university." He banged a fist to his chest.

This man's ego was bruised leading to self-destruction. I could only imagine how it felt to witness the woman you have loved most of your life happy and whole; moving on without you. He was desperate.

"Quinton, please stop this. You are embarrassing the both of us," Jemma pleaded, speaking through gritted teeth.

"I need to talk to you, J. Come on, baby, please," he continued, slightly jerking her arm. She stood placid but I sensed no fear, only agitation.

I maintained eye contact with him but addressed Jemma. "Dr. Holiday, are you ok?" Her eyes softened indicating that she comprehended the compassion in my tone for her and the angst in my timbre for him.

She nodded, then whimpered, "I'm fine. Thank you, Dr. Green. It's just a misunderstanding." Eyes wide with degradation lacing her beautiful face, she lowered her head.

It took every bit of composure not to nudge her chin to lift her head up; catch her crown because it was slipping. This corny ass nigga was only concerned about that fake headpiece she wore earlier during the home-coming ceremony but didn't give a damn about the literal crown... her self-esteem and reputation. She endeavored to pull away from his grasp but he was unyielding. The longer we held the stare the tighter his hold.

"Quinton, please," she whispered, vainly prying his fingers away. He remained motionless, still staring at me.

I brushed a hand down my beard to quell the irritation and fury I was experiencing. Jemma was not mine but I wanted to protect her. Beat the shit out of this punk ass nigga then snatch her up to come home with me. I was educated, polished and professional, but a nigga was a thug. I wanted to beat the brakes off of his ass but there was too much at stake for us all.

"Coach Holiday, I would prefer not to involve campus security since you've been drinking, so I'm going to ask you one time only, please release Dr. Holiday." My demeanor was eerily calm.

"Q, let her go. I'm calling daddy and Mr. Warren. They are going to beat the shit out of you, boy." I heard Quaron say, finally realizing that she'd been standing there the whole time but I was so focused on Jemma.

Clearly the mention of their father and his father-in-law calmed him and he relinquished Jemma's arm. She audibly exhaled, rapidly blinking to prevent the tears that threatened to release throughout this fifteen minute ordeal.

"Jem. J, I'm sorry," Quinton sighed, appearing to momentarily realize he'd messed this shit up… again.

She shook her head, tossing a hand up to cease any further words from him. "I hate you, Quinton. Stay the hell away from me," Jemma hushly spat. Her eyes pooled with tears but she refused to let them fall. She quickly trotted away with Quaron and Maxine following her. Quinton watched, expression downcast, dejected. He quickly turned to me as if his jolt was supposed to make me flinch. I lifted a brow mutedly daring him to fuck with me.

"Let's get the hell outta here, Q," assistant coach Jamar said, guiding him by the shoulders. "Give her time, man," he uttered. Quinton pounded a balled fist against his temple in angst before ambling away.

I circled my eyes throughout the crowded bonfire in search of Jemma. Old school Jay-Z and Wu-Tang Clan boomed through the speakers as various lines of sorority and fraternity members danced and strolled. The uniquely familiar acoustics of George Clinton's Atomic Dog resounded and I quickly moved out of the way of the dramatic hopping and flailing hooked arms of my frat brothers. Back in the day, I would've joined in but today I had to be the astute university provost. Meandering through the crowd, I was still on the hunt for *her*, Jemma was nowhere to be found. *She needs some space*, I thought.

"Dr. Green, can we get a picture, frat?" an older group of brothers asked me.

I nodded and took the picture before joining their conversation. Damn, I wanted to text her and make sure she was good, but I knew I shouldn't. This shit with Jemma was ripping me to shreds. Our relationship… our friendship, lived and breathed in the confines of our phones and unfortunately that was no longer good enough for me.

About an hour later, the bonfire was still going strong but I said my goodbyes. My cell phone buzzed in my pocket as I slid into my truck. *Jules.* My big grown ass was blushing. I clicked to expand the screen and saw that she'd done exactly what I said. *If you ever need to talk, need a friend, just drop your location and I'll be there.* Once my phone connected to the car, I clicked on the map to load the directions in my GPS. It was almost midnight and she was about thirty minutes away but I didn't care. I texted back. **OMW.**

I didn't know where the hell the GPS was taking me. One dark gravel road followed by the next had my ass ready to quickly turn around. A black man traveling on the country roads of Missouri after midnight wouldn't end well. Finally minimal beams of light appeared, directing my eyes towards an oversized boulder with *The Caverns* etched onto the limestone surface.

I drove another half mile before I reached one of the most beautiful sites I'd ever seen. Massive rock structures with hues of orange, red and yellow surrounded a circular patch of bumpy pavement. Cars and trucks were aimlessly parked while bunches of crowds formed throughout the space. The intense glare of the full moon offered the only gleam except for the dull lights built into the artificial rocks sporadically positioned along the walkways. I parked my truck and texted Jemma but after five minutes with no response, I decided to call just as she was calling me. I was tired and slightly annoyed by the obstacle course and it showed in the ruggedness of my tenor.

"I'm here," I answered, offering no greeting.

"Hey. Ok, where are you?"

"Um, shit, I don't know. Near a tree, a rock. I have no clue."

She chuckled. "Is the pickup truck with the speakers to your left?

I circled my head, noticing a tricked-out all black GMC Sierra with two monstrous ass speakers on the truck bed blasting music. "Yeah."

"Are you behind a red Tesla?" she continued to probe.

Growing more annoyed, I sighed, "Mm-hmm."

"I see you. Give me a second." Jemma didn't hang up the phone so I heard her say to someone, presumably her friends, "I'll be back. Don't leave me."

We continued to silently hold the phone until she came into view. Once she saw my car she disconnected our call. She couldn't see me because of the extra dark tint on my windows, but I could see her. Fresh-faced, with a simple black maxi dress, denim jacket, red flip flops and a crown of curls sprouting from a colorful head wrap, she was stunning. Casual, relaxed Jemma was my favorite version.

I opened my door to greet her, but before I could exit the car she muttered, "I'll get in."

I eyed her rounding the front of my car. I had no clue what I was in store for tonight but Jemma looked like she had some shit on her mind. She flashed a slight smile, sliding into the passenger seat and whispered, "Hey."

"Hey," I replied.

"You came," she maffled. The inflection in her voice indicated surprise.

"I told you I would." My damn attitude was shitty and I didn't fully understand why.

"Are you… mad about something?" she questioned.

I shook my head. "Nah, just tired."

"Dr. Green, I'm sorry. I shouldn't have texted you."

"Dr. Green?" I irritably queried, then lifted an eyebrow seeking understanding. "We're on the clock now. Is this official university business or something else?" I probed, turning in my seat to face her.

"Ezekiel, I shouldn't have asked you to come this late," she explained.

"You didn't ask, Jules. But I told you, drop your location and I'm there every time… anytime," I confirmed.

Jemma meshed her lips into a tight line before biting the corner of her slightly more plump bottom lip.

"Are you okay?" I asked, tightening my hands on the steering wheel to prevent from touching her.

She nodded.

"Jules, that was a lot to deal with back there. Trust me, I've been in your shoes. Are you good?" I asked again.

"You've been in my shoes?" She pointed a finger to her chest. "You care to share?" she questioned, folding one leg under her body, positioning herself to face me.

"Answer my question first," I sternly requested.

Jemma leered, her frustration aimed at me. Her irritation with the direction of this conversation was evidenced by her creased temple. "I'm not happy or sad, I'm embarrassed. When Quinton feels backed into a corner he unconsciously lashes out by doing stupid shit. I've seen this movie before and I'm over it." Jemma shrugged.

"Backed into a corner? How? It looked to me like he was the instigator.

The aggressor." My brow furrowed because a part of me wanted that nigga to flex so I could beat those red and white canes right off that punk ass t-shirt he wore.

Her eyes rolled, coupled with an exasperated sigh as she stoically stared straight ahead.

"Really, Jules?" I said, my own indignation building.

I reached across the console and fingered her chin. Reluctantly she focused those glorious orbs back on me. "We can talk about everything when we're on this phone. Texting, FaceTime, almost daily communication other than when you decide you need a break. But you can't talk to me face to face about what I just witnessed; what you're feeling, Jemma."

She audibly exhaled, resting her head against the gray leather rest. I'd begun to master every curve of her face, every joyful and disgruntled expression. This countenance? This was exhaustion and frustration.

"I filed for legal separation and now he's pissed, ok?" She irritably blurted, tossing up one hand. "He's playing games. Quinton won't sign the divorce papers because he knows I can't do anything until it's final. I filed for legal separation so maybe I can get a place without his involvement. But he knows I want to purchase a new house, rearrange investments..." She paused for a heartbeat shaking her head. No tears, just pure rage. "I can't move on with my life. I need him to just let me go," she whimpered.

"I'm sorry, Jemma," I quickly muttered and I meant it. I was disheartened to see her struggling with this. When I said I understood, I wasn't just talking shit. Her situation bore several similarities to my past relationship.

"Hey," I said, cupping her chin to bring her face to me. I leaned over to kiss her temple then coupled mine with hers. "Can you give me a tour of the cave?" I asked, endeavoring to take her mind off of the bullshit.

She nodded.

We followed the less than a half a mile trail into the cave that was the focal point of The Caverns. The bustling of water provided a sense of calm when crossing the threshold to enter. Luminous candescent lights affixed in the rock emblazoned the million plus year old limestone deposits with hues of blue, purple and pink. Man-made bridges arched over the periodic small streams of water that guided the almost four mile cavern system. Holes and dips in the stone created little hideaways on the trail. Jemma unhurriedly ambled, articulating the history of this place as if she was a tour guide.

"When the city neglected the grounds years ago, the university maintained it as a part of the school of anthropology up until ten years ago when they discontinued the program due to low enrollment. The Cavern was neglected again and became a spot for the homeless until about five years ago when the first black mayor in Monroe City committed to finding homes for the unhoused and revamp what was once a historical monument. Now it's a thriving venue. They host weddings, the summer fair, concerts, all types of events here. And once a month during the fall, the locals host a small business Saturday that goes on from the morning to what you see tonight." She clutched her hands behind her back as she continued to saunter aimlessly. Even in the maxi dress, the fullness of Jemma's ass was profound.

"Sounds like you've spent a lot of time here," I acknowledged, playfully bumping her shoulder as we strolled.

"Honestly, I haven't been here since the university relinquished responsibility. But back in the day - " she said animatedly, "you were not a member of the clique if you didn't come to The Caverns. It used to be the after hours spot for college students. All of the fraternities and sororities would meet up here on Thursday nights. It was insane. Somebody would have music blasting from their car but not as advanced as the guy in the pickup truck. Omega oil and Alpha punch would be flowing from random coolers out of the trunk of an even more random car," she chuckled at the memory. "We would dance and stroll... among other things that we probably should not have been doing in public. But it was a good time."

"I'm sure the cops would have a field day with that. Shutting that shit down every week," I laughed.

"Yeah. Unfortunately somebody decided to try to dive in the lake and got hurt pretty bad. It was shortly after I graduated but they definitely shut it down after that happened."

"What is this over here?" I asked, pointing to a large opening in the structure that was pitch black dark other than a faint glare from the moon.

"The historians say that Native American artifacts were found here and they believe that the people rested in this space. That's why it's called The Home of the First People. It's the only part of the cave that offers a glimpse of the outside so it's assumed they slept here to know when the day progressed to night," she schooled me, first pointing to a plaque naming the room in the center of the floor then to the slight opening above. "If you stand in the center of this spot, it is believed that you can hear the echoes of the native people. Come here." Jemma extended her hand, drawing me closer to her. We stood face-to-face holding hands.

"Close your eyes," she whispered, then tickled four fingers down my face encouraging my eyes to close.

Subdued then bizarrely stronger whispers blared. After several minutes, I lazily opened my eyes, experiencing an unexpected peace. Jemma's eyes remained shut, almost meditatively. I regarded her for a lingering heartbeat, enjoying the momentary tranquility. Freckles. At this proximity I could see the freckles again that were sprinkled at the peaks of her cheeks. I grinned a little, as languid breaths slow-danced between us. She leisurely opened her eyes, joining my subtle glee.

"You made me lose count," I whispered.

"Of what," she practically croaked then swallowed as I glided the tip of my bent finger down her face.

"Your freckles. They're beautiful," I declared, scooping her entire face into the palms of my hands. Our eyes chased, frolicking to capture every fleck of coloring.

"You're staring," she giggled.

"Just admiring the visual." My thumbs simultaneously stroked down her rosy cheeks, then swiped across her bare lips.

I bit my lip through a closed mouth smile. Kissing Jemma was all that I'd been thinking about since our first and last kiss weeks ago. Still clasping her face, I softly kissed her, testing the situation to determine if she had any opposition. Her response was quite the contrary, instead she offered a sexy smile. I licked against the seam of her mouth, gently nibbling on that plump bottom lip.

Jemma parted, granting me permission to enter her delicious mouth. My tongue gleefully pranced and twirled; happy to be at home. Jemma was surrendering as she caressed my head urging me closer. Her nipples hardened against my chest while my hands journeyed the length of her body. I'd been watching that ass all night and I desperately desired a handful. Vigorously kneading, I gathered every inch of her fleshiness; every dip and dimple rested in the palms of my hands. Our moans and groans entwined with the whispers of the forefathers as she welcomed each one of my greedy tongue lashings. I knew the origin of my satisfied tenor but was curious about hers.

As I kissed her, I envisioned us lingering in the afterglow that night in my bedroom. Recalling the exact moment when I expelled my dick from her sodden creamy folds. We coalesced as our bodies wantonly entangled and I wanted to do that shit again. I would be a goddamn liar if I said I didn't want to slowly burrow my dick into her sweet ass pussy inch by inch. But more importantly, I simply desired her. What the hell was going on? I had just met this woman a few months ago and I was ready, willing and prepared to give her whatever she needed.

"Jules," I moaned.

"Hmm," she sang.

"Here you go again... giving me a reason, Jemma," I roared, eyes closed, nose nestled into her neck.

"You've said that before. What am I doing? Giving you a reason to what?" she questioned breathily, completely engrossed in the moment.

"You make a man look forward to another tomorrow. You make a man want to snatch you from right up under that nigga's nose. Every damn time I'm near you, you make me want to do so many things," I exhaled against her lips, licking and kissing as I spoke.

"Tell me," she requested as her fingertips delicately massaged my ears.

"I want to take you home with me. Run a hot bath and scrub you from head to toe. Cleanse away all the bullshit from today," I said, circling my tongue behind her ear.

"Then I want to lay you in my bed and rub you down with coconut oil paying special attention to these magnificent breasts and that swollen masterpiece between your thighs." I cupped her pussy through the fabric of the thin dress resting my thumb on her clit.

Her shit was so damn damp and so fat. Sluggish, circular motions paced with the rhythm of our breaths. She gasped, eyes rolling as she tossed her head back.

"After you are good and moisturized, I want to eat your pussy over and over and over again," I professed, orbiting my thumb around her distended bud. Her legs grew weak as she fisted the collar of my shirt, holding on for dear life as the pleasure intensified towards an entrancing climax.

"Then I want you to get a good night's sleep so I can wake you up and do that shit all over again," I said, continuing to mercilessly massage her treasure. I felt the heat of her nectar dampen through the dress as Jemma blaringly bayed her gratification, silencing the mythical whispers in the room.

15

JEMMA

"*As much as I want you... and damn Jules, I want your ass bad, I don't think it's a good idea for you to go home with me tonight. Our first time together was after the bullshit you're dealing with. If you go home with me, it would be after the bullshit again. I don't want that to be the story. I need you to want me because you desire me and me alone... not because you're pissed at him. Baby, Jules, I hope you understand.*"

I lifted my chin as if I could feel Ezekiel's touch against my face like I did on homecoming night when he spoke those words in the cave after giving me the best *and only* orgasm I'd ever had fully clothed and standing on my two feet. When we exited, I had to get myself together because I was walking on wobbly legs like a baby giraffe after that damn orgasm. Thank goodness for the long black dress because the evidence of my trampish ways trailed down my inner thighs spilling from my center.

Ezekiel discreetly placed a hand at my lower back ushering me to the car. He offered me a handful of napkins from his glove compartment confirming that I was a whole entire ho in these streets. We settled in the car for almost another hour and chatted as if he didn't just snatch my soul. His sluggardly circular motions against my clit were my undoing. I wanted him, shit, was a borderline feign for him. But he was right, I had to separate my discontent for Quinton from this looming passion for him.

Our ability to easefully transition into thought provoking conversation was my primary attraction to Ezekiel. Don't get me wrong, the man was fine, but his conversation made love to my mind. With a moist, still throbbing middle, I lazed in his passenger seat considering his every word as he finally answered my question from earlier about understanding what I was going through. He said he'd been in my shoes but I was curious about what that meant. I knew that he'd been married and divorced but never probed for details.

"My ex-wife, Michelle, cheated on me. We were young and in love and had kids way too early. Once we were forced to tap into why we were together in the first place, our juvenile adoration and friendship wasn't enough. So, I understand what you're going through, Jules. The shit ain't easy no matter if you're the offender or offended." I recollected his admission.

That encounter was four weeks ago and I still couldn't cease the echoing of his words or the pulsating sensation in my pussy. We hadn't communicated much since homecoming given his crazy schedule and my desire to isolate. I laid in the bed staring at the ceiling circling my eyes with the motion of the fan. It was the day after Thanksgiving and I'd already planned to enjoy a day of nothingness. Maxi and I had dinner yesterday at one of my favorite restaurants. I'm sure she would've preferred to be with one of her boy toys but she chose to spend the day with me; my first Thanksgiving without my people.

My parents were in southern Missouri visiting extended family and Quaron spent the day in St. Louis with her parents. Shiloh was spending Thanksgiving with Jordan's family in Indianapolis. I did not want her to go but I understood that Shi needed some time away from me and her father's chaos. Thankfully I trusted Shiloh completely so if she decided to make grown-up decisions this weekend, I knew that she was protected. I was unsure of Quinton's whereabouts and I honestly didn't care.

For the past twenty years, the Holiday and Warren families would celebrate together but given the bomb I dropped during homecoming, things would never be the same. To Quinton's dismay, I decided we needed to inform our parents of our separation and impending divorce when they were in town for homecoming. He remained hushed the entire conversation, refusing to disclose the truth. He was placid until my father practically yanked him from his seat after learning that Quinton possibly fathered a child. The patterned knocking against the door disrupted my daze.

"What do you want, Maxi?" I whined, hiding my head under the blanket prepared for her to come into the room and immediately open the blinds.

"Good morning, sunshine," Maxi sang as she opened the door. "I have fresh coffee, croissants, cheese eggs and bacon ready downstairs. And Quaron is almost here."

"I'm not hungry. I will probably stay in this nightgown and in this bed all day," I sighed, rolling away from the gleaming sun beaming through the window. I was in a mood. Quinton still hadn't signed the divorce papers, it had been almost two weeks since I'd talked to Ezekiel, and I was horny as hell.

"Jem, what's wrong, boo?" Maxi inquired but I remained silent. "You miss him, don't you?" she said, placing a gentle hand on my shoulder. I leered at her, angry that she could always read my mind. I didn't need to ask who she was referring to but I refused to acknowledge her accuracy. I did not want to miss him, desire him, but I did - desperately.

"You can stay hushed all you want to, but if I were you I would summon that dick immediately," she chuckled and I shook my head. "That man came as soon as you dropped your location. I'm confident that he'd do it again."

"I haven't talked to him in weeks, Max," I said, now sitting up against the headboard.

"And whose dumb ass fault is that?" She sarcastically asked, rolling her eyes. "My linesister number eight, Destined To Be Great, that's who," Maxi teased.

She was right. I'd been avoiding Ezekiel after what happened at The Caverns. Not because I didn't desire him, because God knows I craved that man. I averted him because I heeded his disclaimer; needing time to ensure that my yearning for him was not rooted in rage or revenge. Admittedly, my one wanton vengeful act felt redemptive at the moment, but thoughts of Dr. Green invaded my psyche well before he ever ravished my body.

"I made peach mango mimosas," she sing-songed before giggling. Maxi knew exactly what was necessary to release me from this California king bed.

"Say less my linesister number seven, Polished Precision," I quipped, dragging myself out of the bed.

"Why are y'all lazy asses still in the bed?" Quaron's raspy voice rumbled from the doorway.

"And here's our linesister number nine," I smirked. "Truth Hurts," me and Maxi blurted in unison, laughing as the three of us ambled down the stairs to eat brunch.

I showered and dressed in a burgundy maxi skirt with a cropped off the shoulder gray Hillman College sweatshirt. Maxi was hosting an old school Friendsgiving dinner with a group of our college friends. Everyone was asked to wear paraphernalia from the eighties and bring their favorite childhood holiday dessert. A feast of traditional and non-traditional food was spread across the oversized kitchen island. Thanks to my mother and Mrs. Holiday, they'd prepared turkey, dressing, macaroni and cheese and sweet potato pie that Quaron brought back with her. I made green beans and my favorite dessert, apple cobbler, wishing I could pair it with some of my grandmother's homemade vanilla ice cream.

"Happy Friendsgiving," voices shouted from the front door. Our friend Adara and her husband, Ken, ambled through the door wearing the eighties movie, The Breakfast Club, branded t-shirt. "I brought my Yia-Yia's baklava," Adara yelped, raising an aluminum pan. In college, family dinner at Dara's house was the perfect Greek-soul food combination thanks to her father's Greek heritage and her mother's African ancestry.

"Girl, tell Celosia Ariti she's still my favorite yia-yia," Quaron quipped, hugging Dara. "Hi Ken," she dryly spoke and he dryly nodded. We adored Adara, but Ken... not so much. He was what we called a local that she met at a party our sophomore year. Five years older than her with a young son and a crazy baby momma that he could not control. The relationship was tumultuous then and remained that way to this day, with them recently reconciling for the third time.

"Ok everybody," Maxi shouted. "Let's bless the food because I'm starving."

At least ten people stood around the island with bowed heads giving thanks for the meal and the hands who prepared it. I peered around the room smiling because I was truly thankful for many of these folks who I considered to be more than friends. They all knew the situation between me and Quinton and never questioned why we were no longer together.

My disposition from earlier improved after talking to Shiloh. Her bright smile and giddiness every time Jordan popped into the frame was cute. "Mommy, try to have fun today, okay. Promise me you'll do something for you," she said, blowing three kisses to signify I love you. My heart warmed recalling her concern for me. I smiled, in a complete daze until the doorbell rang. I continued moving about the kitchen placing serving utensils in the pans when...

"Everybody, this is Dr. Ezekiel Green, the university's new provost and his brother..." Quaron wore a Cheshire cat smile as her raspy voice trailed off trying to remember his brother's name.

"Ezra," Ezekiel's bass-filled tenor sent shivers through me as I peered up at him. "And this is my cousin Myron," he continued, greeting my wide-eyed stare.

"Dr. Green. It is wonderful to finally meet you," Maxine's half-sister Claudia squealed. She chose not to follow the wardrobe directions, opting to wear a skin-tight sweater dress instead. exposing the brand new gigantic booty and double D's she'd recently purchased.

"Thank you. Call me Zeke," he instructed, momentarily taking his eyes off of me to shake her hand.

Maxine shook her head as she settled next to me and whispered, "you texted him?" I nodded. "Damn, bitch. What voodoo you put on that man?" I rolled my eyes at her before focusing back on him.

After hanging up with Shiloh earlier, I decided to follow her instructions, *mommy do something for you.* So I dropped my location to him, followed by a text message with a copy of the invitation we'd sent to our friends. *He* was something just for me. Although he hadn't failed to come when I called, I was still shocked by his presence. Ezekiel wore a vintage Tribe Called Quest hoodie, dark distressed jeans and wheat Timberland boots. He bled Brooklyn today and damn was it fine on him. The two gigantic men next to him were easy on the eyes as well dressed similarly. I observed two sets of familiar orbs who also noticed the intrigue of these mocha-hued Gods. The blush that reddened Maxine's cheeks when Myron complimented her home was comical.

In true Quaron fashion, she couldn't prevent the sarcastic tone layered in her flirtation when she bantered, "Uh, big bruh, the notorious one was not in the eighties," she said, pointing to Ezra's t-shirt with an image of a crowned Notorious B.I.G. Even at her height, Quaron had to toss her head back between her shoulder blades to fully examine his reaction. That nigga was huge. Like John Coffee from the Green Mile kinda big. Ezra shot her a one cheek smile and I could've sworn that heffa visibly shivered. "Neither was House Party, lil sis," he mocked, motioning to Quaron's cropped t-shirt. "You ain't even following the rules of your own damn party, beautiful," he chuckled, bypassing her glare and headed straight for the food.

While the whole exchange was entertaining, I couldn't divert my eyes from Ezekiel. He closed the distance between us while I stood motionless holding a damn serving spoon.

"Happy friendsgiving, Jemma."

"You came," I whimpered.

"I told you I would."

"I guess I thought... since you didn't respond to my text and we haven't talked," I mumbled, completely discombobulated.

"I didn't think I needed to respond, but it's clear to me that I do need to reiterate my stance to you," he rested a bag on the counter before compressing the already minuscule gap between us, disregarding who was watching. He leaned in whispering, "Even when you're in your head, I'm coming every damn time you call, Jules. You don't have to question it, I'll be there. Every fucking time."

I audibly moaned and didn't give a shit. "Thank you," I sexily whispered, nibbling my bottom lip. Motioning to the bag on the counter, I asked, "What did you bring?"

"Well, I wouldn't dare attempt my mother's German chocolate cake, so I decided to bring something I thought you would like."

"Who me," I dramatically pointed a finger to myself as he dug into the bag. My eyes almost popped out of my head when I saw the Straub's Bakery logo and read gooey butter cake on the cover. "What? How? Where did you get this?" I stuttered.

"I was picking up my brother and cousin from the airport in St. Louis when you texted me earlier. And I remembered a picture on your IG page about the best cake you'd ever had. I stopped at the bakery and it was my luck that they had a few left."

Damn I wanted to hug him. Shit, jump in his arms and immediately request he take me upstairs but I acquiesced.

"Ezekiel. I don't know what to say. Thank you." I couldn't control the blush fancying my face.

"Just promise you'll have the first piece with me." He caressed my hand, lifting it to lace a soft kiss on the back.

"I promise." We held the stare for an extended heartbeat.

A couple hours later everyone was fed and full of alcohol. Eighties music from the karaoke machine was blaring on one side of the great room, while a hostile game of Uno was happening on the other side. Ezekiel and I settled on the couch engulfed in conversation. Maxi and Quaron would randomly appear with a goofy, "y'all doing alright," seemingly to play interference when it appeared that we were falling into the abyss of Zeke and Jules land. The more rum punch I drank, the more lax my inhibitions became.

Ezekiel was introduced as my colleague and new to town so a general conversation wouldn't appear strange. However, the distant yet intimate connection we likely displayed probably raised a few eyebrows. But to the two of us, this alliance was routine. The only difference was we didn't have the safetynet our phones created. On Facetime, I couldn't stroke a hand down his muscular arm when he flirted with me. Or it didn't matter how many times he winked at me because it was just the two of us on the screen. But this adjacency granted our bodies permission to absentmind-edly couple like moths to a flame.

When his flesh grazed mine - a simple thumb swipe across my palm or his socked feet playing with mine, we idled in those instances. My damn kitty needed a break from him so we went our separate ways for a spell. Ezekiel played spades with his brother and I joined a few friends in karaoke singing Madonna's Like A Virgin.

I sauntered towards the kitchen to grab a few waters, cracking up laughing at Quaron's very serious rendition of MC Lyte's Paper Thin. Maxine's house was almost one hundred years old so it didn't feature the open floor plans we saw today. Even after knocking down a few walls, the kitchen sat in the back of the home. Walking through the arched entry, I didn't notice Ken seated at the kitchen table.

"What's up, Jemma," Ken said, startling me.

"Oh, shit. Ken," I shouted, clutching my hand to my chest. "Why are you hiding out in here?"

"Sorry. I didn't mean to startle you. I'm not hiding out, just enjoying a piece of cake," he declared, flashing a closed mouthed fake smile.

"Well when everyone is enjoying themselves in the living room and you're the only person in the back of house in the kitchen, one could assume you're hiding from something," I jeered, grabbing a bucket to carry the bottled waters.

"Hmm. You're definitely not hiding with ole boy," he said, forking another piece of cake.

"Excuse me?" I halted, brows furrowed.

"Jemma you know I don't get in other people's business because I don't like folks in mine, but - "

"Then don't, Ken. Especially not my business. And especially when you know nothing about what I have going on."

"Twenty years, Jemma. You and Q have been together for twenty years and you're just going to let that go. Everybody makes mistakes," he explained.

"And everybody has a choice in how they are going to respond to the mistakes," I uttered. "Have you had this same conversation with Quinton? Hmm? Because if you're not, you can miss me with this bullshit."

"I'm just saying... that's half of your life you're throwing away. Y'all were young and didn't get to experience much. He was bound to -" he abruptly paused, catching the words before they spilled from his mouth.

"No. Please continue. It was bound to happen, right? Quinton cheating was inevitable because we were so young and inexperienced, right? So let me get this straight, are you saying I should just tolerate his cheating? Am I supposed to embrace his mistress's child too?"

"That's not what I'm saying at all. You work it out. You don't fall for the new guy at work. Are you really trying to be that cliche, sis?" Ken was going in for the kill, but his *fuck every new piece of pussy at the post office* ass had alot of nerve.

"Bastard," I yelled, as the bucket slipped from my hand. Bottled waters scattered across the floor. "You have a lot of nerve questioning me. You need to tread lightly Ken because I can fuck up your entire world today."

"Fuck up my world?" He stood from his seated position. "How so?"

"Boy please. I know you were more than just Quinton's alibi because he's yours too right? When your new flavor of the month needs some quality time and you suddenly travel for track meets. Ain't that the play?" I scoffed, rolling my eyes as he grew angry.

The crashing bucket and my elevated tone caused Maxi, Roni, Adara and others to start towards the kitchen. I quieted because what Adara accepted from her husband wasn't my business.

"What's going on?" Adara probed, her creased brow laced with concern, eyes darting between me and Ken.

"Nothing," I angrily breathed. "Your husband was just giving me some marital advice," I scoffed.

Ken shook his head. "Sis is just wrong, man," he mumbled to his wife before turning to me. "I'm just trying to tell you it ain't a good look. I get you wanting to have your fun, but not with him."

I lost it. "Sis? Oh I'm sis now. Was I your sis when you were covering for Quinton? Picking him up from other women's homes. Was I your sis then? Were you looking out for me then?" I didn't realize I began aggressively marching towards him until Maxi grabbed my waist.

Adara shouted in disbelief, "Kenneth!"

"Get the fuck out of my house, Ken. You need to listen to Jemma before all of *your* shit is laid bare tonight," Maxi said.

"Ya'll keep talking all that bullshit but you women are just as scandalous as us niggas. Shit, if not more," he hissed. He then turns to Quaron with a look of disgust. "Q is your brother and you ok with this shit?"

"Ken, you are speaking on shit you know nothing about. How about you clean your mutherfucking house before you try to clean others. Nigga your shit is filthy," Quaron spat. Unlike me, Roni didn't give a damn, sparing no feelings.

Ken riled, hurriedly moving towards Quaron when Ezra's monstrous frame stopped him. Ken looked like he just ran into a brick wall. At this point everyone had gathered in the kitchen including Ezekiel. I sucked in my cheeks, unsuccessfully attempting to prevent the flood of tears in my eyes. Embarrassment couldn't describe what I was feeling. Wrath. Humiliation.

"Dr. Holiday, are you good?" Ezekiel bellowed from the kitchen archway with his arms crossed over his chest. He'd clearly heard everything.

"Man, fuck all the formality shit. This is not you, homey," Ken howled like a bitch, pointing towards me. "This ain't your position, dawg. Find another seat. This gonna be my man's seat for life. They got history."

Ezekiel was eerily muted for a second as he ambled towards Ken. Ezra was still holding Quaron's feisty behind back while Myron trailed closely behind his cousin. Ken's aggression quickly quieted. Zeke stood directly in front of Ken smiling with his hands now positioned in his pockets.

"You know, what I love about history is that it continues to repeat itself but takes on new shapes, forms and narratives. History was my favorite subject, especially the stories of battles fought and won. I'm a fan of victorious endings. Reflections of the past, present *and future,*" he stressed, pacing the floor like a professor. Then narrowed eyes landed on me for just a few seconds but his expression made my nipples thump. Ezekiel leered back at Ken. "Yeah... I fucks with history. So I advise you to tread lightly, homey," he mocked Ken. "You don't know me and you don't know shit about what's mine." I was certain the underlying message went way over Ken's dumb ass head, but everyone else knew exactly what Ezekiel was referencing. *Me.*

As several pairs of questioning eyes focused on me, I told myself to run, to get the hell out of there now.

"Excuse me. Excuse me," I murmured, navigating through the crowd and bolted up the steps to the bedroom I'd claimed as my own in Maxi's home. I could hear Adara apologizing to my back as she and Ken grabbed their things to leave but I refused to acknowledge them.

Minutes later there was a light tap at the door but I didn't answer. I figured it was Maxine or Quaron and they would let themselves in. I desperately required air so I settled on the private balcony connected to the bedroom. The french doors creaked and I announced, "I don't want to talk about it."

"We don't have to talk," his throaty baritone surprised me. Zeke's anthracite eyes peeked around the bend of the balcony where I was seated on the loveseat with my feet propped on the ottoman. "You promised me that we would share in this bizarre looking cake," he winked, balancing a plate with a large slice of gooey butter cake and two bottles of water in his hands.

I blushed and whimpered, "hey."

"Hey. You ok?"

I nodded. "I'm sorry you got caught up in that," I said in a small voice. "Honestly I am not even sure what *that* was."

He shook his head. "No worries," he chimed, resting the plate on the table before sitting next to me. "That shit is… what did he call it? History," he teased, forking a piece of the cake.

"It's not funny, Ezekiel. I'm going to have to deal with more bullshit after that." I practically whined, fully expecting for Quinton to be banging on the front door at any moment.

"It's actually hilarious, Jules, and you don't have to deal with anything you don't want to deal with. That's what you're paying a lawyer for, to deal with the bullshit," he pragmatically declared then lifted the fork to his mouth.

I quickly pondered his declaration before blurting, "Wait a minute. Let me do the honors. Prepare yourself for *the* best thing you've ever tasted."

"I don't know about that. I've tasted you, Jemma Jule," he moaned, tickling my cheek as I giggled. I removed the fork from his hand then guided it toward his mouth. I quickly scooped a bite for myself so he wouldn't indulge alone.

"Shit," he exclaimed, retrieving the fork from my grasp to get another piece. I chuckled, "I told you," as we delighted in the gooey goodness. Random gratified groans were the only remarks exchanged between us. We devoured the cake leaving only traces of powdered sugar on the plate and on my face too. He extended his hand towards me to thumb away the remnants but apparently I wasn't close enough.

"Come here," he commanded. I obeyed, opting to straddle his lap.

"Close enough?" I whispered.

He nodded and continued to fondle my lips with his fingers. I licked the sticky sweetness from his fingertips eventually taking his entire finger into my mouth. Sucking and biting, we moaned in unison for a different reason this time. Our lips coupled in a tantalizing kiss, sugar still steeping on our tongues.

Ezekiel's firm hand massaged up my thigh, lifting my skirt to reveal the cotton thong. He cupped my ass, kneading to the dallied pace of our kisses when his tongue replaced his fingers in my mouth. His dick was growing rigid, fighting against the thick denim material. I lifted, reaching between us to release the zipper as much as I could to offer him some relief. I bucked my hips, encouraging the friction from his steely manhood rubbing against my barely concealed clitoris.

Fisting my hair with one hand, Ezekiel pushed two fingers back into my mouth. I welcomed them, sucking and rocking into him had me close to the pinnacle. Interlacing our tongues in a mouthwatering caper, he pushed my thong to the side, slightly ripping the flimsy material. Seconds later, the two fingers that I saturated poked against my ass before acquiring entry into the delicate hole.

"Oh shit!" I yelped, clutching my hands at his nape as I tossed my head back. I was a virgin to anal play so the sensation was new, arousing and sensual as fuck. Ezekiel sluggishly slithered his fingers in and out, twisting and turning as I erratically grinded against his erection. His dick had to be throbbing but I didn't care, the dual stimulation had me too close to stop.

"Goddamn, Jules. Get yours, baby," he requested but I was silent. "Talk to me," he demanded this time, "tell me how you feel," he continued, pausing the stride of his fingers.

"No, no, no. Zeke, please. Don't stop, please. I'm right there, " I whined, digging my fingernails into the thread of his hoodie. He clamped his available hand around my neck forcing me to look at him.

"How do you feel, Jules?" he probed, resuming the felicitous invasion of my unsullied opening with his fingers. "Tell me."

We stared, so many unspoken words lingered. He clamped my neck tighter as I rocked my hips back and forth creating a perfect rhythm. My breathing grew unstable as my rapture approached its peak. Still no words exchanged, just a beautifully silent assault. Zeke closed his eyes and firmly pressed his temple to mine. His muted aggression was my tipping point, my breathless liberation. Winded from his chokehold, my eyes rolled to the back of my head as I crested then hailed, "Free!"

16

EZEKIEL

F*ree.* Such a simple word but it held so much complexity for Jemma. She was free to express herself with me, liberated from the bondage of her past. And unbeknownst to her, *free* was now our safe word in those intimate moments when I needed to take her body to new heights she'd never experienced. I'd told myself not to go there with her but I couldn't resist once she let me penetrate her ass with my fingers. It took her a minute to come down from her high. This was the second time she'd had the most gloriously violent orgasm without vaginal penetration and while her pleasure was my priority, my dick was aching to be inside of her.

Still tightly clutched around me, I carried Jemma into her bedroom. She darted into the bathroom without uttering a word. I flopped on the edge of the bed concerned that I had gone too far. *Idiot! Why did you choke her? She's not ready.* I battled, hoping my actions didn't ruin our night. Clearly Jemma was not a virgin but I was uncertain of the limits to her sexual exploration. About five minutes later, she surfaced in the doorway. A bashful yet brazen expression dressed her pretty face.

"Jules, I - " She swiftly reduced the short span between us, placing a finger over my lips to silence me.

"I've been thinking about what you said at The Caverns and I want you because of you, Zeke. And you alone. Only you," she confidently declared standing between my legs, rubbing the top of my head.

My eyes widened, shocked as shit by her confession. Wrapping my arms around her waist, I pulled her into me, nuzzling my face in her stomach. I trailed kisses across her belly before peering up at her. She was so damn pretty. The expression in her glare was a combination of fear and need.

To my surprise, Jemma pulled her hoodie over her head then unhooked her front closure bra. Her bountiful breasts spilled out making my mouth water. Somehow the scars made the globular wonders more beautiful. Like fingerprints, they were unique to only her. I peeled the skirt and thong over curvy hips, anxious to see her completely naked. She didn't appear self-conscious about her breast this time which I hoped was a sign of complete trust.

"Jules, you are fucking contagious," I growled. She helped me remove my hoodie then my t-shirt before I delicately yanked her down to straddle me. We kissed softly, tenderly, dare I say, lovingly. I guided our bodies to lay on the bed with her on top of me. So fucking eager, my hands frantically roamed because I had to touch her everywhere. Our tongues tussled and frolicked, giddy to be joined again. I stroked my fingertips in pillowy strikes against her velvet skin lacking haste for this moment to end. Closeness was what I coveted.

"I still can't believe you came,"she whispered, tracing her nose against my beard. "Why?" she inquired, almost shyly as she nestled her face into the folds of my neck. Caressing my fingers through her hair, I deeply inhaled the fruity scent. I couldn't make Jemma understand how much I wanted her... even under these circumstances.

"I don't make promises I can't honor. And any opportunity I have to lay my eyes on you, I'm going to take it." I kissed the top of her head, still absently massaging her scalp.

"This can get so messy. So much at stake. I don't want you to -" I kissed her, muting the self-sabotaging thoughts.

"I'm a big boy, Jules. Messy shit don't scare me," I responded, tenderly kissing her lips as the prettiest glossy eyes peered at me.

"Zeke, seriously I don't want you caught in the crossfire of my shit. I can't promise you anything because I don't know what's next for me."

"Stop," I said, kissing against both eyelids. "Stop. I'm not asking for a commitment or a promise of anything other than your honesty. If it gets too hard or becomes too much just tell me and I'll press pause. You're always thinking about everybody else. Do something for you. What does Jules want?" I continued to probe as our fingertips absently intertwined. There was no question what I desired and I was prepared to show her better than I could tell her. With no hesitation Jemma whimpered, "you."

I anchored my hands at her ribcage, directing her body up the length of mine as I sprinkled kisses down her chest. She was confused, curious about my movements. I nudged her again, urging her to keep climbing up my extended frame. Her thighs were on my shoulders as she peered down at me trembling. I massaged the thickness of her hips, planting soft kisses to both inner thighs.

Jemma's eyes were wide and goosebumps cloaked her flesh but she didn't tell me no. "Baby, relax," I repeatedly said, feeling her mellow at the sound of my voice. "I just want to experience you in every way, Jules. If it's too much. If *I'm* too much, you know what to say."

Jemma's brow creased momentarily until realization brightened her face. "Free," she whispered, gazing down at my face tensing in anticipation of my lashing. I devilishly smiled then gently kissed her clitoris before seating her on my face, escorting her dripping pussy to my mouth. I fucking feasted, licking her from front to back on repeat as she danced on my tongue. She had nothing to hold on to but the top of my head as she rode my face to the pace I orchestrated. Her womanhood clinched tighter and tighter the deeper my tongue burrowed inside of her. Incomprehensible words dripped from her mouth as she blessed me with another savory, thirst-quenching crescendo.

My beard was a mess but I was taught to finish my meal. Don't leave a morsel on the plate and I ate the shit out of this hearty feast. Jemma collapsed forward, panting as her head dangled off of the bed. She squirmed, ass elevated and ready for me. I didn't want to be presumptuous when she invited me over, but I'm glad I listened to my brother and brought a few condoms, *just in case some shit pops off*, he announced. I removed my pants and boxers then retrieved the three gold-foiled packages from my wallet, tossing two of them on the nightstand. I intended to deplete the damn supply tonight.

Jemma's body was limp but heaving with need. A bead of sweat trickled down the cave in her back, pooling right above her ass. I licked it, allowing my tongue to prance at the seam of her butt before I drizzled kisses across her back, then whispered against her ear, "fucking contagious."

The mushroomed head of my dick throbbed in anticipation of her sex. I slowly drove my manhood into her dampened essence entering from behind. I slouched my head, temple pressed to her shoulder. I couldn't breathe. The way her pussy hugged my dick like they were long lost friends ecstatic to be reacquainted had me ready to faint. I had to deeply inhale then release before proceeding because my shit was about to burst.

I desired to take my time with Jemma though. Leisurely, unhasty strokes was my preferred tempo. I lazed in that position for a lengthy minute, building towards an accelerated momentum. With one hand, I reached down to spread her legs wider, permitting me to delve deeper. I supplied my dick one inch at a time until I was so immersed that I couldn't detect a variance between her gasps and mine.

Jemma reached behind to grab my nape, drawing me nearer to her lips. I licked the crease before feeding her my tongue. She tossed her head back exposing more of her enticing neck. Shit, what did she do that for? That neck was my fucking weakness. She grunted, flinging her ass back to greet my downstroke then tightened the grip on my nape. I lightly snickered because I think Dr. Holiday was mutedly communicating for me to fuck her, shit, to choke her. Jemma wanted to test out that safe word.

"You wanna be free, baby," I huskily questioned.

She nodded and I happily obliged. Seizing her hips, I pulled her sweaty body onto her knees, my dick still immeasurably embedded into her sodden core. Jemma pawed the sheets, pounding her fist against the mattress as I repeatedly thrashed into her.

"Zee," she loudly moaned then repeated the plea.

I listened carefully, verifying that she wasn't tapping out with her safe word. Thankfully Jemma was graciously taking all of me. I'm sure she would have some explaining to do tomorrow because I was certain the entire house heard her screaming her version of my name. Her back sunk into a perfect arch causing her ass to jiggle and slap against my shit.

Jemma crossed her feet at the ankles then lifted into an upright posture practically seated in my lap. She swayed her hips and rocked against me unhurriedly. I fell back against the headboard and relinquished all control to her. She slow-danced on the tip of my dick then slid all of me into her essence. She did it again. And then again. Jemma was in the zone and I fucking lost it. I gripped her hair pulling her back into my chest giving me access to devour her flesh. That damn neck. I thrashed and pounded and pummeled over and over and over again.

"Jules!" I riotously hollered reaching my climax. Jemma, on the other hand, had enough sense to muffle her screams with a pillow.

Now I would have some explaining to do tomorrow as well. Our bodies jointly shuddered before carelessly toppling onto the bed. Whispers of, "Oh my God. Oh my God," rapidly fell from her mouth. The sporadic quivers prevented me from completely catching the condom as my limpness glided out of her. Yet another mess but we didn't care.

I only intended to close my eyes for a second to catch my breath, but by the time I regained consciousness, it was almost one o'clock in the morning. A plush gray towel was laid on top of the bedspread where the wet spot was, her creamy juices were cleaned from my appendage and our naked bodies were covered with another blanket. *Damn. When did she do all of this? Fucking Jemma Holiday,* I thought as I drifted back to sleep with her nestled in my arms.

I meant what I said when I told Jemma that I wanted to continuously devour her sweet ass pussy. By the time a knock sounded at the door awakening us around seven in the morning, I had treated myself to her deliciousness twice more, depleting the condom supply. The knocking thundered again, then a bass-filled tenor followed. "Zeke, we gotta go, bro," Ezra said. chocolate

I audibly huffed, reluctant to escape the embrace Jemma had on me. Her naked body felt like the softest, sweetest lullaby. I tickled her feet, inciting the cutest blush. The soft hum of her snoring was damn near hypnotic.

"Give me a minute," I grumbled, trying not to wake her.

Peeling out of the bed, I ambled into the adjoined bathroom to wash my face and put some toothpaste in my mouth. I dressed before sitting back on the bed. I contemplated leaving her a note because she was sleeping so peacefully, but I had to see those mesmerizing eyes.

"Jules, baby, wake up. I have to go."

"Hmm," she hummed, fighting with a stray hair that tickled her eye.

"Ezra and Myron are waiting for me. Wake up just for a second," I requested.

I laughed when she pried her eyes open with her fingers. "What the hell did you do to me?" she giggled.

"I put your pretty ass to sleep," I snickered, kissing her neck. I licked her nipple before capturing it between my teeth. "Can I call you later?"

"Mmm… yes," she moaned.

Last night I learned that while she was self-conscious about her scars, licking them unlocked a carnal reaction. I circled my tongue around her chocolate areola then licked and kissed down the perfect imperfection.

"Can I come and see you later?"

Jemma's back arched, sleepy lustful eyes gaping at me. She bit her bottom lip, blushing through a moan. Just the slightest touch to her clit and she immediately grabbed my bald head because the climax was looming, advancing beautifully. Her final crest was exquisite; wearing the afterglow like a gorgeous accessory.

She rapidly nodded in response to my question.

"Nah, be a big girl and talk. Can I see you later, Jules?"

"Yes, Ezekiel. I would like that," she panted, fondling her breasts as she descended from the pleasure.

I scattered kisses over her face and lips then planted one kiss against her dewy bud with a promise to contact her later before she dozed off to sleep.

* * *

"You acting like a man in love, Lil," Ezra barked when he noticed me texting Jemma. "You've been away from her for two hours and y'all missing each other already."

"Nah, Big. It ain't like that," I laughed. "This was actually work related."

"Yeah, ok." He shook his head, unconvinced.

Me, my brother and cousin settled in a fishing boat looking out over the river. It was a beautiful day with unusually warm temperatures for November. We'd planned on being out here earlier but evidently we were all caught up in the webs of three gorgeous women. Ezra and Myron were really hushed about their night but interrogated me about mine.

"But you clearly like her. We dropped everything to go to that party last night. Driving around to find a damn gooey gooey cake. We were supposed to be on some big city nigga shit in this little ass town," Myron laughed. "Trust me, I get it, cousin. She's fine as hell. But... her situation is complicated." He lifted a brow.

I nodded, knowing all too well the situationship I was willingly falling into.

"But I can't lie, I had a good time last night so my ass ain't complaining," Myron snickered, dapping hands with Ezra.

"Yeah, neither of you fools should be complaining. What did y'all do last night while you're trying to get me to kiss and tell?" I smirked. "And Ez, you talking about me in love, what was that shit you pulled last night? Coming to Quaron's defense like she's your woman."

"Nah, that lil nigga was a bit too aggressive for me. I'm not about to let no man step to a woman like that. But shorty looks like she can handle her own," he cackled, shaking his head while biting his bottom lip. "That reckless mouth of hers, those locs and that ass... woo-wee. She bad," he laughed.

"Shit, they're all bad. All three of their lil asses," Myron stressed as we all nodded and laughed at that because it was true.

We spent a few more hours on the water shooting the shit and catching up before heading to lunch at a local brewery and pub. Monroe City was a quaint small town that we leisurely explored for the day. For three New York City boys with fast-paced lives, Monroe offered the calm we needed.

I was dog tired when we returned to my house. After showering, I sprawled across my bed and reached for my phone on the nightstand. I'd texted Jemma to determine if she still wanted to connect tonight but she hadn't responded. I was never one to press a woman so I figured she had other plans. I had to admit, that shit messed with me for a minute but this behavior wasn't foreign. Jemma would go ghost when she was in her head. After what we shared last night and this morning, I'm sure she was all fucked up because I know I was. The booming knock at my door rescued me from my loathing.

"Nigga you sleep?" Ezra thundered.

" Man, come in. Why do you have to knock like you're the police?" My brow furrowed in irritation. "What do you want?"

"We are about to pull up on the living single crew," he cackled.

"Who?" I probed, knowing exactly who he was referring to.

"Us. Them. The ladies. We were invited to movie night," Ezra explained.

"I wasn't invited to shit," I spat much more aggressively than intended.

"Man, please. We're probably getting an invitation because of you," Myron said, walking into my room, making himself comfortable on the lounge chair.

"Speak for yourself, nigga. I'm getting a return invite because of this dick," Ezra declared, grabbing his crotch. "This ain't no one night stand type of penis. They always come back for more," he shrugged.

I released a sigh, rubbing a hand down my face. I couldn't help but laugh at his silly ass.

"Jemma is not responding, man, so I don't feel comfortable just stopping by."

"Man, stop whining and bring ya ass," Ezra shouted.

Thirty minutes later I pulled my truck into Maxine's driveway. Approaching the door, we could hear the melodies of Snoh Aalegra resounding in the house. I hung back a bit allowing my brother to be the first face they'd see. Jemma was going ghost on me again so I was unsure if I'd be staying.

"Hey, hey," Maxi sang, opening the massive antique door. "Come on in," she said with a bright gleam directed at Myron. He clasped his hand to her nape then kissed against her cheek.

I peered around in search of her, but the living room was empty. Quaron sauntered down the steps eyeing Ezra as if she was ready for another round of whatever happened last night. What the hell was going on? I had to be in the damn twilight zone. My brother and cousin came to town for two minutes and immediately made connections, meanwhile, I was entangled with a married, separated, potentially emotionally unavailable woman.

"Hey Zeke," Maxi finally greeted me. "Jemma's on the patio writing," she whispered, pointing towards the back of the house.

I recalled a large four-season patio off of the kitchen. Hesitantly, I ambled through the house reaching the patio door but paused my pursuit. Jemma sat with her legs criss crossed on the couch, laptop resting on her thighs. The faux flames of the electric fireplace flickered in tune with the music. A tall glass of red wine and an empty plate of what I would presume was the gooey butter cake were on the side table.

Heather gray wide leg pants and a matching cropped shirt hugged her frame, while a black turban concealed curly coils and black-rimmed glasses fancied her face. She was so focused and so damn gorgeous. I took pleasure in witnessing *JulesPen* in her creative zone and hated to interrupt. Jemma rapidly tapped the tips of her nails against her chin with her lips pouted as she often did when she was deep in thought. I hushly chuckled, as her face brightened once she gained clarity on her next thought. I could seriously watch her all night.

"A penny for your thoughts," I said, my baritone gruff. I opened the screen door but she wasn't startled, simply glared at me with a one cheek smile.

"A nickel for a kiss," she sang, referencing the old 80s R&B tune.

I playfully searched in my pockets and muttered, "Maybe I can find a dime if you...," I teased, considering the next line of the song was *a dime if you tell me that you love me.* "Am I disturbing you?" I said, quickly changing the subject.

"No, just writing." Jemma closed the laptop but kept her eyes on me.

"About what?" I asked, keeping my distance because if I got too close I couldn't be responsible for my wanton actions.

"Black women and the beauty of their skin," she explained. "Trying to find the best words to describe it besides beautiful," she said, blushing.

I leaned against the threshold with my hands tucked in my sweatpants pockets. "Hmm, that's an easy one."

"Really? Enlighten me," she uttered in a sexy tone. Tossing the throw pillows to the floor, she patted the couch cushion inviting me to take a seat.

I settled next to her and immediately began unhurriedly verbalizing the words I would use to describe *her.*

"Rich, golden, umber, velvet, beguiling," I chortled, biting the corner of my lip as I trailed a finger down her forearm then captured her hand.

The next words were followed with soft kisses against her skin. "Chocolate, smooth, silky, perfect, complex, mesmerizing, captivating," I whispered, kissing against her neck before gazing directly in her eyes, proclaiming, "fucking alluring." I planted one tender kiss on her lips, still capturing her ogle. "So you're not avoiding me?" I asked, despising the melancholy in my tone.

"No, why would you say that?" she murmured, shaking her head.

"I called a few times. Thought maybe you were ghosting me; needing time to process last night."

"And this morning," she sexily grinned. "When inspiration hits me, I have to turn the world off to get the words out of my head."

"Got it. Now I'm aware and I'll respect your process," I said, nuzzling against her ear. "Your Inspiration. Say more." I removed the computer from her lap and guided her legs to relax atop of mine. Aimlessly massaging her socked feet, she leaned back, relaxing against the couch.

"Skin is the largest bodily organ and its primary job is protection. Guarding us from bacteria, chemicals, and harmful elements, right?" I nodded, agreeing with her. "Well for black women, when our skin is not perfect or it's blemished or too dark, the *elements*... our friends, family, partners even colleagues, shame, harm and victimize us with their words or actions, depleting our sense of safety and security, therefore weaponizing our skin," she matter of factly said but in a subdued manner avoiding eye contact with me.

I tickled her toes and she animatedly tossed her head back with a smile.

"But last night, I felt quite the contrary. I've never felt more beautiful and lovely in my marred, tainted skin. So inspiration. I had to write about it. Release it," she deeply exhaled, disconnecting from my hold as she slouched deeper into the couch.

I was about to speak but she suddenly continued.

"It's been a really long time since I've experienced the sentiment of..." I hung on to her every word as her voice stalled. Her vulnerability was arresting.

"What sentiment, Jules?" I probed expectantly.

"Self-assurance, solace." She pursed her lips then shrugged innocently before resting her head against her fist on the arm of the couch. "I don't know why, Ezekiel Green, but I feel safe with you and it scares the shit out of me," she admitted.

I paused my movements, glaring at her in awe. Suddenly, I seized her, capturing her quivering frame in my arms. She was shaking, nervous about her admission and possibly my reaction. Although we rarely discussed it, I was well aware that Jemma had been neglected and dismissed in her relationship so my response to her vulnerability was critical.

I decided not to pacify her with fruitless vocabulary, instead I simply embraced her, settling into content and necessary silence for several minutes. No words were required, my actions, *shit*, the turbulent pounding of my heart was indication enough to demonstrate my adoration. Jemma would always be safe with me given the enormity of my fondness for her, but I, on the other hand, was uncertain of the future condition of my heart. The fact remained, my Jules was still somebody's wife.

17

JEMMA

I awakened to a heated sensation dispersing down my back as a quiver attacked my flesh. My body was confused, shifting between hot and cold sensitivities as Ezekiel tasted, tongued and lapped my pussy in the wee hours of the morning. Last night on the backyard patio, we kissed and fondled and necked like teenagers until my essence overflowed. His manhood sprung to attention tenting the sweatpants requiring me to be his human sheath as we shamefully ambled through the living room and up the stairs. My girls didn't need a visual of his third leg.

Thankfully, Maxi and Myron were asleep on the couch and Roni and Ezra were nowhere to be found. We reached my bedroom but never made it to the bed. Frantically disrobing, Ezekiel hoisted all two hundred pounds of me against the wall as he snaked that anaconda penis against my dripping private lips. The head of his girth loitered idly at my center as if it had no place to be. Sluggish oscillations against my bud where about to make me fucking combust with need.

"Zee," I whimpered, practically begging for the dick. I don't know where that cry came from but it seemed appropriate under the duressed circumstances.

"Condom," he huskily grunted the word as more of a query than a statement.

"No," I whined, desperate for the delicious intrusion.

"Jules, are you sure," he confirmed, dick still dallying at my opening.

"Safe," I mumbled, so bewitched by this man that I could only utter one word at a time.

I had already disclosed that my safety resided in him and at that moment, I craved the unveiled tenderness of him. Ezekiel entered me with measured, dawdling motions. His kisses were passionate yet tender. He took his time with me, building the orgasm one gratifying inch at a time. I obeyed his command, methodically swaying my hips to ensure I didn't neglect one morsel of this man's weighty member.

"Jules," he groaned, carrying me from the wall to the bed. I pounded the mattress in frustration when his heaviness slid out of me. Empty. I was empty without his fulfillment.

"Zee, no. Baby. Shit. I need to feel you," I pleaded, with my back against his chest.

Thankfully the vacancy was only momentary. I happily sighed like a crackhead getting that first hit as he glided back into my essence, lounging there as my saturated walls cuddled his erection. I stood with my backside to him balancing on my tippy toes with my forearms perched on the mattress, settling into a downward dog-ish position. Ezekiel lifted his hands in surrender while I got into formation. I peeked over my shoulder, sexily smiling, giving him permission to proceed. For countless heartbeats he plummeted deep into my ocean rhythmically, repeatedly, inciting a guttural cry that he immediately swallowed with a salacious choke to my neck. He pulled me upright for a kiss. That damn snake-like penis never decoupled from my center.

I was motionless aside from the erratic labored breathing. My body shuddered, the crest of the orgasm wouldn't unshackle me. The evidence of my need drizzled slowly down my thigh like hot molasses. He vacated me again and I think I screamed as he flipped me onto my back and indulged in my honeyed juices. This man was going to kill me if he prolonged my orgasm any more.

He suctioned, siphoned and guzzled my gooey delicacy with his tongue before anchoring his plethora into my sodden center again. Ezekiel was like the Energizer Bunny, he kept going and going and his dick kept growing and growing inside of me until he spread his seeds throughout my treasure. If my uterus was capable, I would definitely be birthing Ezekiel the third. I was swollen, sore and unsettled but he didn't rush me, just affectionately cradled my quivering frame until I mellowed.

"Jemma, baby, let me clean you up," he said, baritone throaty, tired. I nodded, then felt my body elevate from the bed as he transported me into the bathroom. He sat me on the vanity chair before activating the multi-jet shower. I ogled him standing before me in all of his naked wonderment. Ezekiel was a beautifully designed Adonis. Sweet baby Jesus took his precious time assembling this magnificence.

"Do you need something to cover your hair?" he inquired with a serious expression.

I smiled, appreciating his concern for my natural coils, but shook my head, murmuring, "No."

Lathering the sponge with Dove, he washed me from head to toe. I faintly flinched when he stroked my kitty. Ezekiel stared at me questioningly but didn't mumble a word. Realization dressed his face. Was I a little achy? Yes. Did he go too far? He'll no. I loved his erotic dominance, *shit*, craved the pleasurable pain. Ezekiel rested me on the shower bench and promptly began caressing and kissing my pussy in the most delicate tempo, igniting my third orgasm.

I repositioned in bed to view the clock on my nightstand. *4:21am.* Ezekiel was sound asleep laying on his stomach. I gingerly slipped out of the bed, used the bathroom then grabbed my robe to get some bottled waters from the kitchen. I lethargically shuffled down the hallway, my body was exhausted after a beautiful battering.

Focused on my phone, I easily navigated the house in the dark; a clear indication that I'd been living at Maxi's for far too long. I needed a place of my own. As if the devil heard my inner thoughts, an email from my attorney was in my inbox.

Hello Jemma. Sorry to email you so late but I wanted you to have this in the morning. Mr. Holiday is now asking for an inventory of the items in the house. Call me when you get a chance so we can discuss this. It's another stall tactic but the request is within his rights unfortunately. Call me. M. Warren.

I scoffed, rolling my eyes as I entered the kitchen to be startled to consciousness. "Ezra. Oh my goodness. You scared the shit out of me," I huffed, pressing a hand to my chest to calm my thundering heart.

"My bad. I'm an early riser and didn't want to wake Q," he grumbled.

"Q? That nickname is usually reserved for her brother but I like it," I said, giggling at his familiarity with Quaron. "I'm an early riser sometimes too, but this time I just needed water." I moseyed around the kitchen humming as I grabbed a bottle of water from the refrigerator and another from the pantry. Ezra was hushed as he sipped on what smelled like cognac.

"Well, goodnight or good morning," I chuckled, heading out of the kitchen.

"I'm not the type to beat around the bush so I'll just say it," he blurted.

My interest instantly peaked so I turned to face him and took a few steps back into the kitchen.

"Lil is feeling you. Shit, he might be falling in love with you. So don't pull him into your bullshit if he's just the rebound nigga," he growled so nonchalantly.

I cocked my head in disbelief as he tossed up a dismissive hand, noticing I was about to speak.

"I know your shit is complicated and you're working through it and that's all respect, but Zeke don't need to get consumed by you and your man's shit. This provost gig is a big deal for him. He told me how he was ready to buck on that nigga at homecoming and I saw the same shit in his eyes yesterday with the corny dude. You are the common denominator, Dr. Holiday. When Zeke wants something, he's merciless. And right now I think he's willing to fuck up all his shit for you. And respectfully sweetheart, when people fuck with my baby brother, they gotta see me," Ezra paused, his gape indignant.

"I can speak now?" I sarcastically questioned because that dismissive hand from a minute ago pissed me off. But sadly, my vexation was only confirmation that Ezra was right. It wasn't fair to Ezekiel to involve him in my disarray. Clearly he's the type of man who safeguards the people in his life at all cost. I saw it too at homecoming with Quinton and last night with Ken.

Ezra nodded, sipping his drink.

I blinked rapidly to temporarily suspend my tears. I swallowed hard before croaking,

"You're right. I don't want to hurt him because whatever you may believe, I do care about Ezekiel." *Too much,* I silently mused.

"I definitely do not wish to impact his ability to do the job I am confident he will be amazing at. So, you're right. But I've never lied about or sugar coated the complexity of my situation. Your brother is a grown man who is highly capable of making his own decisions. And I am a grown woman, who handles my shit. *Is* handling my shit. So the next time you have something to say to me, rethink your tone. Please do not *ever* speak to me that way *ever* again," I hissed, rolling my eyes as I sauntered away just as casually as I came.

I climbed back into the bed uselessly striving to suppress the impending tears but the attempt was futile. Muted hot tears crawled down my face as Ezekiel snuggled closer to me. I kissed the top of his head and nestled into his embrace. Everything in me felt like I wanted this man for all of the right reasons, but then my thoughts traveled back to the email from my lawyer. Quinton would not depart this marriage easily. Ken's punk ass was guaranteed to spill all of what he thinks he knows. So once Quinton becomes aware of even the possibility of me and Dr. Green, he would cause major disruptions in my life. I had to let this go. I had to let *him go.*

The next morning, Ezekiel kissed my temple, nose then lips before he departed. His brother and cousin were flying back to New York today and he was driving them to St. Louis to catch their late afternoon flight. He endeavored to bless me with a forth orgasm but I pushed him away citing exhaustion, which was not completely untrue. If that man had put his mouth on me again, Ezra and Myron would be on the next Amtrak, bus, shit, spaceship back to the NYC, because I would withhold Ezekiel until I couldn't consume anymore of his goodness.

"Ezekiel, you have to go," I whined, playfully scrambling away from his approaching tickles.

"I know, I know. I don't mean to smother you. It's just..." he halted, exhaling while rubbing a hand down his face.

"What?" I asked, scratching my fingernails through his beard.

He shook his head. "This just feels good, Jemma. Too damn good."

We glared at each other for what seemed like a lifetime but only minutes ticked by. I chose not to validate his sentiment with words. Hopefully the dew misting in my eyes narrated my unspoken adoration.

"I know you need time to process, to escape and I will give you whatever time you need. But can you promise me something?"

I nodded with no hesitation.

"Don't shut me out. Talk. I want to hear the good, the bad and ugly. Even if it may hurt. Ok?"

I nodded again, debating on if I should disclose my *conversation* with his brother but decided against it.

"One more promise?" he asked, disrupting my daze. I lifted a brow, silently giving permission to proceed. "I want to take you somewhere... a place that's still and quiet, just for us. A place where we can just be mindless and *free*," he smiled, then winked. "If I can arrange something like that, can you promise me you will seriously consider it?"

I nodded. So many emotions hitched in my heart and head that I couldn't speak.

"Use your words, wordsmith," he teased, nipping the tip of my nose.

"Yes, Zee. I will consider it."

* * *

"Two more days. Just two more days, Dr. Holiday," I whispered to myself after hanging up with yet another parent who was not aware that their child would not be graduating.

December commencement was in two days and I was looking forward to celebrating our scholars. But more importantly, I was ready to enjoy four weeks of nothingness during the winter break. Turning in my office chair, I leaned back gazing out of the big picture window that afforded me an amazing view of the quad. The trees were bare aside from the traces of icicles from yesterday's rain.

Campus was quiet since the underclassmen wrapped up their finals schedule on Friday. You would think that after more than ten years of working at Monroe University I would be accustomed to the hussle that was required to conclude every semester. However this semester came with personal changes that I did not anticipate. If anyone would've told me in June of this year that I would basically be homeless and filing for divorce, I would not have believed one word. I definitely would've called bullshit on the possibility of meeting a man who could turn my world upside down.

Ezekiel and I had not physically connected since Thanksgiving and my body was aching for him. He'd been busy with travel and getting acclimated to his provost responsibilities. Even our text dialogue was minimal over the past few weeks. Life was definitely lifeing. My schedule was crazy as well; swiftly approaching my deadline for the new book and managing some situations with my student population. The need for increased mental health and wellness support was critical for the university so I'd been diligent about identifying programs to support our scholars. Monroe University's expectations were high and unfortunately many students were not fully prepared for the rigor and demands of a Monroe Jaguar; my daughter included, so this effort was crucial.

"Knock, knock," the familiar rich baritone sound disrupted my musing. He was back. I puffed out a breath to subdue the smile coating my face. "Dr. Holiday?" he said, slowly pushing the door open.

"Dr. Green. Welcome back." I flashed a closed mouth smile.

"Thank you. It's good to be back." He returned the gesture.

"I heard you were delivering holiday cheer today to the staff," I said, motioning my head to the cart filled with small fruit baskets.

"It's corny, I know. My mother's recommendation. Something she used to do for her staff and they loved it." He cutely shrugged.

"I don't think it's corny at all."

"May I?" he asked, pointing to the chair reserved for guests.

"Please," I offered, waving my hand for him to take a seat.

"I was hoping you could help me with a situation with a student, Damien Harris. He was waiting for me when I arrived this morning."

"Oh Damien," I sang in frustration.

"So you know him?" he chuckled.

"Too well," I sighed, rolling my eyes. "Damien has been with us for five and a half years and was scheduled to graduate in two days. However, last week his senior thesis advisor informed me that Mr. Harris did not complete the final paper by the deadline which is fifty percent of his grade."

Ezekiel tossed his head back in amusement. "Of course I didn't get that part of the story. Mr. Harris was petitioning for my help given that we are, and I quote, connected through the fraternity brotherhood."

I boisterously guffawed, shaking my head. "I hope that young man goes to law school because he is as smooth and conniving as they come."

"I told him I would talk to the boss…i.e., you, to get a better understanding of if this can be rectified. I am pretty sure he shed a tear when he walked out of my office," he chortled.

I shook my head. "Mr. Harris will be fine. He provided proof that the paper is about seventy percent done. He claims he was so excited about his offer at Google that he forgot about the paper. I'm going to allow him to walk for graduation but I'm making him sweat a little bit so don't tell him that part just yet." I winked.

"I got you," he laughed, sexily gazing at me.

We settled in agreeable silence for a few moments. We intently surveyed each other. I missed him and by the look of the gleam in those anthracite eyes, Ezekiel missed me too. Neither of us would brave the admittance of that fact. His deep murmur broke the stillness.

"What are your plans for the winter break?"

"Absolutely nothing and I am going to love every minute of it," I giggled and he joined.

"That does sound amazing. But seriously, no plans with your family."

"I'll be in St. Louis most of the time. Annual holiday slumber party with my linesisters and Christmas dinner with family at my parents' home but that's really about it," I shrugged.

"Shiloh is going to Disneyworld with her boyfriend and his family for the new year," I mumbled, snarkily lifting a brow. "I will probably bring in the year with my girls. What about you?" I inquired.

"Same. Just enjoy the downtime. Christmas at my mom's and then vacation with my kids. Like Shiloh, EJ is spending the new year with his girlfriend and Eriya will be with her mom's family."

"The beauty and the curse of adult kids, right?" I said and we laughed as he nodded. "Um, when do you leave?" I reluctantly questioned, not wanting to appear desperate.

"Red eye to New York right after commencement."

I nodded, unsure of what to say next and contemplating a month without seeing him. "Well, let me get out of here. I'm supposed to stop by a lunch event for the administrative staff," he said, breaking our synchronized gaze.

Ezekiel stood to his full height looking good enough to eat in casual attire. Dark denim jeans, camel Polo sweater and brown Gucci loafers had my kitty going haywire. He sauntered to the door seemingly prepared to exit but he closed it instead. My eyes widened, trying to predict his next move.

The thump in my yoni ached for him to grant me access to his countless inches. This desk was often the backdrop of my most lascivious dreams starring Ezekiel. If he asked, I would have happily obliged. He crooked his finger, beckoning me to come to him. I obeyed. Feathering the curves of my face, he pulled me into a delicate embrace and planted a guiltless kiss on my cheek. His nose lightly brushed against my ear, then he whispered, "I missed you."

Once again he was the brave one. I should've said something; offered a retort, acknowledged the sentiment, something, but I didn't. Reticently, I clutched the collar of his shirt peeking from under the sweater. Our eyes dotingly coupled, mutely dialoguing our unvoiced desire. Closing our eyes in unison, we kissed. Soft, dainty, impassioned pecks dispatched heatwaves to my pussy. The steeliness pressing against my stomach was indication of his congruent yearning. I took a step back and opened my eyes, endeavoring to cease and desist before I swiped all of this shit off of my desk.

"I better go. I'll talk to you later," he sighed, laying one more kiss on my forehead then ambled to the door.

"Hey," I bayed and he paused. "No basket for me, Dr. Green," I questioned, licking the remnants of his kiss from my lips.

"Nah, no basket for you, Dr. Holiday. But you have something coming though. Stay tuned." He winked then exited just as sexy as he entered.

18

EZEKIEL

An enormous grin decorated my face as I awakened to the delectable aromas wafting through my childhood home. Since my father died four years ago, me, Ezra and Myron always slept at my mom's house on Christmas Eve night so that she wouldn't wake up alone.

Aside from their wedding anniversary, Christmas was my parents favorite holiday. As kids, our house was the winter wonderland of Bedford-Stuyvesant. No surface was safe from holiday lights, tensile, bows, you name it. We even had inflatable Christmas characters in the front yard of our brownstone. Thankfully we'd finally convinced my mother to forgo the inflatables and paid someone to string lights on the house for nostalgia sake.

I inhaled deeply anticipating a slice of sweet potato pie for breakfast. The melodies of My Girl sounded from my phone causing an even bigger smile on my face. "Merry Christmas, peanut," I greeted my daughter Eriya. She was truly a daddy's girl.

"Merry Christmas, daddy," she squealed. "Thank you, thank you, thank you. I love my LV backpack."

"You're opening presents already, peanut," I chuckled. "You better thank your mother. Three thousand dollars for a book bag is not my definition of being fiscally responsible. I better see a 4.0 this first semester at Monroe."

"No sweat, daddy-o. I got you. And it's a vintage LV backpack, not just a Jansport bookbag, ugghh," she crassly corrected.

"Keep being ungrateful and flaunting that privilege and that backpack bookbag whatever the hell it is will go right back. You know I don't like that, YaYa," I sternly proclaimed. Thankfully my ex and I were able to provide handsomely for our children, but unappreciative behavior was not tolerated. Eriya and EJ had to work for everything they were given.

"I'm sorry, Daddy. I'm not trying to be ungrateful. Thank you again," she whimpered.

"You're welcome, baby girl." Eriya and I talked for about twenty minutes to finalize our plans to meet at the airport early tomorrow morning for our flight to Key West, Florida. After my football career ended, my family created a tradition to visit our vacation home in Key West after Christmas and return on New Year's Eve. My ex, Michelle and I, maintained the routine, alternating years with the kids.

I glanced at the digital clock on the nightstand, *ten o'clock*. I wanted to call Jules but opted to send a simple text instead since it was eight in the morning for her.

Me: Merry Christmas, beautiful. Call me when you get a chance.

I quickly hopped in the shower and dressed in black joggers and a holiday t-shirt that my mother insisted we wear. I always indulged her retro reflections of our childhood. A tap at the door paused my reverie. I knew that it was Ezra and he would only knock once before coming in.

"Bro, look at this shit," Ezra yelped with his arms raised to demonstrate how tight and short his shirt was. "Ma thinks I'm still twelve with this smedium shirt."

"Nigga you wasn't smedium at twelve," Myron leaned against the threshold doubled over in laughter. I vainly attempted to quell my chuckle but that shit was funny as hell.

"Ezra, Junior, Myron," my mother shouted, always in order of age. "Breakfast," she announced.

My cousin Myron became an addition to our immediate family at fifteen years old when his mother, my mother's youngest sister, died suddenly from an aneurysm. His father was a New York City police officer and kept odd work hours so they agreed for Myron to live with us full time. Just like when we were kids, three pairs of gigantic feet trampling down the steps sounded like a freight train running through the house.

"Now I know I don't have to tell your grown behinds to walk in my house," momma fussed. We instantly reverted back to little boys, whimpering, "no ma'am."

"Merry Christmas, Mama," I said, kissing her on the cheek as she stood at the sink cleaning greens for today's dinner.

"Merry Christmas, Aunt V," Myron followed.

"Ma, is this the only shirt they had?" Ezra nagged.

"Merry Christmas to you too, Ezra Victor Green," she chortled.

"Merry Christmas, Mama. But Ma, for real, is this the only shirt they had?" Ezra bantered, kissing her on the cheeks while tickling her waist. She blushed, swatting him away.

At seventy plus years old my mother was still an active beautiful woman. Silver hair with a few strands of black remaining, tawny-hued skin as smooth as silk and the most beautiful light brown almond shaped eyes I'd ever seen.

A feast of scrambled cheese eggs, chicken sausage, fried potatoes, grits and homemade cinnamon bread was spread across the dining room table in white ceramic serving dishes. My mother didn't believe in paper plates or utensils so place settings were arranged at each seat of the eight person dining table. She completed the array with a carafe of orange juice and a pot of coffee. Some would assume that this was special treatment for the holiday, but this presentation was my mother's normal weekend routine growing up. Since both my parents worked in education, mornings were managed like a military camp to ensure they'd get to their respective schools on time. However, on the weekends, we'd spend hours in fellowship over breakfast at the same cherry wood table.

I fixed momma's plate while Ezra doctored her coffee. Myron was on kitchen duty today which meant it was his responsibility to pull her out of the kitchen and force her to sit down and eat breakfast. After stuffing an excessive amount of greens into a pot I always thought was too small, she settled at the head table.

"Ezra, since you woke up with no sense this morning, you bless the food," she jeered.

At least an hour later, we were still laughing and talking over our second cups of coffee with soulful holiday music playing in the background. My phone chimed indicating a text message. It was Jemma.

> Jules: Merry Christmas. I pray you are having a blessed morning with your family.

> Me: I recall a morning a couple weeks ago on the balcony that was a blessing to me too.

I was pretty confident I was blushing based on the glares across the table. Ezra shook his head with a disgruntled scowl on his face.

"Was that the lady doctor friend your brother was telling me about," momma questioned, then passively took a sip of coffee.

I shot fiery eyes at Ezra. "and what exactly did my brother tell you?"

"Nothing really. He said she's very pretty and that you seem to be very fond of her," momma inflected, her uncombed curls bouncing as her head cocked to the side.

"It's not something I really want to talk about, ma. Things are... complicated," I declared, endeavoring to cease the choice words I had for my brother.

"Well I guess a married woman can create some complications for you, son."

I jolted my head to my chatty-Kathy ass brother. "Ez, really man. What are we five? You're running to tell mama my business," I scoffed.

"Whatever, Zeke. That woman has your nose wide open and I don't want to see you hurt," he barked.

"Then talk to me about my business, not mama."

"Boys stop it. Stop it. I should've kept my mouth shut," she sighed. "Junior, don't be mad at your brother. He's only looking out for you and he's concerned. I'm concerned."

I took a sip of coffee, then deeply exhaled to give myself a moment to remove the incensed bass from my voice. "Mama, I appreciate your concern but I have it under control. Jules - Dr. Holiday is separated and in the process of a divorce. We are friends and yes I enjoy her company but I understand the complexities of her situation better than anybody at this table. And to be honest..." I paused, peering around the table when my phone chimed. **Jules:** Mornings on the balcony are my favorite. Repeat?

Her words made me snicker, then I peered at my family and said, "For whatever reason, I'm willing to risk it all for her."

"You need not explain anything to me, son. That's between you and your God. Just be careful, Junior."

Me: Yes, hopefully sooner than later. Enjoy your day, beautiful. We'll talk soon.

19

JEMMA

S unrise service at church truly blessed my soul. I was exhausted after a night hanging with some of my linesisters for our annual holiday dinner but I got up just in time to throw on a red sweater dress and black knee-high boots to join my mother and Shiloh for church. After my mother greeted the pastor, the deacons and every member of the motherboard, we were finally able to meet my father for breakfast before dropping off Shiloh at her other grandparent's house. She opted to spend Christmas morning with her dad and dinner with my family. I hated this new normal for Shiloh.

Since birth, she'd always experienced a cohesive unit between the Warren and Holiday families. We were virtually inseparable for the sake of Shiloh. But now, even at twenty years old, she's being forced to determine custody for the holidays. Divorce was hard, even for me, the initiator. Sometimes I felt guilty for separating myself from everyone because I adored my in-laws, they were like second parents to me. But given the tension between Quinton and I… no, scratch that, given the fact that he cheated on me countless times and now he's fathered a child, my relationship with them would never be the same. At least not while Quinton was around. Just as we pulled up to the glorious home of the Holiday's my phone chimed.

> Zee: Mom cooked enough food for an army and made us wear these corny ass shirts.

Seconds later, the phone sounded again and I heartily chuckled at the site of Ezekiel, his brother and cousin in the Grinch Christmas t-shirts and plaid pajama pants. But damn he still looked good.

"Mommy," Shiloh yelped, interrupting my monetary elation. "You're coming in right?" I nodded and shot a quick text back to Ezekiel.

> Me: Aww, I love it. A momma loving on her babies is never corny.

Nervous jitters instantly flooded my core while ambling down the walkway to the front door. This would be my first time seeing Quinton in over a month since he made another bullshit request stalling the divorce proceedings again. My parents, Shiloh and I approached with cakes, pies and Christmas gifts in tow.

Mr. Holiday opened the door, warmly greeting us as if he and my father didn't just finish a round of golf together. Our parents were friends, so it wouldn't have been fair to ask them to discontinue their relationship just because Quinton and I were no longer together. Mrs. Holiday quickly appeared aside her husband with those beautiful green eyes she gifted her children. They were misty with tears as soon as her eyes landed on me.

"You came, Jemma. You look gorgeous," Mrs. Holiday sighed, embracing with a firm hug. I smiled and nodded my thanks. "And look at my Princess," she said, turning her attention to Shiloh. "Go on and put those things in the dining room, Shi. We are ready to open gifts as soon as your dad gets back from his run."

I hushly breathed a sigh of relief because of Quinton's absence, but it was going to be in vain if my parents didn't stop yapping. Normally, we would have brunch with the Holidays on Christmas, but nothing was *normal* about this situation and I was uncomfortable. We transitioned into the living room just as Quaron sauntered down the hall offering holiday greetings while holding two champagne glasses filled with mimosa.

"Merry Christmas, sis. I thought you could use this," Roni snickered, handing me the glass.

"You be knowing, sis," I giggled, taking a hefty swig of the bubbly. "Merry Christmas," we toasted, clinking the expensive crystal flutes.

"I swear, you two," my mother fussed, shaking her head. "Jemma Jule you just came from church."

Quaron motioned her fingers over her body making a cross symbol and muttered, "Thank God. Praise the Lord, now gone keep the party going, Mama Maureen," she playfully smacked her lips together kissing my mother's cheek. We all emitted a boisterous laugh at her silliness.

"Hey Ma, Mrs. Owens said the cake will -" Quinton's breathy words suddenly became lodged in his throat when he ambled from the back of the house to see us bantering in the living room. I tossed back the rest of the mimosa wishing it was a shot of tequila. "Pops, Ma Maureen," he winced, uncertain if he should still use the loving acknowledgement. "Um, Merry Christmas, Mr. and Mrs. Warren," he nervously mumbled.

"Merry Christmas, Quinton," my parents greeted.

Those widened green orbs observed me from head to toe navigating up my frame before he muttered, "Merry Christmas, Jem." He was uncomfortable too, noticeably swallowing hard and tensely rubbing his nape.

"Merry Christmas, Quinton," I retorted with a faux smile.

Disappointed and heartbroken eyes tossed between us as our family ogled the tortuous discourse.

"Daddy!" Shiloh's screeching cheer saved the day. A silver box in one hand and car keys dangling from her other hand, she squealed, "Are you serious? I have a car. Where?" She leaped in the air, clutching her arms around her dad's neck.

"In the garage, baby girl," he chortled.

"Mommy! Seriously?" she screeched.

I giggled, nodding.

"OMG! Thank you, thank you. Let's go see it before you leave," she practically yanked my arm towards the door to enter the garage. Everyone joined us to admire Shiloh's brand new white Jeep Cherokee as she posed for pictures. I, on the other hand, was ready to go. I was certain that with time this desire to murder Quinton would dissolve, but right now it was ever-present. I tipped out of the garage and ducked inside the house to use the restroom. I needed some space from the cheerful banter. Exiting a few minutes later, Quinton was waiting for me in the hallway.

"Jemma," he whispered, grasping my hand to pause my pursuit.

"Quinton I don't want to fight," I huffed, already exhausted by the impending exchange.

"Neither do I. I want to figure this out, J. Look at our baby girl. This is all that she knows," he said, pointing his finger towards the garage. "This family. Our home and her grandparents' homes are her mainstays. We can't disrupt that for her."

I scoffed and rolled me eyes. "We can't disrupt that? You did that all by yourself, Quinton. Not me, not my parents or your parents, you. The quicker you take responsibility for your actions, the better this will be for everybody," I stressed, attempting to walk away when he grabbed my waist pulling me into him.

"Better? Ain't no *better* in this situation," he began to yell but quickly lowered his tone. "I'm losing my fucking family. How is that better?" he gritted through his teeth, expression strained.

"So because you fucked up, everybody suffers? Namely me? You would prefer to make my life miserable instead?" I yanked away from him.

Quinton stepped back to lean against the wall. Ironically his head was positioned right next to our hanging wedding picture; a glimpse of happier times. I darted my eyes away from the memory to witness the smug smirk on his face; a snapshot of today's reality.

"Nobody told you to leave, Jemma. I'm not losing my family. So now you suffer the consequences. Whatever those may be," he shrugged dismissively.

Fire blazed through my chest as I leered at him. Violent malicious thoughts flashed in my head. I wanted to scratch that fucking sneer from his face, but I considered the ramifications. I considered my Shiloh.

"You're delusional. There's no family for us. Love don't live here anymore, Q," I whisper-yelled, pointing to my chest. "Yes, I left because finally…" I paused, sucking in a deep breath before continuing,"I chose Jemma and now I'm free, with or without your cooperation."

* * *

Christmas was exhausting. Dozens of family and friends were packed wall to wall in my parent's home ambling in and out like an open house event.

My mother spared no expense on food, decorations or gifts to celebrate the birth of Jesus. She even had a basket of holiday cards filled with lottery tickets available for surprise guests. God forbid anyone didn't receive a present on Christmas. Maureen Warren didn't miss a beat. Nothing topped Shiloh's car, possibly except for the Louis Vuitton Neverfull gifted by her Aunties Quaron and Maxine.

I leaned against the cherry wood banister gazing at Shi with a smile because she was so happy under the circumstances. I walked away from Quinton earlier ready to explode. I was so angry, but maintained my composure. I wouldn't disrespect my daughter, his parents or baby Jesus on Christmas Day. I was exhausted and just wanted this day to be over, but I must admit, the pomp and circumstance of the day was a great distraction. The house was finally fairly empty aside from the immediate family. Shiloh was on FaceTime with Jordan, Mommy was feeling good after a few wine spritzers and daddy was on the patio smoking cigars with his brothers which gave me an opportunity to sneak away.

I was stuffed full of dressing, macaroni and cheese, and ham and now it was time for the creme de la creme; a large slice of 7-Up pound cake with the last drop of expensive red blend dessert wine my uncle gifted me. But first a bath. I schlepped up the back stairwell to circumvent any pressure to play Tunk or Phase10 with my cousins.

"Sneaking?" My mother's giddy voice chimed. I halted, snickering because I was tipping away like the Grinch that stole Christmas.

"No, just needing some alone time," I sighed, turning to face her. My mother closed the space between us, extending her hands to clutch my cheeks.

"My light, my sparkle, my Jemma Jule. Have you prayed about it?" Mommy asked, gently stroking against my skin.

I nodded, allowing a stray tear to fall.

"Then what are you worried about? It's already done," she boldly conferred, nudging my chin to lift my head. "You're a fighter, baby girl. It's going to be alright. You, my love, are going to be alright."

I hugged my shero so tight until I was good and ready to release from the embrace. She kissed my cheek then turned to get her own slice of cake.

"Jemma Jule," she called out with her back to me. "You have a secret Santa, little girl. I put the box on your bed," she wryly squealed.

With a closed mouth smile, I nibbled the corner of my lip then muttered, "I love you, momma."

"Mmhmm. I love you more," she tittered.

Turning to head towards the staircase, I forced myself to placidly saunter but I wanted to run. Make a mad dash two steps at a time like a kid on Christmas morning anticipating the gifts they'd prayed for all year. Balancing the serving tray while opening the door to my childhood bedroom, I peeked around the edge with a Cheshire grin plastered across my face. An elegantly wrapped red box with an oversized gold bow sat in the middle of the holiday plaid comforter spread across my bed.

I rested the tray on the nightstand, clicked on another lamp and climbed on the mattress. With criss-crossed legs, I giddily, yet carefully untied the sparkling gold ribbon and opened the box. Concealed by pounds of confetti paper, I lifted a round heavy object as my face scrunched, perplexed. A snowglobe. *Why in the world would he send me a snowglobe?* I mused, making assumptions about the identity of the sender. I thought it was Ezekiel… god, I hoped it was him.

My wish was confirmed as the New York City skyline glinted through the streaming iridescent flakes. I shook it again silently naming the miniature historic structures mimicking the big city. A handwritten note was taped to the box lid and the front of the envelope read, *Jules*. The grin that spread across my face was as white and brilliant as the snowflakes.

Hello Gorgeous. Merry Christmas.

It took alot for me to pull this off but the Junior's cheesecake that I owe Maxi is well worth it.

Jules, as we prepared for another year, I'm pondering on how my life has changed this year. I'm fulfilling so many dreams that I never voiced. One being you. It sounds crazy but I imagined you in my dreams. Your eyes, your lips, your inviting embrace. Come to me, Jemma. Just like that night in the hotel, don't hesitate, don't think, just come. To a serene place where we can be Zee and Jules with no disruptions or disquietude. Check your email for the details. I've taken care of everything. All I need is you, Jules.

You are the first and only person I want to see to start my new year.

20

EZEKIEL

"*D*on't think. Don't hesitate. Just come." Those were the same words I said to Jemma that night in the hotel. The only difference now is that I'd experienced first hand how she felt burrowed in my chest, her taste... the saccharine goodness still loitered on my tongue today.

I sat in my childhood bedroom sipping cognac, glaring out of the window as a light snow began to cover the homes in the distance. It was almost two o'clock in the morning and I couldn't sleep. I kept hearing myself say to my mother and brother that I would be willing to risk it all for Jemma. But why? What was it about this woman that had me behaving haphazardly? I was methodical and logical in my decision making, but Jules... The creak of the door interrupted my reverie. I didn't have to turn around to know that it was Ezra.

"Look, bro. I'm sorry. I should not have said anything to mama, or to Jemma, but I am concerned, Zeke."

"About what?" I swiftly shifted in my chair. "Wait, what the hell did you say to Jemma? When?" I roared, then quickly calmed so I wouldn't wake our mother.

"Thanksgiving. She didn't tell you? I told her not to hurt you or she would have to see me." Ezra's face scowled.

"You fucking threatened her," I said as a statement, not a question. I abruptly rose from my chair, terminating the space between us. I'd never won a fight against my brother but I'd left some scars.

"She's married, Lil," he said, pounding a fist into the palm of his hand. "I know she's getting a divorce but she's been with that nigga for twenty years. Half of her life. What if she decides after the divorce that she wants to get some other experiences? You ready for that? Jemma has only had him and now you. She's still young, fine as hell and has a lot of life to live. Ain't no shortage of niggas vying for her attention. This situation just seems a little bit like deja vu to me."

"Deja vu," I questioned, brow furrowed.

"Michelle," he declared. "She messed you up for a minute and I don't want to see you like that again."

"I appreciate your concern, bro, but I'm not a teenager, Ezra. I'm a grown ass man and I know what the fuck I'm doing. Jemma is not Michelle," I proclaimed with the utmost confidence.

"I know she's not and that's the problem. Michelle never had the power to completely break you, but Jemma…" He pursed his lips, shaking his head. "She's fucking domination and destruction for your ass."

I blankly leered at him, not willing to exhibit that I may agree with his interpretation. "It's under control," I said, jaw tightly clenched.

He nodded. "Ok. Ok, Lil, you got it. Whatever happens you know I'm gonna be here to pick up the pieces." On that note he left my room.

Unfortunately Ezra was right. Jules was my weakness, my kryptonite; the potential to completely ruin me. I was in my head because Jemma still hadn't called and I was certain she'd received her gift by now. Maxine helped me arrange this surprise after I basically begged her for several minutes. She gave me the address to Jemma's parents home where the box from Secret Santa was delivered on Christmas Eve.

Before being rudely interrupted by Ezra, I'd spent the last hour conceiving sane and insane possibilities in my head as to why she hadn't contacted me since earlier today. My brother's declaration didn't make my private musings any less destructive. Gulping down the last sip, I climbed into bed ready to retire for the night when my phone rang.

"Just the face I needed to see," I said with a somewhat faux smile. "Merry Christmas, beautiful."

"Merry Christmas. Are you ok?" she said, eyes squinted with concern.

"Yeah. Yes, I'm good." I smiled but I'm certain it didn't reach my eyes.

"Liar," she chuckled.

"Is it ok if I say I don't want to talk about it right now?"

She nodded, whimpering, "Of course."

"You are gorgeous," I announced, my tenor was a bit too lustful, but lust was one of the many emotions I was feeling for Jemma right now.

"I - I got the gift. The letter," she stuttered. "You really want to spend the new year with me?" she blurted questioningly.

I smiled, wiping a hand down my face to clear the haze of sleepiness. "Oh, Zee, I'm sorry. It's so late and you were probably asleep. We can talk tomorrow," she nervously uttered.

"Baby, Jemma, I always have time for you. I was hoping you would call. And yes, I want you here. Shit, I want you right now," I confessed, staring directly into the camera. "I miss you," I blurted. Damn, liquid courage was something else.

"I miss you too, Zeke," she hesitantly expressed verbally but the glimmer in her honey eyes spoke volumes.

"Was Santa good to you this Christmas?" I asked, watching her prop the phone up on something then rest her head against a pillow like a teenage girl. She was so pretty with a fresh face, glossy eyes and a giddy slur, seemingly from the wine that previously occupied the glass in her background.

"Santa was very good to me. How about you?" she chuckled.

"Same. I had a great time with family. My mother was overjoyed and that's all that matters to me," I muttered. We nestled in tranquil quiet gazing at each other.

"Zee, your letter. Your request..." She was in her head but I quickly disrupted her pensiveness.

"All I asked is for you to consider it, Jemma. You promised that you would so there's no discussion or debate necessary. I promised my kids I'll be offline during vacation so my phone will be off until I'm back in the city on new year's eve morning. The details are in your inbox."

"But Ezekiel -" she interrupted.

"No, Jules. Get out of your head. Stop burdening yourself with what ifs and do what feels good to you. Do what feels right *for you*, sweetheart," he smirked with a raised brow. "If you agree to my proposition, you know what to do, right?"

She nodded, murmuring, "Drop my location."

"And what will be my response when you follow those simple instructions?" I faintly smiled then winked.

"You'll be there. Every time," she whimpered.

"Every fucking time, Jules."

Six days without access to my phone or computer was actually liberating. My family had the phone number to the house for emergencies, but otherwise, me and the kids had a relaxing vacation in Key West. My chilled energy quickly transformed to antsy anxiety when we arrived at the airport to learn that our 8am flight would be two hours delayed. That was an hour ago and we still didn't have an update.

"Mr. Green, I said I would make an announcement when I have an updated status on the flight. Please have a seat," the airport gate agent irritably sighed while staring at her computer screen and avoiding eye contact with me.

"It's Dr. Green and this is passenger service, right?

"Right," she responded, still focused on her screen.

"Well I am a passenger and I would greatly appreciate your services when I am asking a question, Myra." I heatedly stated. That caused the seasoned brown-eyed woman with a spiked-hair wig and hips spread wide to glare up at me.

"Sir -" her words were momentarily lodged as she stared at me with a weird, yet dreamy expression. "Oh damn. You fine. Now, how can I help you, Dr. Green?" she sang, flashing a bright gold-toothed gleam.

I shook my head. "Flight 268 to New York, any updates?"

"The flight crew just landed. Once they make it to the gate and perform the security checks we can begin boarding." She nibbled the corner of her mouth. "Anything else I can do for you, handsome."

I scoffed, peering around in disbelief when Eriya heatedly yelped, "eww, this is my daddy. And no, you can absolutely not do anything for him."

"Girl yo daddy is fine," the woman whispered-yelled, rolling her eyes as my daughter pulled my arm to usher me away from the desk.

Forty minutes later we were boarded and ready for the three hour flight. Once seated in first class, I finally decided to turn on my phone but it was dead.

"YaYa, where's my charger?"

"Didn't I give it to you daddy?"

"Nope," EJ chimed in. "I told you to grab it from that charging station, Ya."

"Oops," she whined, gazing at me with those big, bright eyes resembling her mother's.

"Eriya!" I shouted, much louder than intended.

"I'm sorry daddy. You can use my phone."

If I was a man who rolled his eyes, I would've rolled my eyes at my beautiful daughter. "Do not talk to me for the next three hours," I muttered, plugging my ears with headphones prepared to watch Black Panther for the thousandth time.

Based on my calculations, I would have to drive at supersonic speeds from JFK to get my kids back home and make it to the hotel in Time Square before Jemma's flight arrived at LaGuardia. *Damn I hope she's on that plane,* I mused. Included with her Christmas gift was a ticket to New York. The flight was scheduled to arrive at 4:10pm. By the time she lands, gets her luggage and the limousine navigates holiday traffic, I estimated that she would arrive at the hotel by six o'clock. At the rate I was going, I would be lucky to get there five minutes before her. *But what if she doesn't come?* I continued my senseless, yet possibly realistic pondering. I glared at my useless phone and mouthed, *don't think Jules, just come.*

4:49pm I glanced at my watch, shaking my head as we exited the plane. There was no way I was going to make it on time. I needed to get my phone charged before she thought that I was now the one ghosting her. Sternly eyeballing Eriya, I motioned my head for her to put some pep in her step. "I bet if your lil ass had plans with Pedro tonight you'd be moving faster," I barked, glaring at her over my shoulder as she leisurely strolled.

"His name is Mateo," she corrected.

"Whatever, Eriya. Get a move on. I have plans."

Of course she had to make a stop at the restroom, so I took the opportunity to dart into one of the electronic stores and bought a charger for a ridiculous amount of money. I was edgy and practically snarling at my kids. I couldn't fuck this up. If Jemma is on that plane, it likely took an act of God to convince her. This was probably the one moment in time that I would be able to have her to myself. No text messages, no video chatting, no sneaky glances across the room. I could walk the streets holding her hand, embrace and kiss her at my leisure. On this trip, Jemma would be mine; even if it's just temporary. Aside from that, her trust issues were valid and real. I promised her that I would be there every time she needed me and I refused to be a liar today.

"Dad. Calm down," EJ whispered, placing a hand on my shoulder while we waited for his sister. "Tessa can pick up me and Ya. Go handle your business, " he chortled, nudging me forward.

My brow furrowed, momentarily unable to comprehend his words. Ezekiel Jr. was practically my clone in features and mannerisms. He loved hard and long until you no longer gave him a reason to.

One day on the beach while we drank cognac and smoked cigars, we talked about his relationship with a childhood friend, Tessa, who was now his girlfriend. That discussion led to me disclosing about what I described as a new woman in my life. *Jules.* No details, just the basics, but EJ was an intuitive young man. *"She got you smiling, man. Shit, blushing, Pops,"* he teased and I couldn't deny that shit for one second.

"This new lady sounds really important to you. And you're a man of your word, so go get your girl, man," we laughed before exchanging a special handshake that we've shared since he was a kid. Arriving at the baggage claim, I embraced my two heartbeats, extending sentiments of love before dashing out of the airport.

21

JEMMA

"We are preparing to make our final descent into New York," the flight attendant instructed. I glanced out of the window admiring the snow covered landscape of the city similar to the snowglobe. It took Quaron, Maxine and an act of god to get me on this plane. My heart and head struggled for days in a game of tug of war.

My therapist, Dr. Ray suggested that I make space to find myself. *Settle your heart, Jemma, before matters of the flesh blur the lines.* Too damn late; the waters between me and Ezekiel were murky as shit. We gleefully swam in an ocean of perplexity and pleasure. His ability to demonstrate affection with the utmost simplicity had me feigning for closeness. *He wants me with him,* I pondered, drawing lines through the frost on the window. New York? New Year's Eve? Me? Ezekiel? Together? It was almost too much to fathom, but damn did I want to be here with him too.

"What time are you meeting the good doctor," Maxi questioned, leaning over me to peek out of the window. I shrugged because he hadn't responded to my text. I did know the details but I knew he was planning to arrive back in the city this morning but as of right now he was missing in action.

"Are you going to run into his arm at the stroke of midnight like a sappy love story," Roni teased. I rolled my eyes.

Quaron and Maxi were all too eager to join me on this trip. Since they both fell head over hills for Ezra and Myron, they'd been plotting to get to New York. I wasn't stupid though. Ezekiel had assistance with this master plan he crafted. It was no coincidence that my best friends just so happened to be able to get a first class ticket on the same flight and the same row as me.

"Shut up, Roni," I chuckled. "I don't know anything. He told me to drop my location once I got settled so that is what I'll do when we get to the hotel."

"You haven't heard from him," she questioned.

"Nope," I said, vainly attempting to sound unbothered. But I was bothered as fuck.

"Hmm…," Roni skeptically hummed.

"What was that for?" Maxi said, brow creased. "You know that man is going to come running just like he's been doing for this girl."

"Yeah, I guess you're right. It's just that he's usually more communicative than this. Y'all talk all the time and you mean to tell me that he's been gone with no contact for days and he's not blowing up your phone," she pursed her lips with one eyebrow lifted. "Maybe the disagreement between him and Ezra was bigger than I thought," Roni nonchalantly dropped that intel.

"What disagreement?" I whisper-yelled as the flight attendant shot me a nasty look. I irritably pointed to my seatbelt indicating that it was secured. "Roni, what are you talking about?"

"Well when I talked to Ezra after Christmas he said Ezekiel wasn't fucking with him because he expressed some concerns about his relationship with you."

"What?" Maxi and I screeched simultaneously.

"Evidently Ezra and their mother are concerned about your… marital status," she whispered the last two words. "And Zeke basically told him to go fuck himself," she shrugged, chuckling. But I didn't find anything funny. I leaned back in my seat, refocusing my gaze back out of the window, reconsidering this decision.

I was hushed the entire one hour ride to the hotel, disregarding Maxi and Roni's bickering. They'd been fussing since we departed the plane, only ceasing when they loudly squealed as we approached the driver holding a sign with *Jules* on it. And then again when he escorted us to a black limousine.

Checking my phone, Ezekiel still had not responded to my text messages which made me hesitant to drop my location. I refused to believe that he'd plan this trip and then not follow through. In all of these months he had not given me a reason to mistrust him. But I had to admit that the blemishes from my past were creeping into the forefront of my mind. Especially given the news about his brother and mother's viewpoint about us... about me.

Hovering over the share button, I quickly pressed the pin to release my locale then dropped my phone in my tote. I rested my head against the plush leather rest glancing around the bustling streets of New York where eager tourists geared up to see the historic event tonight. Our driver pulled into the W hotel in Time Square and goosebumps covered my flesh when I saw Ezra and Myron standing at the valet stand. The exuberance was short-lived because there was no Ezekiel. Roni and Maxi couldn't contain their giddiness and I couldn't blame them. These two monstrous men with familiar eyes were glorious and fine as they approached the car door.

"Hey pretty ladies," Myron greeted as he extended a hand to retrieve Maxine. She exited first, immediately snuggling into his embrace preventing us from parting.

"Can y'all step aside," Ezra growled, nudging his cousin out of the doorway. "Hey beautiful," he said, hugging Quaron and doing the same thing he just fussed about.

"Excuse me. I would like to get out as well," I tersely uttered, my leg thoughtlessly shaking with annoyance.

"Oh my bad, Jemma. Let me help you," Ezra offered, extending his hand and I politely ignored it. He snickered, shaking his head.

I glanced everywhere but in his direction as I impatiently waited for the driver to unload the trunk.

"Have you heard from Zeke?" Roni whispered to Ezra but I heard every word.

"Nah, Lil ain't fucking with me just yet," he replied and a little piece of my heart plummeted to my toes.

Where is he? I mused. Hurriedly ambling into the hotel, I tried to disregard the lovey doveyness ensuing around me between the four new love birds. *Gross!* I was absolutely being a hater and I didn't feel bad about it. Thankfully, per Ezekiel's instructions, I was already checked in so I was able to hop on the elevator and proceed directly to the room. I didn't even bother taking a second to wait for Quaron and Maxine because I needed a moment alone to quell the fury generated in my chest. I quickly strolled down the hall, reaching room 1218 as my phone chimed. *Please let it be him.* I closed my eyes and deeply inhaled before opening the text. My face illuminated at the sight of his name.

> The Good Dr. Z: Location from 12/31/20. New York City. This contact is less than a minute away.

I surveyed the attached map and followed the tiny dot that rested next to the words, The W Hotel New York. *Every fucking time,* I ruminated in the promise he'd made to me… and consistently fulfilled.

With labored breathing, a drumming heart and a big ass smile, I glided the key card across the automatic pad to unlock the door. I wasn't sure where he was but I was giddy with anticipation of his face. Stepping across the threshold, a fresh enchanting scent of roses wafted in the air, welcoming me into the room.

I quickly surveyed the space eying dozens of yellow, orange and purple roses and *him.* The bold structure of this man wrapped in a familiar aroma soaked the seat of my panties. Ezekiel stood in the middle of the room dressed in black sweatpants with a *I Am A Man* hoodie and retro black and white Jordans. His hair had grown a bit and beard was full but he looked so damn good. I swallowed hard to prevent myself from drooling at the striking visual. We gazed at each other for the longest moments with an overabundance of questions, uncertainties and passion twirling between us. Then he flashed the sexiest beam I'd ever seen, motioning his finger for me to come to him.

Roni's earlier prediction of my actions seemed absurd, but I did exactly what she said; I dropped my purse, phone, everything and rushed into his embrace just like the sappiest romance movie. Zeke outstretched his arms allowing me to crash into his chest. His tall, imposing frame provided a satisfying solace for me to rest.

"Damn, I needed this," he breathed, nestling into the crook of my neck, tenderly enveloping me. "I've missed you," he continued, trailing a path of kisses across my face until he reached my lips.

"You ghosting me now," I giggled, teasing him with his normal accusation of my behavior.

"Not at all, gorgeous. You know better than that," he declared, ushering me towards the couch, seating me on his lap. He unconsciously fingered my hair as he spoke, "my flight was severely delayed. Once I got to the city I had to make sure Eriya and EJ got home safely. My phone was dead because my wonderful daughter left my charger in the airport. I hauled ass here from the other side of town." He took a breath, nudging my chin to look at him. "Jules, I've been planning for your arrival for weeks and I'd be damned if I was going to miss you." He glided his nose across the arc of my cheek.

"But how did you know I would agree to come?" I breathily whimpered through a moan as his hands roamed my body.

"I just knew that you would." He brushed soft lips across my partially exposed shoulder. "If you were missing me like I've missed you then I figured you would."

I smiled daintily, then whispered, "Thank you."

"For?" he asked.

"Keeping your word," I uttered, blinking back the wetness in my eyes.

"Every fucking time, Jules," he said, licking the crease of my lips then supplying me his tongue. His kisses were brand new every single time we were together. Whether it was the way he found new fascinations with my skin, feathered the oddest places with his fingertips or nibbled the meatiness of my earlobe knocking every hoop earring to the floor, Ezekiel always kept my body guessing. His hands got lost under the fabric of my leggings, manipulating the plumpness of my mound. He tugged at my thong, guiding me towards the couch to mount his lap. The friction from the fabric clutched tightly against my dampened folds collided with his firmness. I was dripping, simmering with need, my erotic fragrance whirled through the room.

"You smell so damn good. You've been waiting for me, Jules? Wanting me, baby?" he probed.

"Mmhmm," I moaned, trailing my tongue down his neck, settling against the small crevice behind his ear that triggered the animal in him.

"Baby, why do you have on so many clothes," he whined in a throaty bass-filled kind of way.

"Because it's thirty degrees outside," I responded in a whiny moan of my own.

"It's been too long, sweetheart. I need to see this beautiful body," he growled and I felt the urgency and stiffness of his desire pressed into my center.

I slowly girated against him. "Zee, we can't. Maxi and Roni will be coming in at any minute now."

"No, they won't. This is *our* room. Me and you," he confirmed, tickling up my back to remove my sweater.

My eyes widened, peering around the room noticing the king sized bed across the room positioned behind a partition providing separation from the living space. "Just me and you?" I inquired with surprise.

He nodded. "I told you I would find a place just for us if you wanted it."

"I want it. Zee, I want you," I admitted, clenching my fingers at his nape as he rested his temple against my chest.

Feathering the tip of his nose against my flesh, his hands massaged up the length of my torso to fondle and knead my breasts. Even through the heavy threads of the t-shirt, my titties were so sensitive. He navigated back to my lips, softly nibbling and fisting my hair as he gazed at me, shit, through me. As convoluted as this situationship was, I was so comfortable with Ezekiel. In Monroe, tension and anxiety were heavy burdens, practically suffocating me. Here, in the confines of these four walls, I'd never felt so unrestrained.

"Jules, can I taste you?" he inquired, peeling off another layer of my clothing.

I shook my head and whimpered, "no."

He halted, shock laced his face as he questioningly clarified, "no?"

"No... because I want to taste you," I said, lust dancing in my eyes and surprise frolicking in his.

I slowly slid off of his lap onto my knees, never disjoining from his gaze. The tent in his pants was more like a damn canopy fighting to maintain that vast, weighty member attached to the milk-chocolate hued God. I tugged at the elastic waist of his joggers encouraging him to lift up.

Desiring to waste no time, I simultaneously peeled his boxers and pants down to his ankles. *Free,* I pondered on our safe word as his goliath dick sprang forward, liberated.

The occasions I'd had the pleasure of experiencing Zeke's manhood, I never took the opportunity to get a good look. *Goddamn.* The up close and personal purview was impressive, shit, dare I say, pretty. Ezekiel's penis was pretty. Smooth unblemished skin offered the ideal canvas for plump veins that charted a path from his perfectly round sacs, across the expansive girth leading to the glistening mushroomed head. And the length? *My Lord today.* The erected length was um, length-ing.

I blinked for a long minute and released a deep exhale. *Just like riding a damn bike, Jemma Jule,* I encouraged myself because it had been a long time since I'd done this. One gentle kiss right on the tip sparked my memory and I quickly advanced from training wheels to a ten speed bike. In sluggish swipes, I circled my tongue around the blooming tip, then tongue-kissed down his magnitude while never relinquishing my eyes from him. Maintaining the dallying pace, I swallowed his dick inch by inch by inch. As his manhood disappeared into my mouth, Ezekiel's orbs expanded with his mouth wide open gazing back at me. He slapped a hand against his forehead and mouthed, *fuck.* The look on his face was bewilderment, satisfaction and... surprise. I guess he didn't think the homecoming queen had a little freak in her.

"Jules, oh my fucking..."

The words got lodged in his throat once I fondled his balls to the rhythmic motion my hot mouth created. I lingered there for several long moments as his body unconsciously slumped further down the couch. I decided to make use of my other hand and wrapped my fingers around his girth, oscillating to the same cadence. My mouth juices lubricated the surface allowing me to smoothly, gently glide over his vast dimensions on repeat. Clearly that did the trick because suddenly two imposing hands firmly clutched fistfuls of my hair guiding the upstroke of his dick to join the downstroke of my lips.

"Jemma, Jule. Goddamn, baby. I'm about to... shit," he incoherently grunted, a clear sign of his forthcoming climax.

I noticed the slight glimpse of disappointment or maybe embarrassment as he fought to withhold his crescendo. He didn't want to come; at least not yet. Zeke had never been a speedy lover. His ability to stave off my orgasm over an extended period of time was uncanny. But today he had the thrill of experiencing this lethal weapon also known as my mouth. I internally snickered when he bellowed at an octave I'd never heard from him, "Dr. Holiday!"

I digested every single drip drop of him. The grip on my hair was still taut as he traversed through the blissful peak. When I attempted to move, his other hand grasped my neck to prevent the departure. I rested my chin on his thigh, planting delicate kisses against sculptured muscles as his breathing stabilized. He shook his head, strained breaths sighing, "you're a fucking seductress."

22

EZEKIEL

The head that Jemma just bestowed upon me was down right lascivious, nasty and fucking sublime. I was a man, so of course I was curious about her head game but I wasn't going to rush and definitely was not in a position to make the request. I could spend the rest of my life pleasuring her, but when she slid off of me moving her body like a damn snake and fell to her knees, my grown ass was jovial like a teenager getting his member sucked for the first time. Jemma was patient and precise in her approach. Her attention to detail was unmatched, leaving no surface untouched. That woman literally sucked my spirit right out of me.

Eight minutes. It took her eight minutes to have me screaming like a punk. Quickies were never my thing because I enjoyed dwelling in intimacy, loitering in the pussy like I was a wanderer trying to find my way. But Jemma had my ass gone. She was a seductress indeed and I wanted to be inside of her so damn bad but we had to adhere to tonight's schedule. Thankfully, we showered together with no incident because if I penetrated her juicy essence we'd never see the ball drop. I stared at her reflection in the mirror as she applied her makeup. Chuckling, I hushly mused, *I got something for her pretty ass tonight.* My plan was to make love to Jemma in a new way to celebrate the new year. I just hoped she was ready.

I ambled into the living area to make us a couple of drinks to go.

Cognac for me, tequila for her. Jules stepped into the room wearing skin-tight jeans, a bright yellow cropped cable knit sweater and dark brown thigh high wedge boots. Her normally curly hair was straightened, topped with a chocolate brown fedora to match her boots. Smokey eyes gazed my way and clear glossed lips smiled at me as I ogled her. Jemma was sexy as hell. It was not her style to conceal the spread of her hips or the portliness of her ass and a nigga was grateful.

"Jemma Jule. Damn, you are trying to bring the Brooklyn street nigga out of me. I may have to hurt somebody over you tonight," I muttered, winking.

"Violence is not necessary, Dr. Green," she sexily sang, sauntering across the room to retrieve her drink and give me a kiss.

I laughed, then questioned, "do you have gloves and a scarf? The temperature is going to continue to drop." She nodded and we ambled out of the room towards the elevator. Stepping out into the hotel lobby people were everywhere. The bar was jumping and crowds began to exit to begin the journey towards One Time Square. Through all of the ruckus, I was still able to hear the guttural thunder of Ezra's laugh. He turned around once Quaron pointed in my and Jemma's direction. Holding hands, we unhurriedly sauntered their way as she watched the giddy passersby.

"What's up, Lil?" Ezra greeted, using my nickname as a test of my mood. If I responded in-kind then he knew our beef was squashed. I narrowed my eyes, studying him and he did the same to me. My brother and I could read each other's thoughts, verbalization not required.

"Jemma -" Ezra tried but she interrupted him.

"Dr. Holiday," she demanded, scowling.

He nodded. "Ok. Dr. Holiday, please accept my sincere apology for stepping to you wrong. I was out of line. Can we cease fire?" Ezra extended his hand to her.

Jemma left him lingering for a long minute then declared, "let the record show that you were the only person spitting bullets. But I accept your apology," she whimpered but I still wasn't convinced although she shook his hand. I decided to call a truce of my own with my brother and address Jemma's downcast expression later.

I finally greeted my brother, "what's up, Big." We dapped and connected in a brotherly embrace.

The six of us leisurely strolled the city streets observing the sights that I hadn't explored in years. We ate from street vendors, the ladies bought souvenirs and took pictures in front of the city's attractions. Being born and bred in New York, Time Square was for the tourists not the locals. But I must admit, the exhilaration adorning Jemma's face was well worth the slow-paced vacationers and overcrowded streets. I kept her close for my benefit and her safety. We reached One Time Square around eleven o'clock for the Dick Clark's New Year's Rockin' Eve event. I had a few friends in high places so I was privy to the performance schedule and VIP access.

Jemma was chatting with her girls, mesmerized by the massive Christmas trees and intricately decorated structures. I beckoned her to me then placed the lanyard over her head. Glancing down, her eyes widened in recognition once she saw the letters V.I.P. Access. If I'm not mistaken her expression transformed from elation to lust. She nibbled the corner of her bottom lip before clutching my collar to pull me in closer.

She whispered in my ear, "You can have whatever you'd like tonight, good doctor."

"Oh, don't worry, beautiful, I will," I teased, smacking her ass. The giggle she released shot darts through my heart. Carefree, unencumbered and lively; this was the Jemma I craved, shit, ached for.

D-Nice was the deejay and we danced through his set and other performances like Travis Barker, The Roots, Lizzo and Mary J. Blige. When MJB sang her hit song Be Happy, Jules was immersed in the music. I intently watched her, sinking deeper and deeper, succumbing to her enchantment. Fingers snapping, curvy hips swaying and that tequila warming her insides, she sang the lyrics from her soul.

> *"How can I love somebody else? If I can't love myself enough to know.*
> *When it's time. Time to let go. All I really want is to be happy. And find a love that's mine. It would be so sweet."*

I nestled behind her, my chest resting against her back with one arm clenched tightly around her waist as we swayed together. I sang the lyrics in her ear because, shit, I wanted to be happy too. Jemma and I were navigating the same narrative, but would we share a happy ending, a cliffhanger or a tragic conclusion.

Ryan Seacrest took to the stage to initiate the countdown... *ten, nine, eight, seven, six, five, four, three, two, one, Happy New Year.* The crystalized glisten of the massive ball illuminated Jemma's alluring brown eyes. I gazed at her while she gawked at it and then closed her eyes seemingly praying. When she opened her eyes, a big smile graced her cheeks just as a single tear released. She turned to me and stroked away the dampness from her face.

"Happy New Year, Zee," she breathed. Reaching her hands towards my face, she captured my cheeks, drawing me closer to her.

"Happy New Year, Jules," I croaked, swallowing hard because there was so much more I wanted to say.

I bonded my temple to hers. Our bodies interconnected in a way that I had not experienced with her over these past several months. The rapid rhythm of our hearts beat faster than Travis Barker and Questlove on the drums. I felt shackled by the words of adoration frolicking within me. I wanted to release them. I needed her to know, so I blurted, "Jemma, baby, I think, I know, I -"

"No. Zee, no. Don't say it. Not now. I think I feel it too, but don't say it. We have so much to think about," she whimpered with her eyes closed tight.

"But you feel it, right? Please tell me you're feeling what I'm feeling, Jules. Tell me I'm not in this alone," I pleaded with my eyes wide open because I had to see her face; discern her expression. She opened her eyes and an eerie sense of calm consumed me.

"I promise you, you're not alone. But let's just be here, in this moment with no complications, no obscure emotions. Can we just bask in our easiness, our simplicity? Please, Zeke," she begged, honeyed orbs darting back and forth to align with mine.

I was muted, no words, except for the adage Jemma would not allow me to convey. So I opted to kiss her instead. I kissed her with a fervor I had not felt in years. Slowly, passionately, lovingly, that kiss was equally hopeful and hopeless. If I couldn't articulate what was on my heart, I would damn sure show her. Thousands of people surrounded us but in that moment it was just me and Jemma, lost and disoriented, yet lucid to the fact that we were in a quandary. There was warfare amid good and bad trouble and right now bad felt too damn good. I swiped another tear away, concealing her face from the onlookers with my arms resting on her shoulders until she stopped crying.

"Baby, are you ok? Jemma, why are you crying?" She shook her head, hiding her face in the crook of my chest. "Use words, wordsmith," I whispered in her ear then nibbled the part of her earlobe I loved so much.

"I want to go back to the hotel." Her voice was so small.

"You sure?" I confirmed.

She nodded, then faintly spoke, "yes."

Jemma was so quiet the entire walk back to the hotel, I couldn't comprehend her mood. I guess her firm hold around my waist was one positive sign. When we entered the hotel, she stopped in the gift shop while I went to the front desk to ensure my surprise was ready. We entered our room and Jule's eyes radiated at the sight of rose petals and luminaires lighting a path to the bed. A bottle of champagne and a charcuterie board was arranged on a room service cart draped with white linen. A box similar to the one she opened on Christmas sat in the middle of the bed.

"Jules, I had this planned but if you're not up to it." She spun around and quickly deleted our distance and placed a finger over my lips to silence me.

"It's perfect, Zee. I just wanted to get away from there because I … I just want to be with you. No sightseeing, no crowds, not even my friends and your family. I want you," she confessed.

I rested my lips on her temple. "Open your box," I requested.

Jemma settled on the bed and I helped her remove her boots, sweater and jeans. She was gorgeous laying against the red roses in only a white tank top and white lace thong. I poured two glasses of champagne while she opened the box. The light gasp behind me made me snicker a little.

"Zee, what is this?" she said, brow furrowed as she lifted the first item.

"You're a smart woman, baby. Tell me what you see."

Jemma was so damn cute and so damn flustered as she named the items. "I see a beautiful piece of lingerie, dark desire eye mask, a command flogger and gentle bondage handcuffs," she squealed a little then paused. Her eyes bulged in shock, but I could smell the sugary desire leaking from her center.

"Keep going," I said, handing her the champagne. She took a long swig before continuing.

"Natural lubrication, clitoral stimulation gel, couples vibrating ring and…" she swallowed hard, lustily observing me, mumbling, "and I guess last but not least, a stainless steel anal pleasure plug." Jemma read the package then peered up at me holding the shiny tool with a look of confusion. "Zee. What?" she stuttered, unable to complete her thought.

I dropped to my knees in front of her, tugging at her legs to pull her closer to me. Resting my lips against her thighs, I glared at her; fear and feverish yearning laced her expression.

"Have you ever used these before?" I asked, sprinkling more kisses against her thigh. She shook her head.

"Do you want to try?" I probed, my nose nuzzling right against her center. She gasped, then nodded with no hesitation.

"I just want to make you feel good, Jules. A heightened experience your body will never forget. Is that alright?" I said, swiping my tongue down the crease of her sheathed private lips. She nodded again.

"What's your word?" I groaned, standing to retrieve the eye mask.

"Free," she whispered, closing her eyes as I covered them with the mask.

"At any moment when you want me to stop, you just say the word."

I grabbed the empty flute from her hand, sitting it on the nightstand. I kissed up her thigh grazing my lips across the lace fabric of her panties then kissed down the other thigh. The song Comfortable by H.E.R. resounded in the background. Jemma panted, digging her nails in my thick coils as I continued to slowly peck and lick her flesh. I stripped her, revealing flawless, unmarred nakedness. The only garment she wore was the face mask. The blaring beat of the music coupled with hindering her sight heightened other physical senses. I layed Jemma across the bed and grabbed the flogger from the box. The satin and leather fringes offered the perfect transition from silky to woolen sensations against her skin. I glided the blended materials across her goosebump-covered flesh, brushing against the bareness of her apex and the peaks of her breast. I was just getting started and she was already flailing from the minimal fondling. The handcuffs were likely not an option tonight.

"Are you going to handcuff me?" she whimpered, as if she read my mind. Unconsciously, she caressed her breast while sliding her teeth across her bottom lip and that shit was turning me on.

"Do you want to be handcuffed, Jules?" I palmed a handful of my dick trying to calm some of the pressure. Thank God for the spectacular orgasm earlier because otherwise I would've detonated at the sight of her intimately touching herself.

She nodded, but quickly responded verbally because she knew I wasn't going for that nonverbal communication. "Yes, Zee. You gifted me these items for a reason. I want to experience everything."

Fuck! I thought, inhaling deeply. I had to settle down but an uninhibited Jemma was a sultry provocative Jules, and I liked that shit. I applied the stimulation gel to her clit right before flipping her onto her stomach. *Swish.* I tenderly swatted the flogger across her ass to the sway of the music.

Retrieving the cuffs from the box, I kissed the span of the most beautiful caramel skin, securing one wrist to the other as her bounded hands rested on the small of her back. With one hand, I maintained a firm grip on the cuffs, while my other hand kneaded the voluptuousness of her ass. I smelled the sugary nectar simmering in her nexus and I wanted a taste. I licked down the seam of her butt journeying toward the pulsating center. I sucked and slurped her pussy, digesting mouthfuls of saccharine juices. But I wasn't ready for her to come yet so I recoiled, hovering over her trembling frame to whisper against her ear.

"Baby, if I let you go do you promise that you won't move your hands?" Jemma was heaving as she slowly nodded her head. "Jules, talk to me. I don't want you to hurt yourself," I commanded.

Muffled by the pillow she was laying on, I almost didn't comprehend her muttering, "I promise."

I wrapped the vibrating ring across my finger and clicked it to the lowest setting to begin. Still positioned on her stomach, I slightly lifted curved hips encouraging her to elevate to her knees. Goddamn she was sexy. A procession of tiny moles lined the middle of her back and I had to kiss them but I couldn't stop there. I sprinkled wet, succulent kisses down the arc of her back and booty before diving in. With dawdling, soft strokes, I circled the vibrator across her fleshy folds to test the pressure. Jemma admitted to pleasing herself with toys but never with a partner so I was curious about how much intensity she could withstand. Her breathing was labored, but controlled. *Click. Click.* I pushed the tiny button activating more force.

"Aah," she lowly panted.

Click. Click. Click. We were at the halfway point and I saw the pressure building. This was the sweet spot. That rotund ass began to stir, tittering back and forth in a provocative sway to Muni Long's song Hrs & Hrs. Jules sensual moans transitioned into angelic singing, *I could do this for hours and hours and hours.* She chanted the same words repeatedly through periodic wanton whispers, grunts and groans as the vibrator continued to massage her bud. I'd beautifully built the orgasm and now it was time to take her to the pinnacle. I delicately pressed her ass down forcing her body to lay flat securing the toy directly between her private lips. I quickly saturated the sparkling silver anal plug with lubrication before rubbing it against her opening. As soon as I breached, her body tensed and breathing ceased.

"Baby, breathe. Breathe," I instructed while sprinkling kisses against her tense flesh. Her body was pacified as I carefully thrusted the plug further into her sodden hole

"Zee," she bellowed. "I don't know. I don't know. Baby," she huffed, extending the last syllable through a sexy grit. I gradually withdrew, then slid the plug back in at the same sluggish pace over and over again. Clitoral stimulation, anal penetration and now the finale. I glided two fingers into the soggiest, wettest pussy I'd ever encountered.

"Shit! Oh my god. Oh my god. Oh my… " Jemma howled and squirmed while she fought against the handcuffs and aggressively bit into the pillow.

I slowly removed my fingers from her essence, then clawed my way under her shivering frame to snag the vibrator. The plug continued to pierce her second hole until she calmed. And just like that… one, two, three, she was down for the count. I eyed her for a few minutes before unlocking the handcuffs. Jemma was a fucking wonder. Body glistening, relaxed and completely satisfied, I could watch her like this forever.

I slithered up her body and was greeted by the softest sexiest pants. I whispered, "you good, baby?" She nodded. "Are you hurting?" She shook her head.

I didn't mean to chuckle but she was so damn lethargic her movements were in slow motion. Removing the eye mask, I kissed her temple, nose and lips.

"Jules, baby, look at me." She opened one eye, then the second. "Was it too much?" She shook her head again. "Words," I demanded.

"No," she drawled.

"Good girl," I said, cradling her limp body in my arms.

We settled in enjoyable serenity for so long that I thought she'd fallen asleep.

"What about you?" she asked, voice at a whisper.

"What about me?"

"You didn't get what you needed," she whimpered.

"Quite the contrary, beautiful. I got *everything* I needed," I said, running my tongue against her lips before slipping it in her mouth. "But don't forget you said you can do this for hours and for the first time we have hours to do whatever our heart desires."

"My heart desires you, good doctor," Jemma proclaimed, sexily smirking as she stroked my dick in the palms of both hands causing my already present erection to stiffen more.

I don't know when I made this playlist but the music whirling in the background was the perfect soundtrack for this night. Tank's When We blared just as Jemma turned over to climb on top of me. She guided my dick into her dewy pussy, slipping and sliding up and down my shaft at a relentless yet slothful pace. Jemma was a good student; she quickly learned the art of constructing the orgasm one stroke at a time. She rocked, swaggered and pulsated on my dick for extended minutes until we both reached an explosive optimum peak.

"Shit, baby. Jules, I, -" I attempted to speak but she swallowed the words with a salacious kiss, terminating my testimony.

Jemma had conquered my heart and soul, shit she had me, all of me. In my mind, she was mine and I refused to let her go. But this was a leased opportunity, short term occupancy because Jemma wasn't mine; at least not how I wanted her. *What the fuck am I going to do?*

The wretched feeling of not having her made me nauseous as she snuggled into my quivering body brushing fingertips across my chest encouraging me to mellow. Lingering tremors invaded me for more reasons than

just the gloriously violent orgasm. I was in love with Dr. Jemma Jule Holiday. Fucking *in love* with somebody's wife.

23

JEMMA

Seven days. I spent seven whole days in absolute bliss with Dr. Ezekiel Green, in his city, in his bed. I woke up on New Year's Day satiated and a little sore. Zeke intricately explored every crevice and orifice of my body unearthing sensitivities and senses that I was still unable to comprehend. I felt like a kid on a colossal roller coaster for the first time; giddy and antsy anticipating the inevitable plummet, yet buoyant and zealous to take another ride. It was official, I'd taken the plunge with Ezekiel. I craved the turbulent craziness of this... him, me, *us*.

Aside from the hours and hours of, shall I say, lovemaking, it was the laze in the afterglow that had my kitty ready to take another joyride. He propped up in the bed resting on one elbow feeding me grapes and tickling fingertips down my cleavage. I gazed up into the most mesmerizing smokey eyes as we talked about the crucial and inessential things but cherished each other's every word.

"I recall the first time we were together you concealed your scars. What's changed?" he asked, involuntarily brushing his hand across my navel.

I shrugged, sometimes feeling reduced to a coy little girl in his presence. "I guess I know that I'm comfortable with you. You don't seem disgusted by them."

"Is that how it started?" he continued to probe.

"How what started?"

"The... problems in your marriage," he hesitantly asked.

We didn't do this; talk about my failing marriage or his failed one.

"I used to think that is when the dissension started, but now I know that after my first surgery I just started paying attention. I was home for almost four months due to complications so the things that would distract me in the past like work, writing or Shiloh's busy schedule were nonexistent. His need for perfection and control became more apparent the more I observed our dynamic," I admitted after recently uncovering that revelation in therapy.

"Do you feel like you were being controlled?" he queried. Surprisingly the inquisition didn't bother me.

I shook my head. "No, not controlled per se, but I was compliant. Doing anything to avoid disagreements or confusion with him. I would pick my battles and stay silent on the things that weren't worth my energy. I didn't see discord and arguing between my parents growing up so I didn't want that for Shiloh."

"You said control *and* perfection. Tell me more about the desire to be perfect." Damn, Ezekiel had all the questions tonight.

"I was a winner. Every competition, every academic endeavor, I won. No one ever told me no, so I was never taught how to lose. And when I found out I was pregnant, I worked hard to redeem myself after the biggest sin in my life at that time," I said, signaling air quotes. "Then I got sick and had to have the surgeries that would forever leave an imprint on my body. Over time I realized that the visible marring was just an expression of the internal scars I'd been hiding anyway."

"Nobody's perfect, Jules, but you're damn sure close to it in my opinion," he whispered, stroking the tip of his nose against my shoulder.

I snickered then turned over to support myself against the palm of my hand, mimicking his position. "I think you're saying that because I just had my mouth wrapped around that monster you call a penis."

Ezekiel boisterously guffawed, pinning me against the bed as he deliciously devoured me well into the late afternoon. I literally did not know what that man was doing to my pussy because the sensual softness of his touch was like the most romantic poem and the sweetest love song. Every instance that he unceasingly permeated me with that dick, that tongue or the whisper of "your contagious" in that throaty bass-filled guttural moan, I widened for him, welcoming him inside every fucking time.

After a week with Ezekiel, one thing I learned was his longing for public displays of affection. Whether it was when we cooked together in one of his AirBNB properties in his old neighborhood, or walking to the park for a run; he snuggled, caressed and downright groped me every chance he got. The night before I was scheduled to leave we had dinner at his favorite restaurant, Bella Italia, that was a few blocks from the house. I finally had the opportunity to taste the black truffle pizza he raved about.

Ezekiel ordered a large caesar salad and two pizzas because he refused to share with me. I chuckled, because his expression was dead serious as he stated, "I'm sorry beautiful, but I'm willing to share a lot of things but this pizza ain't it." A few hours later and two empty bottles of red wine and not a crumb of pizza left, we decided to share a piece of strawberry cheesecake. I was loving this opportunity to explore him - maybe too much.

"Zeke? Sweets, you didn't tell me you were in town?"

Sweets? My brow furrowed as I turned towards the sultry voice to view the mahogany beauty approaching our table.

"Stella," Ezekiel said, standing to greet her. "How are you, sweetheart? You know I wasn't going to leave town without saying hello." He continued, detaching from her embrace to attach to mine. He clasped my hand, kissing the back of it as he pulled me to stand. Wrapping his arm around my waist, he uttered, "Stella, this is my friend from Monroe, Dr. Jemma Holiday. Jules, this is a long time friend of mine, Stella Nolan."

"Hi, Stella. It's nice to meet you," I muttered, extending my hand to greet her.

"Nonsense," she yelped, drawing me into an uncomfortable hug. "Any friend of Zeke's is a friend of mine." Stella bit her bottom lip and winked. *What the hell?* I thought, trying to determine if that gesture was for me or Ezekiel. "She's gorgeous, Ezekiel," she cooed.

"Stand down, Stella. I'm not sharing," he practically growled. The scowl dressing his face indicated no humor.

Stella lifted her hands in surrender. "Ah, that means you're special, Dr. Holiday. Ezekiel only wears that type of scowl when he is truly attracted to a woman. And a beautiful woman indeed," she giggled, playfully slapping against his arm.

A gender ambiguous individual dressed in slacks and a business shirt with a head full of honey-blonde coils approached us and rested a hand directly on Stella's butt, then kissed against her cheek. I was so damn confused but opted not to be disrespectful with my desire to probe.

"Zeke, this is Cora, the woman I was telling you about before you left me here to fend for myself," she said teasingly. Cora nodded after Stella introduced us. Ezekiel offered, but they opted not to join us since they were picking up a to-go order.

I was fairly quiet as I processed what just happened. I had no doubt that Zeke and Stella were a pair at some point. If not in a serious relationship, they'd definitely fucked. But I think Stella was flirting with me and even more baffling, I think she and Zeke have shared a woman or two in the past.

"Stella and I met about five years ago. We had a one night stand that developed into a periodic friends with benefits situation. Stella is...." he paused, cupping his chin in thought. "She would probably say she likes beautiful people, no gender preferences."

I pursed my lips, lifting my brow as I nodded. He halted his stride as we ambled down the road towards the house. Facing me, he nudged my chin to focus my eyes on him.

"Yes, we've had a threesome before. Just once," he said, reading my mind. "I haven't been with Stella since before I left New York. When we're committed to someone, it's one hundred percent. When we're not, we occasionally connect," he explained.

"You don't owe me an explanation, Zeke," I unconvincingly uttered.

"No, I don't. But I want you to know I'm not on any bullshit when it comes to you, Jemma. You don't have to look over your shoulders with me, wondering if someone is going to step to you on some fuck shit about me. Even with our situationship, I wouldn't do that to you. Your trust in me means everything. Do you understand?"

I nodded then blurted, "use my words. I know." I rolled my eyes and he chuckled. "I understand." He stared deeply into my eyes for what seemed like an eternity then kissed me before continuing our leisurely stroll down the sidewalk.

Normally I loved Sunday mornings, but that particular morning I despised Sunday. I was going back to St. Louis after seven days of basking in the paradise called Ezekiel. He treated me with the utmost tenderness and respect. And given the downtrodden expression on his face, he didn't want us to part either.

When making the decision to accept his invitation, it seemed like a good idea and an even better decision when he made me feel like I belonged to him. Like he was my safe place, my home. But leaving him gutted me because I knew when we returned to Monroe, everything would change. I vainly endeavored to smile when he whispered, "two weeks."

I nodded as he leaned his Herculean frame into mine against the car. We were in the airport parking garage because he insisted on walking me in as far as he could go. Our bodies settled there but the pound of hearts were unsettled, turbulent. It was as if the erratic beats were pleading, begging each other not to depart.

"Two weeks," I parroted, not finding anything else to say.

He glared at me, resting his hands on both sides of my face before guiding me to his lips. I trembled from the urge to cry. How the hell was I supposed to behave professionally when we returned to campus in a couple weeks after spending this time with him? I've had a taste of what it feels like to be desired, revered, *his*.

One tender, delicate, heartwarming and wrenching kiss landed on my lips then he quickly recoiled, collecting my luggage from my trunk. Hushed foolhardiness escorted us into the airport with our fingers interlocked. Not a care in the world about who was potentially watching.

* * *

I was ghosting him. School started back weeks ago and I couldn't bring myself to engage with him the way we were before New York. Communicating via video chat was no longer good enough for me so I decided to put some distance between us aside from work responsibilities. I believe he started to get the hint because as the weeks depleted so did the frequency of his attempts to connect. The one constant was his subtle acts of kindness; sticky notes with simple hellos placed on my desk, greeting cards in my mailbox every week and random UberEats deliveries on those nights when I would get lost in my writing and forget to eat.

Even on Valentine's Day I attempted to avoid him but he made it virtually impossible when at least five dozen roses welcomed me home at Maxi's doorstep and another few dozen spread across her living room.

"You need to go talk to that man, Jemma." Maxi bellowed, brows creased in frustration. "It's flowers every damn where and you're not even going to call him?"

I plopped down on the couch and shook my head as she rolled her eyes walking away. Peering around the vintage decor, I reminisced on the last time I walked into a room filled with roses. *New York*. During my visit, he gifted me with a bouquet of roses every day. The various hues carried a different meaning - from yellow roses for friendship to purple for passion and everything in between. But he never gave me any red roses... until today. The collection of roses decorating Maxine's home were blood red signifying admiration, love. I blankly stared between them and my phone for hours, eager to call him. To just hear his voice.

"Max," I called out. "Can I - " I tried to continue but she interrupted.

"They're in the basket by the garage door," she yelped from the kitchen.

I snatched the car keys and hopped in her red Lexus and drove almost thirty minutes to his house. It was after ten o'clock at night but several lights were illuminated throughout the house. He was home but was he alone? I couldn't blame him. It *was* Valentine's Day and it would be all my fault if he was spending it with someone else. I idled in reverse for several extended moments struggling with the desires of my head versus my heart. Deciding to drop a pin to make him aware of my whereabouts, I anxiously perched in his driveway unsure if he would even open the door.

After five grueling minutes depleted, the roar of the garage door jolted me from my daze. Ezekiel leisurely ambled toward the car looking sexy as hell wearing charcoal gray sweatpants, a long-sleeve dri-fit Nike shirt, socked feet and dark rimmed glasses. He halted his pursuit at the edge of the driveway with arms crossed over his chest glaring at me. I swallowed hard because my larynx had dropped to my ass. He was probably going to tell me to take my ass home and never return.

My eyes brightened when he motioned towards the empty garage bay next to his truck. I pulled in then killed the engine, hesitant to exit. The thunder of the door closing caused me to shudder. Gripping the steering wheel, I glanced around the pristine, tidily organized space attempting to ignore his stealthy amble. The reflection of his stately frame flashed in the rear view mirror before reaching the driver's side. *Knock. Knock.* Chocolate brown knuckles tapped against the window.

"Unlock the door, Jemma," he dryly instructed.

I obliged, stepping out of the car and leaned against the ajar door. "You're incognito I see." His voice was throaty, yet monotone, emotionless. He was right about my attempt to be discrete. Not only was I driving Maxine's car, I was dressed down in a hoodie, leggings and Ugg boots with a sorority-branded baseball cap covering my head.

"What are you doing here?" he said with a significant amount of bass in his tone.

"I - I wanted to see you," I stuttered. "To say thank you."

"For what?" he barked. Tension creased his brow. Ezekiel was mad.

"The roses. They are beautiful… and red," I said, nervously fidgeting with my fingers.

"It's Valentine's Day. That's a normal gesture towards a person you consider your valentine," he uttered those words so effortlessly. Even after all of my bullshit.

I blinked back tears then slowly diminished the gap preventing me from embracing him. He remained stoic, arms still tensely crossed. "I'm sorry, Zee," I whimpered, resting a hand on his forearm to determine if he would recoil. He didn't.

"I'm sorry," I repeated, journeying my hands up both biceps to massage his nape.

The tension lessened but he was still unmoved.

"Ezekiel, I'm sorry," I said, rising to my tip-toes to deliver tiny kisses to his neck.

He exhaled, dropping his hand to my waist. I continued my endeavor to gain his forgiveness as I nudged our bodies against his truck.

Whispering, "I'm sorry"on repeat, I kissed him tenderly, deeply until he caved.

Rigidity escaped his body and he touched me like my familiar lover, kneading and cupping my ample behind. Abruptly, he firmly pressed the palms of his hands to my cheeks. The action startled me until I witnessed the dewiness coating his narrowed eyes.

"What the fuck are you doing to me, Jules? I've never missed a woman like I've missed you. This shit is killing me." With his temple rested against mine, he shook his head and audibly sighed, "I'm going to be fucked up after this. You're going to break my fucking heart."

Desperately fisting the fabric of his shirt I whispered, "Zeke, no," because that's all I could muster to say. My body trembled as an ocean of tears soaked my cheeks. I didn't want to hurt him. I only wanted to love him but my shit was so complicated.

"Make me feel something else, Jemma. Take this hurt away. Please baby. Just for tonight," he begged.

I nodded, gazing into his saddened gloomy eyes. Snaking my hands up the back of his bald head, I pulled him into a tongue-kiss laced with desperation and urgency. Our harmonious moans echoed throughout the room. I couldn't believe we were still in the garage. And I definitely couldn't believe what I was about to do in this garage.

I trailed my tongue down his neck, gliding my white-painted finger-nails down the slope of his chest until my hands reached the firm bulge pressed against my stomach. Lifting his shirt, I circled my tongue around his nipples while massaging his firmness for a few moments. That action summoned a low moan. The tip of his monstrous member peaked above his waist band, basically begging me to show it some attention. I missed this man... *all* of him. His dick was fighting to be freed so I conceded. Ezekiel was big and bold and beautiful... everywhere.

With no consideration for our location, I dropped into a squat and ushered his manhood into my mouth. It was as if I was possessed, deter-mined to eliminate the hurt and pain I caused. Deliriously sucking and slurping and licking at a reckless, unabated pace nonverbally communi-cating my apology.

He whimpered lowly, "shit, baby, no."

In one swift move, Ezekiel hoisted me from my position into his arms. I locked my thick legs around his waist as we hungrily kissed. He carefully guided our conjoined bodies into his house. A valiant effort to reach the bedroom was in vain. Ezekiel was like a man possessed, devouring every inch of my flesh on the couch, on the floor, in the kitchen, blessing every square foot. Hours later I awakened on the couch lounger with his heaviness anchored between my thighs. He lustfully smiled, inclined to go another round.

"Happy Valentine's Day, beautiful," he sleepily drawled.

"Happy Valentine's Day, Zee," I retorted before taking a plunge into his salacious sea once again.

* * *

Quinton had been pretty quiet since Christmas, leveraging his attorney to make my life miserable with his unreasonable legal tactics. Today was the fifth mediation meeting since I filed for divorce months ago. Not even the wealthiest celebrities have to endure this type of drama to get a divorce. I had agreed to most of his demands but decided that this would end today. Quinton could have everything. I was exhausted and all I desired was my peace of mind. Not because of Ezekiel or anybody else, but because I deserved to be happy.

I walked into the lobby of Cole and Harper Attorneys at Law about ten minutes before the meeting was scheduled to begin. My lawyer and cousin Mallory Warren was leaning against the receptionist desk speaking to one of the attorneys with her back to me. The flirtatiousness in her giggles couldn't be ignored. The man next to her was fine and big, almost reminding me of the guy who played M'Baku in the Black Panther movie.

"Mallory," I sang, as she turned around.

"Hey Jem," she greeted, closing the short gap to embrace me. "You ready?" she asked and I nodded. "We're ending this today ok? I promise." I flashed a faux smile peering over her shoulder at the gigantic man still watching us. He cleared his throat.

"Oh, I'm sorry. Kyle Creighton, this is Dr. Jemma Holiday," Mallory introduced us. He shook my hand then turned to my cousin.

"Until we meet again next week, Miss Warren," he said, clutching her with a double-handed, intimate handshake.

My brow furrowed in surprise because Mallory Warren, JD, did not mix business with pleasure. She nodded at him before her focus came back to me. "Shall we," she said motioning towards the hallway leading to the conference rooms.

"You're blushing," I chuckled, nudging her with my shoulder as we hurriedly ambled.

Mallory was trying to return to her serious boss-bitch mode. "I'm not," she squealed, an octave higher than necessary.

"Mmhmm," I hummed, smirking at her bashfulness. My cousin was almost forty years old, never married and had no children. She'd been dealt a raw hand with men in the past and it was refreshing to see her spirited and gleeful because of a man.

"Even if I did like him, he's too young," she mumbled, shuffling papers from her briefcase.

"How young? He looks like a grown man to me. And he's a lawyer," I declared, taking a seat next to her.

"He's a third year law student at Monroe, not an attorney. And he's thirty-two," she smirked, meticulously arched brows bunched together.

"So he's grown. You better get yours cousin," I teased, popping my tongue out.

"Like you're getting yours," she retorted with the same gesture. "Mmhmm, don't get quiet now, cousin. Aunt Maureen told me about your Christmas gift and the disappearing act for the new year."

"Mal, it's not what you think. He's just a friend," I mumbled, embarrassed that my mother was sharing my business.

"It doesn't matter what I think, Jemma. You're grown and doing nothing wrong. But you could've still told me as your cousin and friend," she uttered, bumping me with her hip.

"You're right. I'm sorry. After this is over I'll give you all of the details."

"I want all of them shits too. The raunchier the better." We cackled, but our joyous exchange quickly came to a halt.

"What's so funny?" Quinton's gruff baritone inquired.

I hadn't seen him since Christmas and he looked stressed. In past meetings, he was dressed to the nines, but today, he was in a university branded track suit and sneakers with a neatly trimmed beard that I'd never seen before.

"Nothing of your concern," Mallory sternly announced. Disdain marked her pretty face.

He snickered, pulling out a chair to take a seat across from me. "Hello, Jemma," he said, staring directly at me.

"Hello, Quinton," I returned, offering him the same blank stare.

We loomed in that awkward space for a minute. A cloud of bitterness and dismay hovered over him, while sunrays of contentment and joy coasted over me. I was in a good place. Fearlessness and self-acceptance were my new companions. For the first time in a long time, I loved all of me from the inside out, flaws and all.

"Wonderful. The gangs all here," Derek Harper annoyingly giggled as he entered the room holding his iPad. "But unfortunately it may be in vain. Mr. Holiday has some additional items we need the judge to review before we can close out these matters," he nonchalantly muttered as he took a seat.

I was about to speak when Mallory pressed her hand against my forearm, signaling me to let her handle this. "Mr. Harper, we have settled the matter of the primary house, the lake house and the rental properties in St. Louis, Missouri. There are no custody discussions for the adult child so what additional matters could Mr. Holiday have to settle?"

"Well, the appraisal of the two classic cars in storage were higher than we anticipated and Mr. Holiday is asking for the judge to reconsider the fifty-fifty split of the proceeds since Mr. Holiday's efforts are the reason the vehicles are at the higher value."

I leaned over to whisper in Mallory's ear. She immediately directed her focus back to the other attorney. "Mr. Holiday can maintain 100% of the proceeds. Are we done?"

"Well, there is one more thing. Mr. and Mrs. Holiday are under contractual agreement to attend several events on behalf of the university and Mr. Holiday's speaking commitments. The last contracted event is in May, so -"

"Let me stop you right there, Mr. Harper. Mrs. Holiday has not signed any contracts agreeing to participate in *any* events on behalf of the university outside of her role as Dean of Student Affairs. As for Mr. Holiday's speaking engagements, Mrs. Holiday has no contractual affiliation with those events. Therefore, I would advise you not to put this in front of a judge if you want to maintain the minimal credibility you have in the political arena in this town."

"Mallory -" the idiot attorney drawled, stretching out the syllables of her name.

"Please address me as Miss Warren or Attorney Warren. Now, if you are done with these shenanigans, may I address a few matters that we need to settle." The idiot attorney nodded.

"I have filed a petition for the judge to sign the divorce decree today dissolving this marriage effective immediately. I am also prepared to file a complaint against you, Mr. Harper, for neglect."

"Neglect," he shouted questioningly.

"Yes. You have neglected to advise your client in a fair and ethical manner. The fact that my client has agreed to all of the demands presented and we are still here five months later is just plain ridiculous and an abuse of the law," she calmly stated. "And one factor that *we* have not introduced into this case is the fact that your client has fathered a child with an individual who *is not* Mrs. Holiday."

"Allegedly," Mr. Harper retorted.

"Sure, allegedly. I guess Mr. Holiday has also *allegedly* been listed as the father of a child born on February 18th of this year to a Bethany Williamson." Mallory peered at her papers for verification. "Child support documents listed the female child's name as Quinn Holiday Williamson."

I gasped, momentarily dazed because I was unaware that my cousin was going to play this card since I'd been adamant about not disclosing the infidelity or paternity situation. *Quinn.* His namesake and the nickname Bethany used when she approached me that fateful night. Everything around me was hazy. I barely heard Mallory continue her tongue lashing.

"Mr. Harper, please advise your client to settle this matter now, otherwise, we are prepared to petition the court for an emergency paternity test. I am confident that once the results are returned in 72 hours this situation will be resolved for good," she smirked, silently signifying victory.

"We need the room," Quinton said, gritting through clenched teeth.

"Pardon me," both attorneys asked in unison.

"I need to speak to my wife. Alone," Quinton roared, unable to make eye contact with me.

Mallory shifted to me seeking approval. I nodded, still leering at Quinton as they exited the room. The door slammed shut and his gaze remained focused on everything but me.

"Why are you doing this Quinton? Why can't you just let this go… for both of our sakes?" I quickly stood, crossing the room to stand in front of the window.

"Why, so you can be with the new provost?" he questioned.

I snickered, shaking my head as I gazed down at my purple patent leather stilettos. They made me feel powerful, confident, beautiful, and I needed all of the support I could get today.

"Dr. Ezekiel fucking Green. Really, Jem. I can only imagine how long this shit has been going on," he spat.

There it was. Deflection. Redirection. Quinton always had a way of straying from the topic at hand, especially when the main topic was his ass. I knew Ken couldn't wait to run his mouth about what happened on Thanksgiving. I actually chuckled as Quinton continued to rant in the background. He truly believed that this revelation would change something. I didn't care if it took five months or five years, I was divorcing Quinton Holiday. I decided to remain mute and allowed him to keep spewing nonsense.

"I should've known something at homecoming. He gave me that bullshit excuse about protecting his campus when he really was protecting you. You spent Thanksgiving with that nigga. Prancing his ass around our friends like I ain't shit. Fucking disrespecting me. You call yourself loving this nigga, Jemma?"

I whipped around so fast I thought I pulled a neck muscle. Did this man just have the audacity to say I was disrespecting him? While there was a woman with a baby floating around town and *I* am the disrespectful person in this situation.

"You have completely lost your mind. My decision has nothing to do with him and you know it. I refuse to live another day, another minute in agony, Quinton. When I decide to get into another relationship, I want to be with a man who brings me joy. To mend some shit you broke. I want to love a man without shame. Not someone who delivers disgrace and humiliation at my doorstep. And this..." I slid my phone across the table that was open to a text thread that included a picture.

"This was just the final confirmation that this shit is over," I tiffed, witnessing Quinton's realization of the text message from an unfamiliar number to me but clearly familiar to him with a picture of a green-eyed baby girl staring back at him. I received the text a couple weeks ago, but I didn't react, nor did I respond. I simply pressed save just in case I needed additional ammo. If Quinton continued to call my bluff and play these games, I was willing to play my big joker. But unbeknownst to me, Mallory was prepared to run a Boston on his ass before I had the opportunity.

"After all is said and done, you still have a baby. Your silence hasn't been admittance or denial but we both know it's true. Do you know how many times I've looked at the picture of that little girl staring back at me with eyes like yours? Like my Shiloh's," I croaked, voice trembling at the mention of our daughter.

"A living breathing reminder of the hurt you caused, Quinton. In the past when I was unable to see the evidence of your indiscretions I was able to pretend they didn't exist. At least that's the lie I told myself. But this... a baby." I pointed to the picture, shaking my head. "I've already forgiven you, Quinton, for my own sanity. But you made damn sure that I will never forget," I announced, turning to face the window again.

I heard him stand from the chair and felt him terminating the distance between us. His imposing frame pressed against my back as he swept my hair behind my ear.

"I am so fucking sorry, Jemma. So goddamn sorry. I can't believe I fucked up like this. I love you, Jem. What the fuck am U going to do without you?" he said, nestling his face in the crook of my neck.

I was still, motionless - emotionless. "Let me go, Q. Please. If you really love me, you'll let me go," I whispered as my nose brushed the side of his face. Surprisingly, I wasn't crying but the ache in my voice was indisputable, pleading.

"I can't. I'll die without you," he croaked. I adjusted positions to directly face him to see that his eyes were blood red and pooled with tears. "You said you would love me forever, Jemma."

"And you promised that you would never hurt me. So I guess we both lied," I said, shrugging. I sauntered away from him, snatching my Telfar before heading towards the conference room door. I halted before opening it and whimpered, "goodbye, Quinton."

24

EZEKIEL

March in Missouri was quite different from New York. One day the weather was humid and sticky, then the next day there could be a freezing wintry mix. The baffling contradictory weather was reflective of my perplexing relationship with Jemma.

She left my house the morning after Valentine's Day with a pose of doubt and ambivalence. I knew exactly what I'd gotten myself into but I had no dream that it would hurt this bad. We were approaching spring break and I hadn't heard from her. I unsuccessfully attempted to not go searching for her, but it did anyway because I required answers. Ambling towards her office I was quickly intercepted by Maxine.

"Dr. Green, hello. Can I talk to you for a minute in private?" she questioned, scrunching her nose anxiously.

"Hello, Dr. Dupont. Of course," I said, directing her to an available conference room.

"If you're looking for Dr. Holiday, she, um, she's taking a little time off. An extended spring break."

"Is she ok," I blurted, grabbing Maxine's arm causing her to shudder.

"Yes. Yes, she's fine. Jemma just needs some time. Since the divorce is final she's trying to move on and nurture Shiloh through this tough time."

I absently nodded my head. Internally shocked by the news of Jemma's divorce being resolved but externally stoic because she didn't come to me. Not in a celebratory manner but to cry on my shoulder, trust me as her friend.

"Um, thank you for letting me know, Dr. Dupont. Please give Dr. Holiday my best." I turned towards the door because I needed to get the hell out of there.

"Zeke, wait." Maxine lightly touched my arm pausing my departure.

"It was real. It *is* real. This is a new normal for Jem. Give her some time, ok?" She requested.

I blankly stared, clearly unconvincingly because Maxine continued. "She's smiled more with you than she has in years. As much as she may hate to admit it, you put her back together again. Trust me, she'll come around," Maxine said, patting me on my shoulder encouragingly as she left the room.

I rubbed a hand down my face exhaling sharply as I dropped into the conference room chair.

Why did I stay in Monroe during spring break? I should've taken a vacation, been on the beach in Montego Bay with my brother and cousin. But oh, I forgot, they're with the women that I technically introduced them to.

Instead I was sitting in the coffee shop, Rise and Grind, alone. It was one of the mysteriously warm days so I opted to perch outside on the patio. I bidded hello to a few students and staff members who evidently had no plans for the break as well.

A slightly familiar woman walked by pushing a baby stroller. She paused, apparently waiting for someone. "Did you grab her bag," the woman asked, then a very recognizable tenor irritably responded, "yes, B, I told you I would." *Coach Holiday.*

I snickered, shaking my head directing my attention back to my book. This man really had a whole baby with another woman. That's the fucking ultimate betrayal."

"Ezekiel Green," Coach Holiday smugly sang, interrupting my reverie. He postured with his arms crossed over his chest blocking my damn sun.

"Coach Holiday, how can I help you?" I inquired, settling my book on the table and crossed one leg over the other prepared for the bullshit.

"Nigga, how long have you been fucking my wife," he whisper-yelled, slightly minimizing the gap that stopped me from choking the shit of him.

"Wife?" I smirked, unflinched. My questioning tone indicated to him that I knew that wife shit was a rap.

"I'm starting to think this interview over dinner was all bullshit. That the two of you had been fucking all along. You run in the same circles so it would be hard to believe."

I scoffed, shaking my head. "I think you know Jemma better than that." I sipped my perfectly brewed java. "You see Coach, it's niggas like you that like to talk alot of shit about there wife, there woman, but don't put in the work to maintain ownership. Exhibit A," I said, motioning to the woman holding a seemingly newborn baby.

"After the dust settles, the tears dry and you continue to wonder about me with Jemma, you, Coach, still have a brand new baby. A constant reminder that you fucked up, my nigga." I'd quickly transformed from Provost Green to a hood nigga Zeke from Bed-Stuy.

"Jemma is not the type of woman you allow to collect dust on the shelf. You polish that shit... daily. Niggas wait a lifetime to be in the presence of a woman like Jules and you let her slip through your fingertips. "

"Jules? Mutherfucka, she's my wife. Always will be," he gritted through his teeth, jaws clenched tight.

"Nah, not anymore," I cooly stated.

"Man, my dick has a twenty year imprint on that pussy. Shaped to fit only me. You're reaping the benefits of what I taught her," he spewed quietly.

"Things change, playa. And I think we both know Jules is a very good student. Always willing to learn new shit," I chuckled and he jolted, clearly understanding what I was inferring. The unmoved snarky expression on my face let him know that I was the new instructor in town.

A stare down ensued for an extended moment. His breathing was labored, unhinged lunacy burned in his eyes. Quinton was about to go ballistic. If I had to guess, at this moment, coach Holiday's head was spinning with the soundtrack of Jemma's beautiful carnal moans in response to my dick and it blared like nails to a chalkboard.

To add fuel to the blazing inferno brewing in his soul, I continued, "you know what they say, one man's trash is another man's treasure. What you deemed useless and blemished, I regard as valuable and a fucking marvel. But I should actually thank you, Coach, because the trash you left on the sidewalk is my perfect treasure. I love every beautiful flaw, every imperfection on that woman's body. Every scar tells a story that you chose not to read. But I take my time to digest every single word, every fucking paragraph. And if one day she grants me the opportunity to worship and adore her, I'm coming when she calls every damn time."

I fully expected Quinton to throw a punch in response to the gut wrenching blow to his ego I just delivered. But the cries of his new baby and her mother beckoning, jarred him from the ensuing rage.

"We'll meet again, Dr. Green," he muttered while walking away.

"Indeed," I declared, lifting my coffee cup to bid him farewell.

* * *

"Big, it's one o'clock in the morning. What the hell do you want?" I groaned, responding to my brother's call.

"Lil, have you been on IG?" he thundered over the music in his background.

"No, man, I'm sleep," I yelped.

"You're going to wanna wake your ass up for this. I texted you the link. Look at that shit now," he instructed, then mumbled something to who I assumed was Quaron. I heard her slurred drawl say, "right now good doctor."

"Alright," I shouted, then hung up the phone. Taking a deep breath, I turned onto my back then navigated to my messages.

I clicked on the IG link that navigated to a video. It was Jemma. She was speaking on a podcast about her new book and she was so pretty. Faint nude makeup and wavy reddened coils brightened her already gorgeous face. *Damn, that face.* She wore a black t-shirt with the *JulesPen* logo, seated in an unfamiliar background. The overly dramatic moderator danced in her chair welcoming viewers into the chat before she proceeded with the interview.

"Hey everybody and welcome to the Black, Bold and Beautiful podcast.

This is your girl, Golden, and I'm excited to be speaking to one of my favorite authors, JulesPen. Hey lady. It's so good to see you," the moderator said.

"Hey Golden, it's good to see you too. Thank you for having me. Hey everybody." She waved and the biggest, brightest beam fancied her face. She appeared, tranquil, happy.

"Well, you know how I do, girl. We are going to get right to it because we have a lot to talk about. Earlier this week you disclosed to your fans that your marriage of twenty years has come to an end. I am so sorry to hear that," Golden compassionately expressed, pressing praying hands to her lip. Jemma flashed a close mouth smile but no retort.

"In your post you encouraged women to be bold and be brave. Make decisions that are good for them, no matter what others may think." Jules pursed her lips, nodding as Golden continued. "So JulesPen, what prevented you from following your own advice.

"Whew, you are getting right to it," Jemma chuckled.

"Complacency, fear, denial. I became a wife and a mother before I truly became a woman. At twenty years old I had no clue what it meant to be brave or bold when deciding the next steps in my life. Even after graduating top of my class with a two year old on my hip, finishing my doctorate and establishing my own success, I was afraid to take the risk because I was afraid of failing. My parents have been married for over years. They were my roadmap, my aspiration, my muse and I didn't want to disappoint them. The threat of being a disappointment can handicap you in ways you never imagine. Then I looked around and suddenly I was married for twenty years and had no clue who I was."

She shrugged, exhaling deeply as if a weight was lifted with that confession.

"So what changed? What or *who* is your new motivation? Cause I'm liking this new bold and brave JulesPen." Golden smacked her lips.

Jemma nibbled her bottom lip through a sultry smile.

"I decided to choose peace, happiness. Honestly, I decided to choose me. A very special friend of mine told me that *I* was an experience. That my personality was contagious. I couldn't comprehend that and didn't perceive it as a compliment. It wasn't until my therapist encouraged me to rid myself of guilt and shame. And more importantly to forgive those who betrayed and hurt me. This friend also told me to get out of my head. Don't think, don't hesitate, just do it. Do whatever my heart desires. So that's what I'm doing." Jemma released a coy, yet guttural giggle.

"Well, girl, I cannot wait for your new book. It's releasing in two weeks, right? Tell us about it," the moderator inquired.

"Yes, I am so excited about my new project which will be released on April first. It's raw, authentic, personal and it's called, Woman Without Shame. The title was inspired by Nikki Giovanni's poem Woman. Reading it changed my life and allowed me to share my own revelations about finding myself at forty years old and absolutely loving who I am."

The moderator started to take questions from the attendees via chat. One question in particular piqued my interest. *JulesPen, will you marry again?*

I sat up in the bed, eager to hear her response. She chuckled at that question but my heart sank to my toes. I had no intentions of marrying again anytime soon but it was not completely off the table for me. One thing's for certain is that I desired a relationship and companionship with *her*... only her. I momentarily lost my breath as she answered.

"Golden, I was somebody's wife for so long that I never had the opportunity to spend some time with myself. And right now, this self-exploration journey feels really good. But I will say that I want friendship and companionship in my life. I desire to love a man who brings me joy, stimulates my mind and my body."

She sexily jested, lifting her brows for emphasis.

"A man who I can love with no shame. Who shares everything with me, maybe except for black truffle pizza," Jemma chuckled, reminiscence intensified the gleam in her eyes.

"A companion who debates about which Friday movie is the best and loves neo-soul music just as much as I do. Right now, I kinda just want to be somebody's girlfriend."

"Ok fellas, you heard it here first. The beautiful JulesPen is on the market and wants a boyfriend y'all," Golden quipped.

I'm thankful I was alone in my room because I couldn't control my euphoria if I wanted to. *Jemma Holiday wants a boyfriend*, I thought, happy as hell because in my world she was already my girlfriend.

My inner musings muffled the moderator as she concluded the podcast instructing viewers to follow Jem's Instagram page to get a sneak peek of her new book cover.

I quickly pressed the heart button to like the video then typed a comment.

> @JulesPen Black truffle pizza is my favorite. [wink face emoji]

I clicked into her IG page and my lungs lodged in my throat. The book cover was me and Jules. A black and white image of us on New Year's Eve. The details had been edited and our faces weren't identifiable but it was us. A reflection of the moment I knew I was in love with Jemma.

I remember how she gazed in awe of the crystalized ball; how my heart drummed in response to her touch and how we made love all night long with muted whispers of I love you whirling on our tongues.

"Fuck, Jules. Where are you baby?" My shout echoed throughout the vaulted ceiling.

I wanted to call her but it was now almost two o'clock in the morning. Tussling in the bed, there was no way I would fall back asleep now. I perched on the edge of the mattress and watched the video at least five times. I forwarded to listen to her lyrical affirmation on repeat. *I want a man who I can love with no shame.* My phone chimed and I reluctantly rolled my eyes from her face. I knew it was Ezra but I was wrong.

> Jules: Thanks to you, black truffle is my new favorite pizza too.

I heartily snickered, sliding my teeth across my bottom lip as I considered my response. I ceased, anticipating an incoming message as the three dots bounced.

> Jules: Location from 3/18/2021 at 2:08am.

The map pinpointed an area in Monroe that was not too far from where Maxine lived. I furrowed my brow wondering where she was at this time of day, but I hopped my ass up to go find out. Although Jemma avoided me for weeks, nothing had changed, I was going to her every time she called.

I washed my face and brushed my teeth then scrambled through the bedroom to find a pair of sweatpants and a hoodie... no underwear. Grabbing my wallet and keys, I jumped in the truck and journeyed to find my Jules.

About twenty minutes later I turned into a new construction community called Redwood Trace. Some builds were still in the framing phase while a few homes were occupied. The GPS directed me to 13 Red Dawn Court. A ranch style home with terra cotta colored stone and the signature oversized red front door came into view.

I pulled into the driveway lined with solar powered lights. One dim light gleamed from inside. I opted to knock instead of ring the doorbell. Why was I so damn nervous when I heard the lock disengage?

Jemma appeared to glow standing in the doorway fresh-faced with a yellow nightgown. Her hair was a brighter hue of auburn and she trimmed a couple inches, plump coils settling below her ear. Ample breast spilled from the deep v-cut gown, while her nipples protruded against the cotton fabric.

"You just keep showing up for me," she whispered.

"Every fucking time," we chimed in unison and then faintly smiled. She leaned her head against the ajar door gaping at me. Apology and reparation flickered in the umber of her eyes.

"Is this your spot?" I asked and she nodded. "Can I come in?" She stepped aside, giving me space to enter the foyer. I peered around admiring the high ceilings, the detailed crown molding and freshly painted walls.

"Excuse the boxes and paint smell, I just moved in a few days ago," she casually muttered as if we'd been communicating. When the hell did she do all of this? Jemma hadn't uttered a word to me about looking at homes, let alone building one. I was equally aggravated and enamored with her.

"Jemma," I whimpered, grabbing her arm, ushering her into me under the archway. "Baby, talk to me. What the hell is going on?"

She clutched my hand, escorting me into the great room decorated with hues of ivory, blush and midnight blues. All of the furniture appeared brand new except for decorative items and memorabilia. We walked to the couch where she offered me a seat. I perched on the lounger part of the sectional, immediately pulling her to straddle me.

"I know I have a lot of explaining to do," she bashfully declared. *You damn right*, I thought but wouldn't bicker with her in this stimulating position. My dick was hardening at the mere graze against my core.

"Are you ok, Jules," I asked, fingering a loose curl from her face. She nodded. "Words, wordsmith." We laughed and she rested her forehead on mine.

"I missed you," she admitted. "I'm sorry for evading you all these weeks. I just needed some time to process all of the changes."

"Changes?" I probed, motioning around the room at one major adjustment; a new home.

"I'm divorced. Quinton has a new baby girl. Shiloh is devastated. So… changes or what I like to call the abnormal normal." She shrugged.

"Baby, I'm so sorry. This shit is never easy. Why didn't you come to me? Trust me with all of this, Jules," I interrogated, clutching her nape to draw her closer but there was no available space between us.

"I needed to ensure that Shiloh was going to be ok. But most of all, I had to navigate this on my own. Make my own decisions with no influence from anybody… including you." Jemma's syrupy brown orbs moistened.

"You told me in New York that I wasn't in this alone. That what I'm feeling isn't partisan. Is that still true because what I think I'm hearing in your voice is going to fuck me up. What are you saying to me, Jules?" I clenched my teeth, bracing for the devastation.

"I'm saying that I am no longer somebody's wife. I'm saying that I can't do another day without you. And I'm saying thank you, babe." We harmoniously discharged the breaths we'd held captive for what seemed like eternity.

"Why are you thanking me, baby?" I inhaled her rosy scent, feathering my nose down the crease of her cleavage.

Jules cupped my chin, stroking her finger across my lips. "Because you put me back together again, Zee."

I gazed at the most fascinating human I'd encountered in a very long time; possibly ever. Jemma's complexity was captivating. Her courage, inspiring. And she was all *mine*.

"I love you, Jemma. I am in love with you. I've known since the night I walked into that restaurant. As fucked up as the shit sounds, I was in love with you before I ever fathomed that you could actually be mine," I confessed. Gliding my lips against hers, our tongues collided in the most delicate, sweetest exchange. I fisted handfuls of her hair drawing her nearer to me as I laid back on the couch deepening the kiss.

"I -," she stammered, word stalled in her throat. The emotion glistening her orbs contradicted her stifled disposition.

"Don't think. Don't hesitate. Just come," I whispered, reasserting the sentiment that initiated all of this.

"I love you, Zee," she palmed my cheeks, staring directly into my eyes.

"I was hoping you would say that," I chortled, grinning against her lips. I reached in my pocket to retrieve an envelope then handed it to her. Jemma's brows crashed, puzzled. "Open it," I encouraged, gently brushing my fingers down her face.

She perched upright in my lap and unfolded the paper. Jemma spiritedly tittered, laughing uncontrollably.

"What does it say? And use your words, love," I said, joining in the jeer.

"Somebody wants you to be their girlfriend. Who will it be? Ezekiel, Zeke, Zee or all of the above," she giggled, shaking her head at my shenanigans.

"So what is going to be, Jules?" I snuggled into her neck, trailing kisses up its length as I pawed and caressed her swelling titties.

Jemma breathily sighed through a moan, "mmhh, all of the above, baby."

The End

The Robbi Renee Collection

www.robbirenee.com

Join the private Facebook Group - Love Notes.
Follow me on Facebook and Instagram